BODIES BLADES & RITUALS

A Walt Asher Florida Thriller

ANDREW ALLAN

Copyright © 2018 Andrew Allan

All rights reserved.

This is a work of fiction. Names, characters, places and incidents are used fictitiously.
Any resemblance to actual events, or persons living or dead, is coincidental. All rights
reserved. No part of this publication may be reproduced, or transmitted in any form
or by any means, electronic or otherwise, without written permission from the author.

ISBN-13: 978-1-7321385-1-3

THANKS

To everyone who reviewed and shared the last book.

To my friends / first draft readers / error spotters.

To you, for reading this book.

Cheers!

To Leslie, my wife.

The book is ready when it gives you the willies.

Also by Andrew Allan

Killers, Bikers & Freaks
(Walt Asher Book 1)

Temples, Tempests & Blood
(Walt Asher Book 3)

Sell Shock
(Walt Asher Short Thriller #1)

Walt's Fault
(Walt Asher Short Thriller #2)

Passport
(Walt Asher Short Thriller #3)

The Pimp's Henchman
(Grindhouse Pulp #1)

The Unpopular Sheriff

1

The moment DG dumped a Coleman cooler full of baby alligators into the backyard mud pit atop the naked, oiled-up, wrasslin' bodies of Dee Dee and Marva, was the moment it became evident to everyone this would go down as his most legendary party ever. There was no disputing it. No one could believe he did it. And, no one was sorry he did it.

Except maybe the two women in the mud pit. They flailed and flopped, each attempting to pin the other face down in the slop; Wet slop that molded to the curves of their slim, sexy bodies and gleamed beneath the fiesta lights strung between towering pine trees. They were too distracted to notice the cute, scrambling reptiles.

But then, a pair of those tiny gator jaws snapped around Dee Dee's wrist just as she was about to pin Marva. She saw the critter and screamed as she drew her hand back and attempted to shake it off. The little sucker held on tight.

Then, Marva screamed. Another gator had her by the seat. She slapped at it as she tried to get out of the pit. "Get it off me!"

I reached down, grabbed her hand, and pulled. My shoes slipped and in I went. Me, two naked women, and a litter of baby gators. Everyone howled.

Dee Dee slammed her gator against the muddy ground. It let loose and crawled away. She ran away.

I kicked at a gator about to crunch down on my ankle while I simultaneously prodded Marva's backside until she was out of the pit.

She still had the gator swinging from her ass. Drunk tears ran down her mud-slathered face. Her hands waved in panic.

I grabbed the gator by the tail and yanked it off. Dots of blood bloomed on Marva's muddy ass in the shape of the gator's jaw. I tossed the gator in the pit.

DG walked up, grabbed me by the shoulders, and laughed right in my face as he handed me a glass of clear, home brewed liquor.

Fun times indeed.

2

The record settled. The turntable spun. The needle dropped. Piano...harmonica...drums...voice...

Side one, cut one. Beach Boys "Holland" LP. My current musical obsession and the perfect soundtrack to wind this evening down. Inside my car was trashed and muddy from the drive home. But, at least I was home and showered, with cocktail in hand, a record on the player, no alligators in sight.

Home was Dunnellon, Florida, right on the Rainbow River. Prior to DG's mud bash, I had spent the day swimming and floating with the fishes and birds and otters and gators; Feet dangling, reeds from the riverbed wafting between my toes. The perpetual 72-degree water soothed my body and bones as golden sunlight beamed between the tall oak, pine, and palm trees running along the riverbanks. A fine kind of paradise.

My fiancé, Ilsa, was in the Netherlands tending to her sick mother. Barring any last-minute miracles—and I am not a religious person—these would be the last weeks they'd spend together. I told her not to worry about anything here. I'd manage everything, including her bars in Gainesville.

But, it had been my day off from that. I was a free man. Free to eventually fall in the mud at DG's. I hadn't decided how much of that story I'd share with Ilsa. Not that she'd mind. It just made me look like an idiot. But then, she'd probably say 'a chivalrous idiot.'

Midnight approached. Too late to work, which still involved writing infomercials for an array of 'As Seen on TV' products. Although these days they were being seen less on TV and more online. Either way, I was up to my neck in projects. Fine by me. Work kept my mind occupied so I wouldn't dwell on my recent near-death experiences. That's right, plural.

It was only a few months ago that I was accused of murder, chased across the state by the police, attacked by a Senator wielding a fireplace poker, and hunted by a trio of ruthless executioners...all while trying to find out who was responsible for killing my friend Ken. I found out. And, I got them before they got me.

My body had healed fast. My mind took more time. It was a traumatic experience that left its share of psychic scars. Killing people was something I didn't care for, even though it saved my own life. What hurt most was being responsible for an innocent man's death.

Teddy.

I had enlisted the promising young journalist to help me discover the killers and in doing so ushered him to a brutal death no one deserves. I didn't kill him. But, it was my fault. There was no denying it. That was the hardest part to handle.

Enough, Walt.

I was letting my mind wander into those dark, regrettable places. Something I knew would continue for the rest of my life. A distraction was needed. And, one was waiting on the DVR: The game. UF versus Ole Miss, men's college football, recorded while I was at the party. Perfect brain sorbet.

TV on. Lights off. I kicked back on the couch, remote in one hand, whiskey in the other. The recording started to play as the game's broadcast announcers were finishing up their opening statements and promising the kickoff, right after these messages. I nestled into the cushions content with knowing I'd be asleep before the first quarter ended.

A political advertisement played on the screen. They were unavoidable this time of year. The main race was for the Governor's seat. Voting was a month away and the contest had gotten ugly.

This ad slammed incumbent Republican, Gordon Vissel at the behest of challenger Emiliano Abrantes. He was a Democrat who had made a fortune in palm trees. He owned profitable nurseries across the state, but his bread and butter was down in South Florida. He was Miami's "Palm Tree King". And, he wasn't happy with how the state had been run, in particular on matters concerning the environment. There had been too many contaminating accidents that should have been prevented. I agreed with him. But, I didn't have the desire or moxie to run for office.

As a rule, I don't put much faith in politicians. Far as I could see, politics was the biggest of all infomercials. "They're the problem. We're the solution. Send us money!" No thanks.

And, I had good reason to be jaded about politics after dealing with State Representative Trip Wingart and his brand of governmental corruption first hand. But, Trip was out of office for good, and I dug what the Palm Tree King was saying. Like many of my fellow Floridians, I was hoping he would get the job and clean house. Seemed he had a legitimate chance. He'd already earned my vote.

Enough of this. Get to the game.

After a few more advertisements—car dealership, Bucky's Riverside Cafe, Jacuzzi clearance sale, "Everything must go!"--a promo for the 11 o'clock news played. And, their lead story was sinister.

"I'm Geraldique Tremain. Coming up tonight, we're unraveling the mystery behind a gruesome discovery. Why was this semi truck abandoned on the side of I-75. And, why were dozens of dead bodies inside? We'll have more at 11."

Red and blue police lights flashed and flickered across the crime scene in the background. The footage cut to a shot of technicians in Hazmat suits hauling bodies off the truck and onto stretchers. A frail, brown arm flopped out from under the discreet sheet. That's when I saw it.

The symbol.

It was branded into the brown arm of the dead body. One of the rubber gloved techs grabbed the wrist and tucked the arm back under. It was gone in a flash.

But, the significance lingered. Maximum Freedom. It was the same symbol on the ring I had removed from Doug Tanjeris, the man who tried to murder me.

3

I fast-forwarded the DVR, tossed the remote onto the couch, ran to my desk, and opened the drawer. It almost fell out. I ran both hands through the clutter inside until I felt the ring.

Back to the television. I snatched up the remote and watched the game play out at triple speed. Second quarter, third quarter, fourth quarter. News.

I hit the play button and the on-screen action slowed to normal speed. On my knees, on the floor. I leaned in close, not wanting to miss a thing.

Carol Barbour, news anchor most noted for her Farah Fawcett inspired hair forty years after that style went out of style, set up the lead story: "Gubernatorial candidates on the campaign trail."

No. Fast-forward. Next. Crime tape and a dead body chalk outline graphic appeared on-screen next to Carol. "Hit and run driver left a man dead."

Shit, no. Fast-forward...school meeting, outrage parents...commercials. Back from break, weather. Break. Sports. Bucs on the practice field, speculation about the upcoming game. "We'll see you tomorrow. Have a good night."

What? Where was the truck story? Did I miss it?

I hit rewind and travelled back in time at double-speed...receiver throws to the quarterback...toppings fly off a burger...a hurricane swirls back towards Africa on the Doppler radar...no, no, no...run and hit.

I paused the television. I didn't miss the truck story.

It wasn't there.

Where the hell was it?

I felt the ring in my hand. It was heavy, thick, and imposing. Brushed platinum with fluid lines that wrapped and twisted to form a strange symbol. The symbol was impressed upon my palm skin from gripping the ring so tight.

A recollection: the battered Mexican girl at Tanjeris' house had the same symbol branded on her arm. Melted skin, discolored dark and bumpy. She had been Tanjeris' sex slave.

I looked at the ring.

This was the same symbol I had just seen on the dead arm in the news promo. There was no mistaking it.

It was the symbol of the elite, maximum freedom secret society that had fueled Doug Tanjeris' killing-for-hire spree. The one that killed my good friend, Ken, orphaned his kids, disabled Ilsa, blew up DG's house, launched a manhunt for me, and beheaded poor, innocent Teddy. All for...nothing?

I had stopped Doug and Ken's duplicitous wife Karen. But, I hadn't stopped *them*.

I fell back against the couch and stared at nothing.

Wait, you fool.

They don't make secret society rings for just one person. Of course, there had to be more members. And, if they were all enjoying the charmed life Tanjeris had been living—the maximum freedom life— they wouldn't stop just because he was dead.

Maybe I knew that all along. In my gut. Was that why I had kept the ring? How many more of these rings were out there? And, which of those ring-wearers had left their truck full of dead bodies by the side of the road?

Ever since I had left Tanjeris' house, amidst the roar of DG's cycles and Doug and Karen's anguished cries, I had wanted to understand what drove these people to such extremes. Just like pitching a new product in infomercials, I needed to know how it all worked.

I had spent time digging around online, researching at the library, trying to discover what the symbol on the ring meant and who was behind it. No luck. But, the curiosity lingered.

I never mentioned it to Ilsa. She wanted to put the entire encounter behind us. She *thought* it was all behind us. I knew she considered me lucky to survive at all, so why go picking at old wounds? She'd tell me to let it go.

I couldn't. Some nightmares you never forget. Not when they're stitched to the emotional fabric of near death and savored survival.

More than that, I had to do it for Teddy. His death weighed on me more than any bitterness I could have had about almost being killed myself. He had been innocent. I coaxed him into helping me out. I got him killed.

There I go again.

With a gruesome five-second news tease followed by a complete absence of that very story on the eleven o'clock news, my fears had new life.

I knew why there was no lead story about a truck full of bodies by the side of the road. It was the same reason my face had been plastered across the media as a murderer. The phantom forces Tanjeris ran with possessed unlimited reach and sinister connections across all industries. The phantoms were everywhere. A corrupt, invisible brotherhood that believed in maximum freedom. If they were related they'd be kin. But, they weren't. So, they were what, kith?

The Kith.

And, the Kith had to wield that power tonight. The dead body truck story wasn't on the late-night news *because they didn't want it there.*

Break it down: Something went wrong. The truck and the bodies were discovered. It was reported over signals. News showed up to capture the story. The promo ran.

The Kith saw the promo.

The Kith made a call.

The Kith made sure that story was squashed.

Sometimes you just *know.*

I went to my desk, flipped open the laptop, clicked on the browser. I checked the news sites. Not just Channel 12, which I'd been watching, but also Channels 8, 10, 13.

Nothing.

No one was covering the truck story. Nothing was mentioned on any other local news sites, television, newspaper, radio, alternative weeklies...nothing. Had they clamped down on all the local media? Or, did the media bosses know not to mess with such a story?

News 12 didn't get that memo. Whose head would roll for the brief television report? What the hell was going on?

I started to dial DG, but stopped. He was in party mode. No way he saw the news. I called anyway.

"DG, indeed." he said.

"DG, it's Walt."

"You get the mud off your ass?"

"Yes. Listen, we gotta talk. It's an emergency."

"You're right!"

I didn't expect him to agree with me.

He continued, slurred, "Patty has gator bites on her butt and I need to kiss them away. And that I shall do with these royal, redneck lips. I'm already puckered up and, hey don't run…"

He hung up.

Couldn't call Ilsa, she was in Europe and didn't need the extra stress.

Tom, the inventor. He was a homebody. Good chance he saw it. But, his machine answered. Now, what?

A question bubbled up in my mind: What the hell was I going to do about this?

The pros and cons started to form...

Don't get involved, Walt.

I need to do it for Ken. For Teddy. For Ilsa. For...me.

They almost killed you before, many times, Walt.

But, they didn't succeed.

They're tough sons of bitches, Walt.

I proved to be pretty tough, too, didn't I?

You may survive them, but Ilsa will kill you for it, Walt.

What, with my charm? I'm a very persuasive person.

Despite your lucky heroics in the past, you're still just a lowly infomercial writer. Why not simply continue raking in the money and let others worry about it?

Because.

Ken's murder taught me a valuable lesson. Sitting on the sidelines was as bad as perching in the assassin's crosshairs. If they want to kill you they will. If you don't do something about it, they will. Most importantly, caring hurts if you're doing it right.

I hadn't answered the question. What the hell was I going to do about it?

I'm going to do what I always do. Make a pitch. Persuade someone to pay me in answers. And, work it from there.

The ugly truth crystalized in my mind's eye: This new development, this lead, was exactly what I had been wanting. A direction, any direction that would lead me to answers. To the truth. The trail was hot again. I couldn't let it slip away.

What was that reporters name? Geraldique?

4

A call to News 12 proved fruitless. They couldn't connect me to Geraldique. I considered driving down to Tampa, but figured it best to wait until morning when I was fresh and not wiped out from messing around in a mud pit.

Sleep was lousy. Adrenaline rush had zapped all relaxation benefits the alcohol would have provided. I was up before eight, and the first thing I did was step on Tanjeris' ring.

My heel was still tender when I arrived at DG's, now clean, fed, and swollen-eyed. Getting inside his house was always tricky because he had armed bikers standing guard at all times. It was a necessity due to the business he was in—crime. However, security had become top priority after the Gagnon executioners blew up his house a few months back. It had been rebuilt in short order. But, you couldn't just go up and ring the doorbell.

Although, it did help to be a recognizable face. The biker guards on duty had fond memories of me slipping into the mud pit last night. How much of a threat could I be after looking so silly? They waved me in with a smile and a pat on the back.

DG was awake, in the kitchen, and trying to make a sandwich with two pieces of toast and four eggs over medium.

"You're up early," I said.

"Didn't sleep," he said.

"I slept like shit."

"You look like shit."

"Because I'm tired as hell."

"Speed? Pick you up."

He held out a small, quaint tea tin. Tea wasn't what was inside it.

"Thanks. I had coffee."

"That's what it's for. Sprinkle it in."

He gave the tin a shake.

"I'm good."

He shrugged and set the tin on the counter.

"Let me know when your coffee wears off."

"Okay."

"Are you back for the gators or the girls?" he said with a smirk just before chomping onto his four-egg sandwich. Yolks squeezed out of the toast, through his fingers, and into the hairs of his forearm.

"Neither. Look, we gotta talk..."

"'Bout?' He set the sandwich down, pulled a towel off the oven handle, and wiped his arm.

"The morgue," I said.

He held two hands around his cup of speed-laced coffee, sipped it, and savored it like a thousand different moms in coffee commercials. The only thing he was missing was the fluffy pink bathrobe.

"Go on," he said with a salacious smirk as he leaned against the counter.

"Know anyone who works there?" I said.

He looked at me odd, no longer celebrating the moments of his life.

"What the fuck for, Walt? And, cut to the chase." DG could be an impatient friend. It was a strength and a weakness.

"There was something on the news last night."

"I didn't see it," he said, interrupting.

"I know. That's why I'm telling you. Would you listen?" I said. DG responded best to tough talk. "Channel 12, last night. Story about a semi-truck trailer full of people. Looked like immigrants. Mexican, I presume."

"Sounds like a party," he said and raised his mug in salute.

"They were all dead," I said.

He lowered his mug, less enthused. "What'd they say on the news?"

"Nothing. They promoted the story. But, then there was no story."

"You lost me," he said. "There was or was not a story on the news about a truck full of dead Mexicans?"

"They said the story was coming up but they never ran it. Why would they do that?"

DG appeared flummoxed, caught between sleep and his speed kick-in.

"And, why would there be a truck full of dead Mexicans on the side of I-275?" I said.

"Illegals, like you said. Being shipped," he said. "Trafficking. Happens all the time."

"They get shipped by tractor trailer and end up dead on the side of the road?" I said.

He set his mug on the counter and studied me. Like he was sizing up my ability to handle what he was going to say next.

"Every business...sometimes inventory gets damaged," he said.

That had to be the coldest, most inhumane statement I had ever heard.

"DG, are you serious?" I said.

"Entirely."

"Those are people!"

"Absolutely. But, what you need to understand is this: To the people who own that truck...they're product. They either make them money or cost them money. That's all."

I wasn't naive. But, the thought was revolting. That wasn't what was important right now.

"Where you going with this?" DG said.

"The bodies had symbols branded on them." I held up the Kith ring. "This symbol."

DG took and studied it.

"This from Jax?" he said.

Jacksonville. Where the bad times with with Tanjeris went down.

"Yes," I said. "Same ring. Same symbol on the body. On TV."

"No thanks," he said, then slapped the ring back into my hand.

"What?"

He snapped quick and pushed his fist into my chest.

"They jacked me up bad. And, I am just now getting my shit back together."

"Believe me. I don't want you involved. I just need to see the people at the morgue," I said.

"Living or dead?"

"Living. If you know someone--"

"Why?"

"The bodies from the truck should be there now. I need to make one hundred-percent sure I saw what I saw then see if I can find out anything else. But, I need you to get me in. That's it."

"No way."

"They blew up your house and killed your men. You hate these guys as much as I do," I said. Then, I leaned in for the kicker. "And, it drives you crazy knowing there's a big-time underground operator in the state that you know absolutely nothing about."

He simmered.

"You're a good goddamn salesman, Walt."

"I know." I pulled out my keys. "I'll be waiting in the car."

5

"The hell's a kith?"

"You know how you have kin?"

"My kin are solid," said DG.

"It's like that. But with people who aren't blood. Just bonded by belief," I said.

"Belief ain't as strong as blood."

"Just listen. I don't know their real name. But, they're still functioning and people are still dying. It didn't stop with Tanjeris."

We were in my car, driving down to Tampa. DG was studying Tanjeris' ring.

"I seen a lot of gang symbols, but never this," he said.

"I'm sure it has some meaning." I turned on to Bushnell Road in Florida City. Small, pretty town.

"Maybe sex trafficking is all it is," said DG. "You've heard stories like that. How them billionaires who own islands have sex parties and they ship in all kinds of people for their rich friends."

"Never heard of them dumping the bodies by the dock afterwards," I said.

"They're not gonna advertise it. Could be what that Kith is doing. God, I feel stupid just saying that!"

DG dropped the ring into a cup holder.

Beams of sunlight flickered through the trees that hung over the tight, two-lane highway. A clunky old Chevrolet pickup rambled past.

"I met guys who deal in trafficking," he said. "They snatch 'em, hook 'em on horse, maybe something cheaper to cut costs, and put 'em on the circuit. That circuit covers the entire state. A week in Sarasota, couple weeks in Lauderdale, and so on. They move the girls so no one gets attached and the customers don't get bored." he said.

"You sure know a lot about it."

"You know my work takes me into interesting territories. I see lots of things."

"And, you think this truck was delivering to the circuit?" I said.

"Be my guess," he said. "They're some bad dudes, Walt. If I had a daughter, I wouldn't let her out of my sight," he said.

"You probably have fourteen daughters who have never been in your sight." I couldn't resist.

"*En guard,*" he said and pointed at me.

"You mean *touché.*"

"Right. But, the joke's on you. I ain't getting involved after today."

"Fine by me." My neck stiffened as Dead Teddy flashed through my mind. "To be honest, I don't want to get involved. Life's been good. I don't need the hassle again. I just want to get enough info to pass it along to someone with more resources than I have. Someone who can stop all of them this time."

"I do appreciate your earnest desire to make things right. You're a good man," said DG. "Dumb sometimes, very dumb, but good. Your buddy Ken rubbed off on you."

I didn't quite know how to react to that. But, okay.

The Interstate 75 overpass appeared in the distance. Beyond that, stood the small town of Bushnell.

"If the news killed the story, think the police will kill the investigation?" DG said.

I didn't like that idea one bit.

"You know these people have deep connections. They're dangerous," he said.

"We either pass the information along or get involved," I said.

We reached the I-75 on ramp. I flipped on the turn signal.

"Well, we got time to think about it," he said, casual.

"What? We're an hour away from Tampa."

"It's Sunday. Morgue's closed."

I flipped off the blinker and swerved hard out of the turn lane. The minivan behind me screeched in panic.

God dammit.

6

My mind was made up. Before returning to DG's, I decided to drop him off and leave town again. I was too restless to sit alone in the river house. So, I figured I'd give myself plenty of time to think with a nice, long drive.

"You'll want to speak to Coroners Al Trotter and Jeremiah Lo. Respectively," DG said as if it was the most natural fact in the world to have at the top of mind.

"You don't even have to look it up?"

"My work takes me into interesting terri—"

"Yeah, yeah. Give me their numbers," I said.

DG had exhausted me.

Back on the road. I took the Turnpike and called both coroners' offices. No answers, messages left on the off chance they were in today. Wasn't unreasonable to think a semi-truck full of corpses would trigger some overtime.

As disappointed as I was not to go to Tampa earlier, I was relieved DG wasn't with me. It was so natural to ask him for help and bring him along. But, that was contrary to keeping other people out of it. No collateral damage. Not this time.

If I wasn't brave enough to pursue the Kith myself, then I needed to just let it be. That was the litmus test. It was fine for me to do a little snooping on the sly. As much as a non-detective infomercial writer can. I just couldn't do anything dumb to draw the bad guys attention. And, if things started to look dangerous, get the hell out. Pass the information along and disappear back into the peace and quiet of river life. *Deal? Deal.*

My new destination was West Palm Beach. Four and a half hours away. I wanted to see Ken Kerenz's kids. The boys had been orphaned by violence several months ago. Their father's murder started my journey towards discovering the Kith. Their mother, Karen, had been one of the participants behind it. And, I let her pay for it. Did I feel guilty? No. It would have been worse to let those kids continue living with her. She and Tanjeris had a sex slave for god's sake.

Even as she pleaded with me in the last few moments of her life, I got the sense Karen didn't care all that much about her children. She'd had her sights set on a new, elite world where dreams came true for those willing to create a few nightmares. She was a murderer who got what she deserved. But, I couldn't say that to the kids if they asked what happened to their mom. So, I was hoping the topic wouldn't come up.

I remembered watching them play with Ken in the Rainbow River, paddling boards past my backyard. They loved him and he adored them. I wanted to do my part to ensure Ken's positive spirit remained in their lives as a guiding light. It did in mine.

"How's my favorite Dutch lover?" I said, answering the phone.

"Favorite? You have more than one?"

That's my Ilsa.

I wasn't quite to Orlando when she called. It was late afternoon Netherlands time.

"Absolutely. There's regular you. And, feisty you. And, frisky you. And..."

"Okay, enough. We're paying international rates, weirdo."

"How's your mom?"

Her words came out in a sigh. "Not good, Walt. The end is near."

"Sounds like you should be wearing an apocalyptic sandwich board sign," I said.

"Don't joke," she said in a flat tone.

"Just keeping it light. You can't keep all that stress wound up inside."

"There isn't much I can do for her. She seems to have made peace with her time."

"Too bad we all can't do that while we're young."

"She is handling it with grace, despite the pain."

"How much longer, you think?" I said, not wanting to sound anxious for her mother to die. But, I did miss Ilsa. She'd been overseas nearly two months. I flew over for a quick visit a couple weeks ago. If I only had to worry about my writing work, I could have stayed and helped. But, the bar business needed supervision.

"A few days or a few weeks says the doctor," she said.

Ilsa was no bullshitter. She'd prefer silence instead of hollow platitudes. I kept quiet.

"Did you make the most of your night off living like a bachelor?" she said.

I had to measure my response. I didn't want her to know anything about my looking into the Kith. But, I didn't want to lie either. So, I only told her what she'd approve of: "I watched female mud wrestling in DG's alligator pit."

""I'm sure you loved it," she said.

"I'd rather wrestle with you."

"Put it on our 'to do' list."

Man, she didn't even hesitate. God, I loved her.

"I'm driving to West Palm to check on Ken's kids," I said.

"Kiss their foreheads for me," she said.

"I'll probably just tell them you said 'hi' and wish 'em well."

"Hmmm."

A weird thought hit me. Here I was preparing to dig into bad business again. And, if things went wrong, I could slip off beyond the blue horizon in time to welcome Ilsa's mother to the other side.

"I love you, Ilsa."

"Where'd that come from," she said.

"My heart. I love you like crazy. No matter what happens."

Shit.

"What do you mean?" she said, already sounding suspicious.

"With your mom, I mean."

""Well, we know what's going to happen, Walt."

"True," I said.

"I love you, too," she said.

"Kiss your mom on the forehead for me," I said.

"Okay. I'll call you tomorrow."

It's a special kind of lonely when the person you love most in the world is on the other side of it.

7

West Palm Beach, you crowded, crazy, heathen with your balmy breezes. I cut across town and over to the beach and the house where Ken's kids were now living. It belonged to their grandfather, Oren, Karen's father. It was a spacious home in a well-appointed, gated neighborhood. A bit much for my taste. And, Ken's taste. But, the kids were safe here. I rang the doorbell. The boys, Kelvin and Kory, reached the door first and opened it.

"Are you taking us to the river?" said Kory. He was trembling with excitement.

"I just came from there. Tried to bring it with me, but it wouldn't fit in the car," I said.

"You'd get all wet," said Kelvin.

"As soon as it starts to warm up again, let's get you guys up there. I'll toss you both in the river just like I'm throwing out the trash. Then, *you'll* get all wet."

They laughed and that made the entire drive worth it.

"Want to see our new pool?" said Kory.

"Let's check it out," I said.

A woman appeared in the hallway and walked over to us. She looked like Palm Beach personified—a healthy glow, stunning figure, and fine threads. A natural beauty with effortless style. I estimated early twenties. She looked like she could handle any man of any age or stature.

Her bright smile contrasted against the dull dishtowel she slapped over her shoulder.

"Hi, Walt," she said.

I nodded. "Indeed."

19

"Nice to meet you. I'm Gale," she said.

I shook her soft hand.

Kory tapped me. "She's our nanny."

"Hands off, Asher. She promised to marry us," said Kelvin.

I gave a surprised look.

She blushed and laughed.

"Don't worry. I'm already attached. You remember Ilsa, right?" I said.

The boys nodded.

Gale balled a fist on her hip and pointed up the stairs. "I'm calling off the wedding if your rooms don't get cleaned up right away."

Kelvin shook his head and looked at me. "Already nagging. But, I love her."

My laugh echoed down the marble foyer. Now, that was funny.

"Go clean. Now," said Gale.

The boys plodded up the stairs less than enthusiastic.

"Good kids, even if they are a little sexist," I said.

"I'll break 'em of that habit," she said. "Come in. Oren's around the corner. Would you like a drink? You had a long drive."

"Sure. Water, whatever."

Gale led me into a vast living room. It had a stunning view overlooking the Atlantic Ocean. She pointed out Karen's father, Oren, who was sitting on the couch watching an old history program. The décor was Native American inspired—spears, a wall tapestry, even a framed scalp?

"Hi, Mr. Denner," I said.

Oren glanced over and smiled. He was looking weaker than when I'd last seen him. Losing his son-in-law and daughter had taken its toll. Good thing he didn't know what his daughter-in-law had been up to. That would have killed him.

"Hello, Walter. Good to see you." He started to get up but I waved him back down and shook his hand.

"All well?" I said.

"As well as can be. The children are doing alright, which is what matters most."

"True." I looked to make sure they were still out of earshot. "They ever ask about their parents?"

"Oh, here and there. I think they unload most of those questions on their therapist."

"That's a good thing," I said.

He nodded.

"Gale seems nice," I said.

"She's a godsend," he said.

"Talking about me?" said Gale, now at my side and offering a bottle of water. Cold, but dry on the outside. Wiped down. Courteous. Class. I took it and drank.

Oren waved his crooked forefinger at her. "Neighbor's daughter. Rance Williams. Good guy. Know him from the country club."

"I didn't know you golfed," I said.

He waved me off. "That dumb game? Please. I'm just a social member."

"Never could get into it myself," I said.

"She was gonna go up to Harvard, study international finance and wealth management. But, we talked her out of that."

"When I learned the kids needed help…I just couldn't go."

"Cambridge is a great town," I said. I'd spent plenty of time in the Boston area.

"We're paying her way through U.M.," said Oren.

Gale revealed a hint of embarrassment.

"I study when the kids are at school. And presuming I graduate, the idea is for me to manage the kids' finances and affairs, after you know..." she said, nodding over at Oren. She was implying his death.

"So, you're like a nanny deluxe," I said with a smile.

"I suppose so."

The boys rumbled down the stairs, ready to play.

The day went fast. I hopped in the pool with the boys. My visit seemed to help everyone forget about Ken and Karen. I was grateful for that. Grateful I could make even a small difference in their lives.

I felt reassured that the boys were going to be fine. They had an environment where they could thrive. They were surrounded by people who loved them. And, they had enough money in the bank to follow their dreams. And, if all else failed, I'd watch their backs.

I finished drying off from the pool, clothes back on, when I felt the phone in my pocket. Two calls from numbers I didn't recognize, both 813 area codes. I checked my voicemail. Two messages from two coroners, both saying the same thing.

No truckload of bodies was ever delivered to their offices.

8

The car was pushing ninety miles per hour.

Cop.

Behind the cluster of pine trees in the highway median. My foot leapt off the accelerator. But, I just tapped the brake. Stomping it too hard would have been a dead giveaway I was speeding.

"Shit."

I gripped the wheel, glanced at the mirrors; my shoulders crawled up my neck.

The cop stayed put. No ticket this time.

I exhaled deep and continued along the flat stretch of westbound Interstate 4, south of Lakeland.

I had zoned off and wasn't paying enough attention to the road. But, I just couldn't believe what I'd heard in my voice mail. If the truck full of bodies hadn't arrived at either the Hillsborough or Pasco county coroner's offices...where could it possibly have gone? Polk and Pinellas counties were too far away, not jurisdiction.

In my heart, I knew what had really happened. No truck, no bodies, no problem. It had become a phantom. Classic Kith. They tried to do the same thing to me. Flip the police from protectors to pursuers and use the media to flush out my location. If they could harness all those resources to make me disappear, there was no reason they couldn't make the truck and the bodies disappear.

These creeps had juice with the cops and the television stations. I had to presume they were entrenched deep in those businesses. Their police reps would be high-ranking administrators, not beat patrol cops. They'd be station managers and executive producers, not field reporters. And, they were always on call, poised to eliminate problems like unsavory stories that might embarrass their members. Or worse, bring their organization out of the shadows. Indeed, remaining secret was their strongest source of power. They would protect their identity at all costs.

Sure makes me sound like a paranoid lunatic. But, the ring in my pocket was proof. And, if I could find that truck and report it anonymously to several entities, then maybe it couldn't be covered up. Maybe. That was the most I could reasonably expect to accomplish. And, that was fine. Good citizen work.

I was so dumb. Of course no big truck full of dead bodies showed up at the morgue. I had seen them wheeling the bodies off separately. So, if all the police shows I'd ever watched were right, the truck would have been taken to wherever the police store case evidence. Duh.

But, I would never get in to see it. What police officer, crooked or not, would allow that to happen? Evidence was protected to prevent tampering. To see anything, I would need credentials. Requesting credentials would put me on the radar. Too dangerous. Find another way.

The Tampa skyline appeared orange and glimmering on the horizon. The sun was setting over the Gulf of Mexico in the distance beyond the small cluster of skyscrapers.

I needed a witness. Who knew the most about what was going on besides the people who were trying to prevent everyone from knowing what was going on? Who was at the scene and could talk about what went down?

9

"I have no authorization to let you in, sir."

The security guard was standing arms akimbo behind the monitor-filled front desk. Big sucker. He looked like he enjoyed tearing heads off for sport. His voice echoed throughout the large, marble foyer of Channel 12 Studios, Himes Avenue, across the street from Raymond James Stadium, where the Bucs were currently playing. The game was on the monitor the guard kept glancing at.

"Can you get him on the phone?" I asked.

"No, sir. I'm going to have to ask you to leave, please."

He looked past me. I followed his gaze over to a Florida Highway Patrol officer standing near the far wall. Eye contact, nods.

Only one option left. Sell him.

"Well, I'm an infomercial guru he was hoping to do a story on. I agreed to come down here, at this late hour mind you, to interview with him."

No reaction.

"You know the commercials you see on television late at night?"

He gave the slightest of nods.

I gave an enthusiastic one. "Yeah, that's me. That's my work. You've probably seen..."

The FHP officer didn't so much release me as he shoved me away like I was carrying a plague. We were outside the studio.

"We've been patient with you so far, sir," he said.

"Kind of you to escort me out," I said.

"Get in your car and leave before there's a problem. Understand?"

The stadium across the street exploded with cheering.

"I do," I said as I pulled keys out of my pocket. I found the key fob and unlocked the car. It bleeped. The officer clearly wasn't going to leave until I did.

"Shame about that truck full of dead bodies, huh?" I said.

"Excuse me?" he said.

It was on the news. I gestured to the building.

"I missed that report."

"Oh," I said. I studied his face to see if he was covering up. It was like studying a rock for feelings. Nothing.

What now, 'detective'?

Four hours and a stomach bloated with fast food later, I saw my man. Geraldique's Chevy Acer pulled out of the gated studio parking lot and merged into stadium traffic driving south on Himes. I followed.

He didn't appear to be in any hurry. I presumed he was off the clock. Geraldique sped past the tailgaters down to Cypress Street, which he took all the way across the Hillsborough River into downtown Tampa.

Ten minutes later we were on foot. He was a block ahead of me. I had an idea where he was going.

The Hub was hopping, as it does most nights, considering it was one of Tampa's greatest dive bars. Smokey, dingy, and loud. A big circular bar with a very active bartender.

Geraldique was on the far side of the room, near the darts and the darkness. The gleam of his tumbler gave him away. He finished his drink in one shot.

I took the seat next to him and waited for the bartender to look my way.

"Don't worry, he'll see you," Geraldique said.

"Good to know," I said. Then the double take. "Hey, you're the guy from television, aren't you?"

He nodded.

"Reporter, right? Channel 12," I said.

He stuck his hand out for shaking, "Geraldique Tremain."

"Walt Asher. Good to meet you."

"Likewise," he said.

"Whatcha drinking?" said the bartender.

My standard drink is a Boulevardier. I suspected he knew how to make one. But, probably a bit fancy for this place.

"G&T," I said.

"What Gin?" he said.

"Boodles?"

He shook his head. "That's for the old schoolers."

"Sapphire."

He nodded and waddled off to work his magic.

I turned back to Geraldique and said, "I saw you reporting the other night. Crazy story. The one with the truck on the side of the road."

He sipped his whiskey.

"That was some fucked up shit," he said. He was off the clock and out of his reporter character. Even better, no denial.

"Oh?"

"I didn't get the final tally. But, I counted fifty-four bodies getting pulled out," he said. "And, they had already started unloading before I got there."

My astonishment was interrupted by the bartender. He set my drink down.

"Tab?" he said.

I nodded, took the drink, and turned on my seat to face Geraldique.

"You have my complete attention," I said.

"Wasn't much more to it than that."

"What do you think happened?"

He killed his second drink and shrugged and got up. Wallet out. He looked dejected. "Who the hell knows?" he said as he tossed the bills on the bar, saluted me, and moved to leave.

I grabbed his arm. He looked at my hand then me like was I crazy?

I released. "Sorry. It's just such an insane story. I'm curious to know more."

"Ain't much more to know. They unloaded the truck, drove it off, took the bodies away, and that's that."

"Where'd they take 'em?" I said.

He shrugged. Who knew?

"You didn't follow—Are you guys doing a follow up story?"

"I was about to, but I got a call from the station manager. Had a different story for me."

Interesting. And, I doubted a coincidence.

"Aren't you curious to find out what's going on with it? I mean fifty some dead people..."I said.

He shook his head. "No. I just go where they say to go."

"Wouldn't a story like that generate huge ratings? Kind of odd your boss re-assigned you.

He made a curious expression.

"Huh. Hadn't thought of that."

But, he carried the thought no further. This was the least investigative reporter I'd ever seen. I stood up, getting irritated.

"You went on the air and shocked the whole West Coast of Florida with a truck full of dead people on the side of the road. And, now you don't even care what happened? Don't you want to see who or what's behind—"

Something stopped me.

I realized what it was as I looked into his eyes. He was just an innocent guy doing his job. Reporting the news he was told to report. And, here I was trying to enlist him.

Just like Teddy.

"You finished, man?" he said, sounding aggravated.

I dropped down on my stool. My gaze drifted over to a neon Pabst Blue Ribbon sign. I nodded, still bewildered.

"Shit," he said and strutted out of there.

10

Geraldique killed the story. Scratch that. His boss did, the station manager. Didn't get his name. Was he worth pursuing? I stewed on that for a moment. My gut told me 'no.' He might have information, but that would put me too close to the radar.

A full day of stress and driving had me wiped out. The hour and a half trek up to the river house seemed daunting. So, I had set course for my place in Clearwater, just on the other side of Tampa Bay. It was where I stay when I'm in town hanging with the kids or working on infomercial productions.

Ever since Home Shopping Network started there back in the late Seventies, St. Petersburg/Clearwater (as they are commonly linked) has been Infomercial, USA. And, if you get close enough to the action, it sucks you in. That's what happened to me. And, I couldn't be happier about it.

Wait.

I was going the wrong way.

Instead of heading south on I-275 towards the bridges and beach, I was heading north towards the edge of Tampa. While I had been lost in thought, my subconscious set the course.

It didn't look like a crime scene anymore. No yellow tape, nothing cordoned off. No cops, no bodies, no truck. No one passing along this part of the interstate would have fathomed the atrocity parked here the night before. But, I recognized it from the news and its proximity to the Highway 56 overpass.

Road gravel crackled under my tires. Traffic whipped past.

It looked like any other easement off a major highway. Dirt, rock, trash, glistening glass shards, and weeds leading down into a grass covered ditch. My footsteps kicked up swirls of road dust. The scene brightened and darkened with the passing cars.

A set of large tire tracks. A scattering of footprints nearby. Then, thin wheel tracks, from gurneys. An echo of the previous evening's clean up effort.

I stood still and took it all in, waiting for something to jump out. I needed to keep this lead hot. A panel van raced past, its drift blew my hair. I squatted and let the light from my phone illuminate details across the ground. Nothing dropped, discarded or lost.

Made sense. The cops would have scoured every inch of the area. And if the cops didn't, the crooks behind it all would have.

I stood and walked the twenty feet past where the front of the truck had been and back. And, then again.

There.

Weeds and grass were matted down. The grass was green and hadn't withered into a brown, crunchy husk. It was recent. There was another imprint two feet further. Then another. Footprints forming a trail into the ditch and up the other side towards a cluster of woods.

At the edge of the trees was an opening in the brush. The footprints stopped at a broken twig just inside the opening. My guess: The truck's driver ran this way. It was the closest, fastest escape. And, a dead end. But, I was too tired to feel frustrated.

I turned to the highway. Traffic whizzed by. People talked, texted, drummed their steering wheel to music. Their cars whisked them through this weird world. I was ready to get back to my part of it.

First step down the ditch bank and I landed on my ass. At my feet was an old, plastic soda cup. Like most things in Florida, its colors were faded by days spent under the harsh sun. But, I could still read the logo printed on the flattened packaging: Flying J truck stop.

That gave me an idea.

11

The Flying J truck stop was six miles north up I-75. Dade City exit. Aileen Wuornos' old turf, as I recalled. Won't find that in the tourist guidebook. I circled the parking lot twice before pulling into a vacant space, where I sat and took in the scene.

The place was hopping. Tourists hurried in and out of the convenience store. Truckers moseyed around. Cars, trucks, and RVs were gathered under the tall sodium lights.

I was reminded of my childhood and playing the license plate game on road trips with my parents. No time for that tonight. I was looking for a truck.

I didn't believe the Flying J cup I had seen by the roadside belonged to the driver of the body truck. And, I didn't believe the body truck would be here. I did believe, and hoped, someone here might recognize the truck if I described it. Perhaps they could let me know where it came from or where it was going. Shit, it was all I had to go on.

I walked inside the convenience store and bought a bottle of water. As the clerk rang my order up I considered asking if she had seen the truck. But, she looked annoyed and the line of anxious patrons was growing behind me.

A retired couple, which I silently named Gladys and Harold, rushed in the door before letting me out. A scruffy dog barked on the front seat of a dumpy Camaro. A trucker belched.

Dozens of semis filled the lot ahead. More swarmed in and out in almost continuous fashion. Some of the truck cabs were dark and empty. Others had people tooling about under the dim ceiling light inside. A trucker turned his light off and closed a privacy curtain leading to the back of the cab.

I spotted a trucker sitting behind the wheel, door open, a map spread across his lap.

"Evening," I said.

He sized me up over smudged, thick-lensed glasses.

"Help you?" he said.

I pegged him in his early sixties, a lifer. He had one of those enormous bellies that protrude at such a distinct angle it looks like it was hung on a skinny man by two hooks over the shoulders. His black suspenders stretched and bent in odd arcs over and around it.

"I was hoping you might be able to tell me the name of a company for a certain type of truck."

His expression made clear he thought the question odd and perhaps, pointless.

He shrugged, "Maybe."

He didn't say 'no'. That was good.

"Well, it's a green truck, not a flat front, but you know with the long...snout," I said, mangling the trucker terminology.

"An 'aardvark'," he said.

"Yes."

"You're gonna have to narrow it down, son," he said.

"White lettering on the sides?" I said. I realized I could barely describe what the truck looked like. Did it have the Society symbol on it? I couldn't remember. I only knew for sure that I had seen the symbol on the arm that fell from under the gurney sheet.

"It might have had a symbol on the side of it like a--"

He interrupted, "You're better off talking to her."

He pointed past me to a middle-aged woman stepping out of the passenger door of a parked tractor-trailer. She clop-clopped in chunky heels over to the convenience store.

"Who's that," I said.

"Oh...she works here. Probably the most familiar with what trucks drive in and out," he said.

"Thanks."

I hurried over towards the woman in an effort to catch her before she entered the store.

"Excuse me," I said from a distance. I waved her way.

She glanced my way and appeared to speed up, not wanting to be bothered.

"Hey, can I talk to you for a moment?"

"Easy, buddy. This ain't the best spot for it," she said. "I gotta hit the little girls' room."

She yanked open the door and went inside.

I hovered next to the magazine rack. This month's issue of Backyard Chicken didn't call to me, so I picked up a copy of Black Belt magazine and skimmed. Chuck Norris retrospective, an ad for a newer, better throwing star, and Top 5 quick strike moves. In that short span, I went from thinking this magazine was a relic from the early 80s to thinking I might need to read it given my current pursuit.

She was taking forever. Had I missed her coming out when I glanced at the Roundhouse Kick How-To Pictorial? I set the magazine down and peeked around the next two aisles. The ladies room door swung open. She appeared, saw me, looked annoyed, and walked my way.

"Come on," she said without breaking stride.

I saw her pocket a warm Mountain Dew from a soda pallet and slip fast out the door. I followed her over to a picnic table and benches set up a few feet from the truck wash. There was just enough light to see the basic details of each other's faces.

She sat on the table, feet on the bench.

"Open this," she said.

I took the soda from her and twisted off the cap. She took it back, swigged it, set it down. "Got smokes?"

"No," I said.

She shook her head and pulled out a crumpled pack of off-brand cigarettes from her purse. She lit one, inhaled, exhaled. The smoke was backlit by the high light attached to the outside of the tuck wash.

"So?" she said. She rested back on her arms as if she might stay a while. But, her face showed impatience.

"I need to ask you about a truck. A semi," I said.

"You mean, what you want me to do to you in a truck. My eleven o'clock's gonna be rolling in soon. I can stall him for a few as long as you can be quick. Real quick. But, we gotta cut to the chase. Where'd you park?"

I laughed, nervous and awkward.

She took another puff and seemed more relaxed now that the scope of the encounter had been established.

"I'm not looking for sex," I said.

"The hell we talkin' for then? If I'm off the cock, I'm off the clock. And, that don't pay."

She stepped down from the table and dusted the back of her shorts, cig dangling from lips.

"I need to know if you've seen a certain truck," I said.

"Well, two problems. One, I seen hundreds of trucks everyday. They all kinda blend together. And the other, I mostly just see the insides."

She cocked her hips.

"I'm sorry, I didn't get your name. I'm Walt."

"I'm Love-Mart," she said, a sly smile on her face. "Everything you need. Always low prices."

She sex pitched out of habit. The light hit her face and I caught a glimpse of the cute kid she must have been. What went wrong? Maybe things had actually gone right. You never know.

"Okay. Love-Mart, I'll wrap this up. Have you seen any semi trucks that are green, aardvark front, white lettering on the side, and maybe a--"

"Weird symbol on the side?" she said.

"You know it?"

"Uh, yeah. Not it, them,"

"There's more than one?"

"See 'em all over the state. And, I'm not messin' with them ever again. You shouldn't either."

She moved to leave. I grabbed her wrist.

"Love...Mart, I need to know the name of the company on that truck."

"Why?"

"It's important."

"But, why?"

"They're into some bad stuff. I've dealt with them before and I'm trying to stop them."

"You a cop? I really hope you're not..."

I shook my head and released her wrist.

"They messed with me in the past. I'm...considering messing with them," I said.

"You ain't kidding. They're evil. Tried to kidnap me once. I had to slash the guy's arm with my blade and jump out of a truck rolling down the Interstate. That's how I got this," she said, pointing to an ugly scar along the back of her right thigh, all the way up inside her very short shorts.

"I believe that," I said. "Do you remember the name of the truck company?"

A truck rolled up and hissed to a stop ten feet from us. The passenger window rolled down and the burly trucker inside leaned out, leering.

"Go ahead and park, baby. I'll be there in two shakes," she said to the trucker.

I looked away, not wanting to be introduced.

When I heard the gears shift and the truck rumble off, I turned back to Love-Mart who was getting up, again dusting off her backside.

"Do you know the name of the trucking company?" I said again, worried she was going to leave me hanging.

She looked down at me. She was all business again.

"What's in it for me?" she said.

I checked my pockets. "I don't have any cash on me."

She shrugged and I thought she was going to take off, so I spoke fast. "But, I can help get your prices up."

"Mean what I charge?" She looked her most skeptical. It spoke to deep-down self-doubt.

"I'm in sales."

"Go on," she said as she looked over my shoulder, at her waiting john's truck, I presumed.

"First, you gotta go in knowing that if those guys have money to load up on half gallon sodas, heart-clogging sausages, audiobooks, booze, and coffee, they have cash to pay for what I can only imagine are your fantastic services."

She smiled, flattered.

"If you know that, then you won't fall for their hard luck money sob stories," I said.

I could see the epiphany blooming in her eyes. "Good point."

I continued, "Are you clean? You know..."

She struggled with giving an affirmative answer. "As far as they know."

"Keep it that way and remind them of that. That's a selling point. Tell them the other girls aren't."

"There ain't no other girls here."

"Good. You have exclusivity. If they don't want to pay your higher prices, they can move on down the road. But, by the time they're talking with you, they're probably already settling in here, yes?."

"I never thought of that." She looked bewildered, inspired. "But, what if they haggle? I can't really afford to say no."

"Then, you do two things. First, you tell them the price is based on experience and you have tons of it," I said.

"How'd you know that?" she said with genuine surprise.

"Just a guess. Then, you say, 'But if you don't want to feel what it's like to...' I gestured for her to fill in the blank. It took a beat, but she got it.

"You mean, I should say 'If you don't want to feel these soft lips sliding up and down that hot meat. Or, you don't want to slide it deep in my—'"

"You got the idea. Walk them along, give them a glimpse of their sex-filled future," I said.

She nodded and looked the happiest I suspected she had been in a long, long time.

"Wow, that's brilliant. You think it'll make me more money?"

"I guarantee it. I use those same tactics every day on television."

"You'd make a great hooker," she said, and patted my shoulder.

First time I had been told that.

"Thanks," I said. "Now, can you give me the name of the trucking company?"

She pointed past me.

"There's one's leaving now."

A truck just like the one I had seen on television was exiting the parking lot. And, it had the Kith symbol on it.

12

I couldn't understand what she was yelling. My eyes were locked on the truck and my heart was pounding in my ears as I ran to my car. The truck had stopped at the exit waiting for traffic to break, ready to pull out. I had a chance.

Keys out of the pocket, hands shaking, keys dropped. I scooped them up. The truck pulled into traffic. It wasn't two hundred feet to the interstate. My lead would be lost if I couldn't follow it.

I dropped into the car, turned the ignition, and ripped into reverse. Honk.

I stopped hard. My bumper inches from a bumper sticker-covered junker with an irate driver yelling at me. He shook his fist. I yanked the car into drive and floored it and swerved around a truck pulling a horse trailer. Parents yanked their kids back onto the sidewalk as I raced past. Their slushy drinks spilled. "Oh, man!" one said.

Damn!

A car cut me off at the exit. Geezers in a Chrysler Beige Bland. The cotton-topped couple was Florida's state bird.

Honk! One, two, three and held it. They startled and their startling made them stop and look around to see who was honking. Like it couldn't possibly be at them. I cut around them onto the main road. Look both ways? Please.

A loud honk-honk-honk startled me. Semi truck lights blasted my eyes via rearview mirror. Flat front, not an aardvark.

My truck was just ahead in the turn lane to get on the interstate. Same direction the other one had been driving the night before. That might matter. The light turned red. I hoped for the truck to stop and wait for the next green light. Son of a bitch ran the red.

I accelerated. Traffic cut me off at the intersection. My tires screeched and stopped. I squinted. Shadows obscured the wording on the truck until it passed under a streetlight. The truck rumbled up the ramp and out of sight. But, I had seen what I needed to see:

Groveland Trucking

Bartow, FL

An eternal minute later, the light turned green. I gunned the car up the ramp and onto the interstate. Fifty, sixty, seventy...eighty miles per hour and pushing. I swerved across lanes and cut around cars. Up to ninety miles an hour now.

There was a cluster of semi trucks a hundred yards ahead. I closed the gap and cut between them. None were my truck. I looked all directions. Nothing. I passed an exit ramp. Had the truck gotten off there?

My car passed the roadside where the bodies had been found. The road forked just up ahead. To the left, I-75 continued south. Not quite to Bartow, but in that direction. To the right, I-275 snaked into Tampa.

I took I-75 and regretted it right away. Very little traffic up ahead. No semis to be seen. He couldn't have gotten that far ahead of me. He went the other way. The chase was over. For tonight.

13

I had a company name. I had a city. Wasn't much. But, it was enough to savor on the drive back to Clearwater.

The house was hot and stuffy. But, it was home and I was beat. What a strange, stressful, exhilarating day. I drank whiskey on ice in the shower and was amazed when I realized it hadn't even been twenty-four hours since I'd see the news promo about the mysterious truck. My bed felt like heaven.

I turned out the light, ready to forget everything and sleep. But, a minute later I was waiting for my eyes to adjust to the brightness of my phone screen. I pulled up the browser and punched in Groveland Trucking. A link to a website popped up. The site itself was unremarkable. It informed me that Groveland Trucking was "one of the Sunshine State's premier trucking companies, serving the entire state...and beyond!" Their specialty was agricultural shipping. Made sense. Groveland was in the heart of Florida orange country. There was a contact number. No contact name. Informative, but not revealing. No sign of the Kith. No Kith logo.

I woke up nine hours later feeling sore and groggy. An adrenaline hangover. Deep fatigue from the stress. Based on past experience, I'd need at least one more great night's sleep to fully recover.

But, that wasn't going to happen anytime soon. As I walked from the bedroom to the kitchen to get the coffee started, I found something that startled me out of my haze. Something terrifying.

A dead body on the couch.

I knew the face.

I knew the scar up the leg.

Love-Mart.

A chill hooked into me and I stopped breathing.

Her face was slashed. Her hands bruised and deformed like they'd been smashed with a hammer. A big one. She wore a necklace of crusted blood from ear to ear.

You poor thing.

She hadn't been there when I returned home last night. She wasn't there after my shower when I walked out to get a drink before bed.

She'd arrived during the night.

While I was sleeping.

A folded note was safety pinned to her lip. Miniature doilies of blood garnished the pin's entry and exit points. The paper had my name on it.

"Mr. Asher..."

I scanned the room. Doors and windows were locked and closed. Was someone here? I held still. The house was quiet. Birds chirped outside.

The note wafted in the breeze from the air vent above. I attempted to peel it open. No luck. Shit. This might get messy.

I pinched the paper and pulled, hoping to tear it from the pin. But, the pin pulled her lip. The willies hit. I was going to have to touch her.

The wood floorboards creaked under my feet as I steadied my weight against the couch. I pressed thumb and forefinger against her lip to hold it down and tore the note free.

The message inside was typed. Seven simple words:

STOP NOW OR WE WILL KILL YOU.

14

The world stopped. My lungs emptied as my stomach knotted up. The notecard fell from my fingers and landed softly on the kitchen floor.

Cold air hit my skin, hair, leg. I was still naked. Too vulnerable. I ran to the bedroom and threw on clothes. I grabbed my phone off the nightstand. Then, I grabbed a stun stick from deep in the closet, top shelf. I purchased it years ago. The marketing materials said just a touch would drop a man to the ground on contact. I hadn't been able to test it. And, it had been a couple years since I charged it.

The stick click-clacked out with a pull of the trigger. Electricity sizzled across its metal surface. Still charged.

I held out the stick and started searching rooms. Kid's room #1. I scanned around then focused on the closet. I slid the door open and swung the stick in. Nothing.

I nudged the shower curtain open with the stick. It melted the plastic liner where it touched. Hot, plastic stink stung my nostrils. No one was there.

And, so it was with the rest of the house. That almost made it worse. They weren't in my house. But, they were in my head.

How did they get in? How did I not hear it? How did they know I was home? I haven't been here for months. Did they follow me? Yes. They had to. From where? They knew about Love-Mart. Saw me talking to her. Wouldn't have been hard to get her to talk about our conversation. But, they had to have followed me to her. From the accident scene? Very possible. Where else had I gone?

Geraldique.

He reported the story. They knew he knew about it. They had to be watching him. They saw us talking.

A presumption: They'd kill him if they could. But, he was a television personality whose death would be noticed. Maybe. He was third tier at best. These guys were pros. They'd find a way to kill him and get away with it.

I had to presume they viewed my contact with Geraldique as no coincidence. And my continuing interest in them would have been proven further if they saw me chasing their truck out of the truck stop. So, they left me a warning.

A dark thought: Why didn't they just kill me? They had the chance. Why wait? A guess: They wanted to know what I know. Maybe they had seen what I'd done to Luther and Tanjeris and didn't want to confront me directly? Calm down, hot shot. You're not that intimidating. I couldn't find a good reason for them to wait. In their shoes, I'd have killed me.

So, now what?

They had to be watching me. Was my phone tapped? Was the house bugged? Mail being checked? Hidden cameras? I had to presume yes to all of the above.

I looked around the room. No way I could stay here. Paranoia sucks.

But, what would happen when I left? A car tail? They'd follow me on foot? Where would I go? It seemed logical to think they already had my River House under surveillance. I couldn't go to a friend's place. That would drag them into it.

My god. Just that small bit of snooping around and I've already gotten another person killed. Teddy and Love-Mart. This had to stop.

I felt stuck. Like my next move, no matter how slight, would trigger painful events. As if I would seal my fate and nothing I could say or do after that point would save me.

Then again...what if I dropped this whole secret society business? I'd be doing exactly what they asked. Wouldn't that mean I could leave, see friends, work, live my life? Business as usual. I'd be fine.

I'd never know for sure.

They could come for me once I let my guard down. Any day, night, or location. They weren't in the business of people knowing their business. They were in the business of tying up loose ends. Every single one of them. Being docile wouldn't guarantee my safety.

And, never being sure would drive me crazy.

It wasn't just the paranoia rankling my nerves. I hated being shut up. I hated being told what not to do. I hated not being able to persuade in my favor. That pressed my button. If you told me not to do something, you'd make me want to do it. If a client got on my ass about a deadline, I'd hit the brakes and their project would drop to last on my list. Never knew why. But, I've always been that way. These guys had just pressed *my* button.

After months of searching, I had a lead on them. Now, I had a decision to make. Was I going to obey these creeps who had killed my good friend to save myself some hassle? Or, was I going to bring that truck full of dead bodies to their doorstep and let them know it's time to pay? Seemed more than fair considering they'd just killed this poor girl and dropped her body on my couch. Tossed there like a television remote.

Ilsa would be pissed if I chose to go after them again, to stir old shit up. But, she was more than a thousand miles away. And, these guys were closing in.

Enough. In truth, I had no choice. Either they came after me or...I went after them.

15

"Yeah, I got ways to hide dead chicks. Of course."

DG said it as if I were asking if he'd ever heard of football.

"Okay, good. Take her there. Bury her. Maybe say a few words," I said.

"And, you didn't kill her. There just happened to be a dead hooker in your living room when you woke up this morning. While your wife is with her dying mother in Europe. Right..."

"DG, come on. This is serious. You need to go to my house, get her body, and get rid of her."

"That's cold, Walt."

"Do it nicely. But, do it fast."

I was in no mood to debate or have my balls busted. I had to get Love-Mart out of my house fast. If I could have done it myself, I would. But, I'd have been clueless where to take her. So with great reluctance, I called DG.

I needed him to move Love-Mart for two reasons: One, he'd know where to bury her where she'd never be found. Two, I had to pull the watchers away from my house for him to do it.

"You at the house now?" he said.

"No, pay phone," I said.

"They still have those?"

"I had to drive all the way to downtown St. Pete to find one."

"Why not just use your phone?"

"DG, they're following me. I bet my phone is tapped, too. They want to know what I know and what I'm doing."

"Makes sense."

I was relieved he agreed, but let's go. I was getting impatient.

"I'm at the payphone to pull them away from the house. I need you to take care of this while they're following me."

"I can't be down there for like two hours," he said.

"So, you'll do it?"

A long pause.

"Yeah. But, you owe me. Again," DG said.

"I paid you back last time."

He was reluctant to acknowledge I had saved his life and his entire criminal enterprise not that long ago.

"I'll call you when it's done."

That's what I needed to hear. DG could be trusted to take care of the body business in discreet fashion.

"No, I'll call you once I get a new phone. A disposable," I said.

"Save your money. I have about fifty burners in my desk, ready to go."

"That means we'd have to meet up. If they're following--"

"Fuck them. You think I don't do shit like this all the time?"

Good point.

"Give me 'til nine o'clock tonight. Then, meet me at Foster's in Gibsonton. It's on 41 before you cross the Alafaya," said DG.

I scanned the block. Ninth Street, across from the legendary Coney Island Hot Dog joint. No one in view looked suspicious. No one seemed to be watching me. I was sure that was by design.

"What if they follow me there?" I said.

"Lose 'em."

16

The basic street grid system and lack of people out and about made St. Pete a tough place to lose a tail. I stepped into stores, peered out windows, acted like I was lost. Quiller I was not. It took pretending to forget something in the car and making a quick turnaround to finally catch a glimpse of the car following me.

It was a Hyundai minivan painted forgettable brown. I recognized the curb scrapes in its front, passenger hubcap. The van had been parked in the Coney Island parking lot across from the pay phone where I called DG. That was back on the other side of town. Now, it was here. Too coincidental. It had to be them.

I walked the boardwalk. To my left, joggers, bikers, and moms with strollers passed in both directions. To my right, the seawall. It was about three feet high and ran along a patch of seaweed-covered beach exposed by the low tide.

I glanced again at the van. No action. But, I knew they were watching. So, I smiled right at them as I jumped off the seawall, onto the sand, and out of sight. I walked fast along the seawall back towards the park pavilion.

I wasn't stupid enough to think they'd come running in a panic just because I'd disappeared from sight. They knew my car was still there. But, I did want to confuse them enough so I could get to my car before they expected it. With luck, that would give me a few precious seconds to lose them on the nearby neighborhood streets.

I hurried past sunbathers, beach readers, and a pair of fishermen who simply drank beer while PVC tubes jammed into the sand held their fishing poles. Unless the Kith had a man on foot, they wouldn't be able to see me from where their van was parked. The trick now was to get to the car before they realized what was happening.

A street freak pedaled up on a tricked-out bike and stopped at the water fountain. Tube socks up, no shirt, and a small boom box wrapped with duct tape played warbling classical music. The guy muttered to himself like a coked-up DJ, his mind caught in a flashpoint of nostalgia. He sipped water and hopped back on his bike, like he had an urgent appointment. You couldn't miss him. He'd make a great distraction.

As he pedaled along the boardwalk, I gambled he'd catch my tail's eyes. That freed me up to run alongside a Kia Optima as it pulled into the parking lot.

A kid looked at me out the back window of the moving car, too fascinated to let his mom know something weird was going on. The car accelerated too fast for me to keep up so I tapered off and stopped next to a parked Camaro.

I snuck a view of the van. They weren't getting out, but they were looking for me. I had been out of sight too long.

My car was fifteen spaces down and two rows over. I ran towards it, hunched down. Seven, eight, nine, ten rows down. Five more and two over. A quick peek.

Van gone. Where the hell did it go?

I chanced a better look. It was driving into the parking lot, right towards me.

I ducked fast and scrambled across the five remaining rows.

The van's engine rumbled closer. Its clean growl confessed serious automotive modifications. I crawled around a Camry and stayed hood-level with it.

The van slowed. Its engine throbbed just on the other side of the Camry. *Had they seen me?*

The van drove past. But, it would soon reach the end of the aisle, turn, and drive past the alley between the cars where I was hiding. If I didn't move soon, I'd be toast.

I cut over to the aisle where my car was parked. The van had made the turn and was rumbling my way. Moving faster. Close. Closer...too close.

I dropped flat, belly on the pavement and watched under the cars as the van pulled to the far side of the lot. They could either circle back around or drive out.

They drove out and I sighed with relief.

But, then they parked along the street, this side of the street. They maintained a clear view of my car.

Damn.

If I couldn't fool them, I just had to be faster than them. Speed was the key.

Keeping low, I ran over to the car next to mine. Hand in pocket, grab the keys, and...

Beep Beep.

Wait. I didn't press the key fob.

The car I was crouched behind beeped.

"Can I help you," said a voice behind me.

I turned to see a guy in his thirties, sweaty, and holding a volleyball and a sports bottle.

"Uh, I'm just..."

"You stealing my license plate?" His fist clenched.

Time to go.

I hit my key fob and ran to my car. Door open, slide in. Start it up. I peeked out the window.

The van driver saw me. He reached to start the van.

Shit.

Mr. Volleyball pounded on my window. "What the fuck were you doing to my car?"

I ripped the gearshift into reverse and backed out. One hand spun the wheel. The car turned towards the lot exit.

Floor it!

My car shot across the street and blasted down one of the tiny neighborhood side roads.

The van tried to U-turn and follow. Oncoming traffic cut it off. The driver pounded his steering wheel.

Left then right then left again. No van in the rearview. I raced down to Fifth and floored it up the 275 on ramp. I was outta there.

An hour later I was still flicking nervous glances at the mirrors and checking for the van.

The coast was clear.

17

The Kith weren't going to leave me alone. At least not until they knew for sure I was going to leave them alone. Even then, I still didn't think they'd let me live long. Not knowing what I know. I had to take action before they did.

But to do that, I needed information. And, the only lead I had for acquiring more information was Groveland Trucking. Their office was in Bartow, forty-five miles east of Tampa. It was just after two. Seven hours until I was due to meet DG in Gibsonton.

For the briefest moment, I tried to guess where he would hide Love-Mart's body. Did he have a regular spot for that sort of thing? Best if I never found out.

It sure helped to have a friend as resourceful as DG. But, I hated getting him involved. With any luck, this would be the last of it for him.

The drive east was peaceful, un-crowded, and didn't take as long as expected. I didn't want to get to Groveland Trucking before five, which I hoped was quittin' time for anyone who worked there. It was quarter of four. Time enough to eat and find a perch to scout the location before going in.

The sun was shining golden-hour orange as I pulled into downtown Bartow. Unlike nearby Lake Wales, which had a touch of charm, Bartow struck me as unremarkable. A former cow town that had grown into a rural economic crossroads. It appeared to lag in culture relevant beyond its city limits. But, I didn't live there. What the hell did I know?

"I'm trying to find the main office for Groveland Trucking. It's on Foot Long Road," I said to the man behind the convenience store counter.

"Welp," he said then paused for a moment. His expression was contemplative, like he was trying to remember how to get there or trying to decide whether he should tell me anything.

"I think it's still just off 60, twelve miles down. Know how you'll know it?"

"How?" I said.

"There's a 'bandoned gas station on the north side and they're always having a garage sale in the parking lot. All kinds of junk. Mex'cans is always shopping there. Foot Long Road is just past that," he said."

"Thanks," I said and hustled out of there.

He was right. There was an abandoned gas station. And, there were Mexicans shopping the garage sale in the parking lot. Looked to be mostly worn out baby toys on offer. Just beyond that was Foot Long Road, which was much longer than its name implied.

I pulled into a nearby church parking lot and waited for the sun to go down. For the next forty minutes, not a single vehicle entered or exited Foot Long Road. Seemed odd for an active trucking company.

The sun dipped below the oak trees on the horizon and the sky approached a mix of deep navy blue and lusty pink. I reset my car's odometer and started driving down Foot Long Road, lights off. There was no break, no side roads, no intersections. The odometer read four-point-four miles when the end of the road arrived and revealed itself in the form of the Groveland Trucking warehouse.

I yanked the car onto the soft sand shoulder then backed in amongst the orange trees.

The Groveland website boasted one of the biggest truck fleets in the Southeast. Why would they list their headquarters address at this tiny, one-dock dump? The land around the building was not paved, but flattened shell and sand. The only light came from two fixtures atop a pair of tall loblolly poles. And, the place looked deserted.

Just a front? Maybe Groveland wasn't even a real trucking company. Just a private transportation fleet. One that traffics in bodies. The website was window dressing.

Shell crackled under my shoes as I walked along the tree line towards the warehouse. Even in the low light I could see wide tire tracks running to and from the loading dock. The place was still being used. Otherwise, rain would have washed the tracks away by now.

Enough sightseeing.

Focus. Scan. Assess.

No signage, no symbols tying this place to the Kith. No truck, no bodies, dead or alive.

There.

Near the loading dock. An entrance with long, plastic flaps hanging down. Possible access. One more glance across the grounds. Clear. I ran from shadowed area to shadowed area, until I was able to belly up onto the dock platform.

The kind of door you'd find on refrigerated storage unit was behind the plastic flaps. I put my hand on it. Cool to the touch. They had power.

Open it? Sure.

Alarm?

I pulled.

The door hissed open. Amazing.

It was dark and cool inside.

Don't go in Walt.

If someone was here, they could slam that door shut when I wasn't looking. Then, that'd be that. Dead and done.

I pulled out my phone and flipped on the light. The room ahead was a cold-storage area. And, it was empty. But, there was discoloration on the floor. It was reddish and it could have been blood. I jumped to the worst, most logical conclusion: Bodies are stored here before loading or after unloading the trucks.

18

Heebie-jeebies hit me. I doused the light and backed into a dark corner, watched, waited, listened. Still as could be.

Don't lose your nerve now, Walt.

The last time I faced these creeps and their hired executioners I didn't have time to think, worry, or second-guess. I just had to react and defend and save my life. Maybe that meant I worked better under pressure. *Don't fool yourself, Walt. There's plenty of pressure. Your life is at stake.*

True. The Kith were just waiting for me to slip up. When I did, they'd kill me. That thought was enough to re-calibrate my fear to the proper levels. I was refocused.

Bugs chirped, frogs croaked, a breeze blew the leaves in the night. No movement on the property.

Now what?

Information. Get it and get out.

A plastic bin hung on the opposite wall. There was a clipboard inside it. I stepped out of the shadows, grabbed it, and squatted down behind a crate near the edge of the loading dock. Phone out, pressed against my leg to reduce the throw of the glow.

Tell me something.

I flipped through pink and yellow inventory slips. These guys are organized, mobilized, and they keep records.

The first sheet gave me shipment numbers, delivery locations, unit sizes, but no description of the cargo. Pre-printed Groveland Trucking logo at the top of each sheet. Note to self: Check state Sunbiz records to see who owns the company. Also check Whois for the domain owner, too. Although, it's easy to obscure ownership there. Maybe they forgot.

Keep reading.

My fingertips tinted blue from the carbon copy printing. All of the sheets were the same form. The details showed different times, different delivery locations, different unit sizes.

So, they're shipping from here. But, not delivering here? Then how does the inventory get here? How long does it stay here? Enough to bleed all over the floor of the meat locker.

Check dates.

Today was the twenty-sixth of October. The body truck was discovered on the twenty-fourth. I flipped fast through the papers. None had that date. The closest match was the eighteenth. Six whole days before.

The delivery locations were all over the state. Bunnell, Ormond Beach, Jacksonville, Lake City, Live Oak, Chiefland, Spring Hill, and Tampa. If a truck filled with immigrant slaves leaves Bartow on the eighteenth and is found abandoned on the twenty-fourth how many bodies will be left alive?

Answer: Zero.

Were those people stuffed in the back of that truck the entire six days? Were they alive when they left here and dead before Tampa? How did they die? Starvation, lack of air, or pure misery? Were some dropped off alive at those different cities? Was it just the Tampa-bound suckers who lost it all? What the hell was going on?

A dark thought hit me. Tanjeris had a sex slave at his house. She'd been roughed up. And, it looked like Tanjeris had planned to do more. What if...god, no.

I tried to block the thought. But, it was too horrible to simply blink away. I took a deep breath and as I exhaled the thought I was trying to block seared onto my brain: What if the bodies on the truck were the society members' scraps. The worked over leftovers. What if the truck was just picking up the trash from their sadistic slave buying clients?

This was madness. It was nauseating to think about these people as commodities on the supply chain. Goods to be delivered, garbage to be picked up. Some serious organized crime shit. I'd expect to hear about it happening in the war-torn cities of Eastern Europe. Countries that ended in -stan. Maybe South America. Like the exploitation movie tag lines say...where life is cheap.

No. It was happening in sunny, bring your kids to the beach Florida. And, it was revolting.

Squeak.

Sounded like a floorboard being stepped on.

I slapped the phone against my thigh to hide the light. My eyes weren't adjusted to the dark. I blinked away the light trails, but it still took me a moment to see. I could only hear my heart pounding.

Time to go.

I wanted to take the clipboard. Each of these sheets represented a new lead to pursue. And perhaps, proof to convict if it came to that. But, if all the sheets went missing, someone would get suspicious. I didn't want them to know I had been here. I pulled the sheet dated the eighteenth from the clip, folded it and slid it into my pocket. They wouldn't miss it. At least not right away.

Another scan of the land. No movement. No sound. I slid off the loading dock and dashed through the shadows.

It was safer to stay off the road. So, I trudged through the sand and the grove. I needed a drink. No oranges to pluck. These trees wouldn't bloom for another month or two. I'd have to get a drink back in town. And, that might be a while.

Two men were standing next to my car.

I stopped and dropped.

One man was positioned near the hood, the other at the trunk. I didn't need to guess who they were. They were trouble.

And, here I was, un-armed in the middle of an orange grove. Not even an orange to throw. I looked around for any kind of weapon. Stick, no. Root, no. Possum, no. Shit.

"We see you, Asher."

19

"Stop calculating your options. We are only here to have a few words with you," the same voice said.

I found that hard to believe. They'd been tracking me since I left my house. They knew I'd have no other reason to be in these parts, so they knew I hadn't heeded the warning in the note.

I was busted. I could either go to the car or...

I ran.

They chased.

The warehouse might buy me some time. I could lose them and double back. Maybe find a weapon there.

Or, more thugs could be waiting for me.

The warehouse lights glowed ahead, past the silhouettes of trees. I could hear them running behind me. They were fast. I ran faster.

I broke out of the grove and ran to the rear of the warehouse, towards the loading dock. They'd see my footprints. Couldn't worry about that. I needed shadows...find the darkness...

The thugs ran into the light from the dark of the grove. Shell dust clouded around their feet as they stopped to fire their guns.

I ducked behind a metal power box.

Bam! Bam!

I forgot how much I hated this stuff.

Sparks rained over and stung the back of my neck. But, their bright burning revealed a path forward, under the loading dock.

I crawled with abandon. Knees, elbows, hands, all scraped by sand and shell. Rodents skittered away as I scrambled between the wooden pylons holding up the dock.

What was that? A floor hatch above me. It had to lead into the warehouse. I got on my knees and pushed up with my hands and shoulders. The hatch lifted part way. Something was on top of it. I pushed harder and it opened and I climbed up into total darkness.

Where was I? Hard to see. Heart pumping. Could only hear blood pounding in my ears. *Slow down...breathe.*

They could be crawling under the building, headed my way. The trap door was still open.

I needed a weapon. But, I needed light first. I felt along the walls and found the light switch.

No! Skip it. Use the phone.

My hands were shaking, lungs tight. I was scared. I shouldn't have—

Quiet. Focus.

My hand was cupped over the phone screen. It threw a small bit of light, just enough to reveal surroundings:

Oh, god.

I was in a small office with piles of clothes and purses. Items that belonged to people who no longer needed them...who would no longer need anything. On the floor: A stack of blue jeans and a box of watches, rings, and pocketknives spilled onto the floor from when I had opened the hatch.

I grabbed a fat, deer skinner of a knife. A weapon, sure. But, little use against guns.

I swung the phone around the room, casting light across piles of t-shirts, sweaters. I found a stack of wallets, grabbed one, flipped it open. No license. No money. A Walgreens card made out to Hector Marquez. I tossed it down and checked another. Nothing. I checked another. Its lone possession was a green card belonging to Orqueño Maya.

Mind flash: The body in the news report. The arm dangling out of the stretcher. The Secret Society logo on brown skin. What is the Mexican connection? Maybe DG was right and these guys were trafficking illegal immigrants.

But, the green card...not illegal.

They're kidnapping, too.

A clanking sound. Something heavy tumbled onto the ground.

"Shit!" a voice said in a half-whisper.

They're in the building.

I ducked down, slid the phone in my pocket, and held still.

I had my information. I needed to get out of here. If they're here, they're not at the car. The coast might be clear.

The soft, muted sound of something sliding. Shhht. Shhht. Shhhhht. Thump. It was coming from below. One of the thugs was under the building, sliding towards the open hatch.

My escape route, blocked.

A light beam shined up through the hatch. I backed against the wall and hurried to pile sweaters and jeans and boxes on top of myself, quiet as possible. I clutched the hunting knife.

The light from the hatch went out.

Bam! Bam! Bam!

I startled as orange blasts flashed through the hatch. I heard the thug grunt as he climbed up into the room.

Please don't see me.

His hard sole shoes clicked across the hollow wooden floor as he stabilized his balance.

I set my feet against the wall, knees bent. That was my one chance. Please work.

I pushed off the wall. My arms wrapped around his legs and I tackled him into and down through the hatch. He gasped as impact with the ground knocked air out of his lungs.

The gun fell hard against my head. Where did it go? I scrambled off him to find it before he did.

He punched. Landed a good one in my ribs. I stabbed the knife. Don't know where it hit, but he wailed.

The stirred up dust and dirt was enough to make me choke as I searched for the gun.

There—

Bam!

Dust and dirt exploded next to the gun. Sand grit stung my cheeks. Wait—the shot came from above the hatch.

A hand grabbed my ankle. It was the guy on the ground. I kicked at his face. His lip split and bled. His teeth smashed into his mouth like an old, sagging fence. He rolled onto his back.

The other guy reached down through the hatch and pointed the gun in my direction. I rolled my guy on his side just as the gun fired. It blew his brains out and bloodied my shirt.

No more fighting.

I scrambled out from under the building. Another shot fired, dirt sprayed against my legs. I didn't look back, just got up and dashed into the orange grove.

It took the breeze blowing against my face to feel the cool of soot-tinged sweat running down it. My adrenaline was on full blast. Trees blurred past as I ran. My eyes, well-adjusted to the moonlight after being under the dark building, were laser focused on a path ahead. To my surprise, I ran with precision, not panic.

20

No headlights in the rearview mirror for several miles. They weren't following me. But, I had to stay alert. The point of no return had been crossed. They knew I'd been snooping. And now, one of their guys was dead. They were going to come after me with everything they had.

Goddamit. Life had been great. Why the hell did I get involved again? *Shut up, Walt. You know why.*

I'd just had a face full of why I got involved. That room. That room with all the personal belongings. It wasn't a lost and found. It was detritus of an underground holocaust in progress.

That seemed melodramatic. But, hell. The Kith were killing people. And, they were kidnapping. None of that had stopped when Doug Tanjeris died. It wasn't going to stop. And, I best shut the hell up about it.

No way. That's why I got involved. Every good infomercial product needs to do one thing: solve a problem. That's what infomercial makers do. We solve problems. This was the biggest problem I had ever known. And, I was the only one who could solve it because I was the only one who knew what was really happening. Well, me and DG. And, I was ready to limit his exposure.

The good news was I had another solid lead. Eight leads to be exact. Eight addresses where I could presume people had been delivered by Groveland Trucking.

I pulled the sheet out of my pocket and unfolded it. Yes, eight addresses. Most of them on the East Coast and in North Florida. But, there was one in Tampa and that was the closest. Made sense to check it out first. Those thugs didn't know what I had discovered at the warehouse, so they couldn't know where I was going, unless—

I almost didn't see the tracking device inside the grill panel. It was a small, black half sphere attached to the car's metal frame. That's how they found me in the orange grove. So, why the chase panic back in St. Pete if they knew they'd be able to track me? I got spooked with the realization they had been there to scoop me up and dispose of me. That's why they needed the minivan. But, I had screwed up that plan.

Back on the road, Tampa via Brandon. What type of person pays to have people delivered? How sick do you have to be? And, how do you find those services in the first place? They don't advertise this stuff. It all went back to the Kith. Tanjeris had talked about unlimited privilege that came with membership.

Did that mean there were secret society members in eight different cities around the state? More if you factor in the other delivery sheets on the clipboard. How depressing. I wished I had those sheets now. They could be important. More leads in case the eight I already had didn't pan out. But, I couldn't risk going back to the warehouse.

What did those eight addresses have in common? Farms were a popular destination for immigrants, forced or otherwise. That theory didn't hold water because the Tampa address on the shipping sheet listed Kennedy Boulevard, one of the city's main thoroughfares. No farms there. And, no sense in speculating. I wouldn't know more until I visited each address.

21

Gibsonton was situated southeast of the Port of Tampa, just north of the Alafaya River. But, its real claim to fame was its history with the carnies and sideshow freaks who made it their winter quarters. Percilla Bajano the Monkey Girl lived there. "World's Strangest Couple" Half woman Jeannie and her husband Al Tomaini owned a trailer camp there. And, Grady "Lobster Boy" Stiles lived and was murdered there. Truly like no other place on earth.

Given its inherent outsider status, anything went in Gibsonton. That meant drinking establishments could get rough. I expected as much from Foster's. Especially if DG frequented it. What remained to be seen was whether it was carnies that raised the hell or bikers. Two very different types of trouble.

If I hadn't been looking for it, I would have passed it. Foster's was off the main drag and set under a cluster of palm trees that swayed in the breeze. Choppers of all kinds surrounded the dingy, brown cinderblock building. I pulled in and parked.

A short, ancient man hobbled out a side door carrying a bag of trash. His face was shadowed from a bright, moth-swarmed light on a wooden pole. He hobbled towards a dumpster on the far side of the property.

The creaky screen door slammed behind me and I got all the looks. They weren't inviting. More like, they were expecting a goddamn answer—who the hell are *you* walking in here??? And yet, The Go-Go's were playing over the sound system. No a/c.

DG waved to me from a second bar at the back of the room. I nodded and walked past the dirty looks. I noticed out the corner of my eye that once they saw I was DG approved, they let it go and got back to business. For some, that was drinking. For others, it was darts. For a trio at a table in the corner of the room, it meant fondling a mama. She appeared blitzed enough to enjoy it.

DG gestured to an open stool. The bartender arrived on cue. She was leathery with bleach blonde hair that took years off her appearance from a distance. But, up close she was scarred and packing fists of mangled fighting knuckles.

"PBR," I said. Drink to match the establishment.

I turned to DG, "Well?"

He nodded and looked at his hand. It was wrapped in crumpled, blue shop towels. Blood had soaked through.

"What happened?" I pointed to his hand.

He finished off his whiskey and waved for another. His delay worried me. The bartender brought his whiskey and my beer.

"They had cops waiting," he said.

My stomach sank. If that had been me, I'd be in jail now with no chance of explaining my way out.

He continued..."Maybe they were cops. Pulled us over. Rapped about some bullshit violation. Insisted on searching our rides. That'd be a no-go even if I wasn't cleaning up your mess. But, because I had the girl in there, there was no chance of it happening."

I appreciated his discretion.

"We resisted, they attacked. It got ugly. Real ugly."

I wished he'd just spit it out.

"We buried three bodies."

I wished he hadn't spit that out.

"Jesus..."

What did this mean? Were the police now after DG, which lead straight to me?

"Ask me, I think they were imposters. They wanted to get rid of the girl and us. Anyone who knows what's going on."

"If they were real cops we're in the deepest shit. If they were Kith, we've pissed them off," I said. The beer wasn't making a dent in my nerves.

"I gave those motherfuckers just what they deserved." He downed his whiskey. "They picked the wrong man."

"Think you're on their radar now?"

"They're on *my* radar now!" He thumbed to his chest as he said it.

Shit. I wasn't much in control of the situation before. But, whatever I had was being lost before my eyes. I couldn't have DG on the warpath.

"Look, don't worry about it. I got some new leads before I came here. I can handle it."

"You can't handle shit, Walt."

"I handled it last time," I said with defiance.

"They expected you to die, not fight. You surprised them once, but they're ready for you now," he said and held up his slashed hand. "You need my help."

"Look, DG. I still feel awful about getting you involved last time. And, for what happened to Teddy. I can't have that happen again. Even if it means...things get dicey for me," I said. As absurd as the notion was, I was dead serious. I wanted this fight for myself.

"Well, that's dumb. You don't stand a chance without my help."

I sighed.

He continued, "Look, I am sick to death of these assholes. We're gonna track their asses down, flush 'em out, and take 'em down for good. Send a fuckin' message, you dig? That way you can get back to writing your little scripts and I can get back to running my business," he said.

"This is my fight."

"Not anymore. I knew that girl." His fist pounded the table.

"Who?"

"Love-mart," he said.

"You did?"

He nodded. "Friend of the family's."

Was he joking? What the hell could I say to that?

"You're getting my help, like it or not," he said.

I was damn good at persuading people. But, if this had become personal for DG, there was no talking him out of it.

"Now, tell me about your new leads. We have some ass to kick," DG said.

22

A slob of a man waddled into the windowless building with the pagoda-style roof. Sizzling green neon trim accented the structure, while a giant Buddha statue smiled because a neon female hand was reaching under his belly. It was the Ancient Delights Massage Parlor, and it belonged to the Tampa address listed on the paper from Groveland Trucking.

On the drive over, I determined the truck full of bodies had to be found. It was the only tangible proof of the Kith's guilt. Everything else I had discovered—the shipping slips, the warehouse filled with piles of clothes—all seemed circumstantial at best. They could weasel out of that. But, they'd have to goddamn answer for a truck full of dead Mexicans.

"Call me crazy, but if I were a practitioner of Maximum Freedom, I'd go for more than just hand jobs in this scum pit," said DG.

"Maybe they just deliver the girls," I said.

"Or, they own it. You can make serious cheese off a dump like this. Almost invested in one once."

Of course he did.

Ancient Delights was just one of many massage parlors lining Kennedy boulevard. Aside from the Asian decorative flair, all the parlors looked them same. No windows, painted in dull colors with small signs, and front doors located in the back of the building. Anything to not attract attention, except from fellas looking for that kind of good time.

We were parked across the street in a strip plaza parking lot. The empanada bakery, used clothing store, and barbecue grill outlet were

63

closed for the night. DG rode with me so his guys could take his van back to Dunnellon and purge any dead body evidence.

A paid political message for Emiliano Abrantes played on the radio. The ad was hopeful in tone. He was taking the high road, whereas his incumbent Republican opponent, Governor Vissel, was slinging as much mud as he could. I recalled seeing an article stating polls showed Abrantes' approach was working. He had the momentum and was closing in on his opponent. Most local political pundits pegged the debate, scheduled two weeks from now, to be the moment he—

A man walked out from behind Ancient Delights.

His hands were in pockets, head down to avoid eye contact with anyone. He shuffled down the sidewalk.

"Time to go in," DG said.

He looked at me. I looked at him.

"What?" I said.

"Get going," he said.

"I figured you'd know how to handle this kind of place better than me."

"I'll be here watching your back because I don't trust you to watch mine."

Okay, then.

"I'll find out what I can," I said.

"Just get a read on the place."

"I wanna talk to one of the girls."

"Oh, I'm sure you will."

"Funny."

The sound of a gong played when I opened the door to Ancient Delights. The smell of Nag Champra incense mixed with a flowery plug-in fragrance was enough to choke on. That much fragrance had to be covering other odors.

Two guys sat in the waiting room. One was a red hair, freckle-faced guy in cargo shorts and a Rays ball cap. He had an Ohio State tattoo on his shaking leg and a lusty, eager smile on his face. The other was the slob I'd seen waddle in moments earlier. He looked fresh out of an insurance convention. Sweat rings discolored the underarms of his sport coat.

It wasn't until I arrived at the chest-high reception counter that I saw the tiny, kimono-clad Asian woman standing behind it.

"Good evening," she said, surprising me with her complete lack of an accent.

"Hi," I said.

"You would like a massage this evening?"

"Yes, please. The usual."

The usual?

"And, what is your usual?" she said, a polite smile under her inquiring eyes.

I was getting nervous. I didn't want to attract any attention but now I felt like every eye in the room was on me, as well as those behind the security cameras.

"Well, I mean, you know. The basic. The basic massage," I said.

She gave a courteous nod. "Your name?"

"Uh...Arthur."

"Sit." She gestured to an empty foldout chair.

I sat and took in the room: Gold foil wallpaper depicted a quaint Asian village filled with blossoming cherry trees. A small sign, handwritten in thick marker read "Massages $50/half hour. Consult massoos for menu – Management." Spelling wasn't a prerequisite for the job. Stapled to the wall behind the counter were several state business licenses. At least, that's what they looked like. If this place was dealing in trafficked women, I couldn't imagine they were up to date on licensing.

"Been here before?"

It was the freckled face guy. He was leaning forward, elbows on knees, looking right at me. Awkward.

"Uh, no," I said.

Big mistake. He got up, walked over, and sat next to me. Super awkward. People communicated less in doctor offices. He leaned over as if to whisper something confidential but still spoke at full volume.

"This place is great. The girls, top notch." His hands waved with excitement. "Now, look...they don't advertise it on the sign up there, but make sure you ask the girls about the *special* menu. They got all sorts of exotic treats on there, if you know what I mean." He served up a huge grin.

"I think I do," I said.

"Good, good. See, I like 'em a little freaky. Best is when they look like good girls, but then do the weird stuff. That's my kind of kink. And, this is the only place in town that serves up the full buffet. It's like the Golden Corral of smut. You get where I'm goin' with that?"

I nodded. He smiled and looked at the opposite wall, lost in the recollection of good times.

"And, it's cheap. Well, cheaper than you'd expect," he said, leaning in closer. "After she gives you the basic rub, make sure to kind of wince and tell her there's still some deep pain that needs relief. That'll give her the signal that you ain't here for just a back rub, understand?" He giggled, as if he'd been waiting years to tell someone that secret.

"I appreciate the advice," I said.

This guy was crowding me and I was already feeling off-kilter and anxious. But, I had to get to the girls.

"Hey, any time. I'm kind of a regular here. And, at just about all the other parlors." He let out a big laugh and slapped his leg, which was still shaking. "This fella does not discriminate. But like I said this one's the be—"

"Doctor Rodrigo?" said the tiny Asian woman.

"Ooh, that's me!" He stood up and walked over beyond the counter. He looked back at me and spoke confidentially behind the back of his hand. "And, no that ain't my real name. Have fun!"

More laughter as the tiny hostess led him through a jade bead curtain. Good riddance.

The grease ball across from me looked down at his twiddling fingers.

The hostess re-appeared from behind the curtain and walked out into the foyer. She was followed by a large, brute of a man with hair in a tight perm. He wore a sweater with a gold chain on the outside of it, shorts, and loafers.

He gave the hostess a shove and a scowl.

"Gentlemen?" she said, both hands extended, inviting us to come forward. We rose.

"You guys come on. Special event coming up. You're gonna have to make it quick," said the man.

What kind of special event?

"After you," I said with a wave of the hand to grease ball. He nodded and waddled. I got caught in the wake of his ripe body odor.

The hostess led us down a hallway lit by dim, green lights and lined with doors on each side. She stopped and gestured for grease ball to enter a room on the left. Once he did, she led me two doors down and gestured for me to enter on the right. It was time for my massage.

23

The room was empty save for a waist high massage table, a small dresser with a towel, and a bottle of rubbing oil. No 'massoos'. The walls were painted green with red trim. One wall was covered with mirror. I grew uncomfortable thinking it might be a two-way set up designed to film clients or keep track of the girls.

Worrisome question: If this place was owned by the Kith and they knew I was here and they made a move, how would DG know? And, how would he be able to back me up? I needed to keep my guard up.

I sat on the massage table and texted DG: In room. Waiting on 'massoos.

A gong rang and plucky oriental music started to play out a speaker mounted in the corner above the door, through which my girl appeared.

She was short. Long, black hair, tan skin. Full-blooded Mex.

"Good evening," she said with a bow. The accent confirmed her heritage.

I nodded, "Hello."

"Please remove your clothes to where you feel comfortable."

"Okay," I said.

I hopped down from the table. Just removing my shirt made me feel vulnerable. But, I had to play along. Off went the shoes and the pants. Not my underwear. All the while, I watched her out the corner of my eye. Her back was to me as she prepared a towel and oil.

"Please you lay down," she said.

I did.

67

She dropped her smock and stood next to me one hundred percent naked. I couldn't resist looking at her body—pert breasts, smooth tummy with a slight pooch, discolored stretch marks around the thighs, and a groomed black bush. Attractive enough to make me feel like a creep.

She smiled. No life in her eyes. Her spirit had been snuffed out long ago.

She stepped closer and put her hands on my shoulders to guide me down onto my back.

Hold on.

The Kith symbol. Branded into her left shoulder.

"Just relax. I rub," she said.

There was no feeling in her words. She had said them a million times to a million men whose faces had long since melted into one generic customer.

I nodded.

She started rubbing my chest. I was surprised by how soft her hands were and how fast they started to untangle the knots in my shoulders. But, I couldn't relax.

"That's interesting. What does that symbol mean?" I said. I nodded towards the brand.

She glanced at her arm then looked at me with a blank expression. She shrugged.

"Does it mean anything?"

Shrug. Head shake.

"Do you not know how to say it en ingles?" I said.

She just stared at me, still rubbing my shoulders.

I got a slight nod out of her. Then, she put a finger over my lips to quiet me as she used the other hand to rub further down my body.

"Look, is it alright if we just talk for a few minutes?"

She glanced back at the mirror. Two-way monitoring confirmed. She gave me a look. A scared one.

I peeked at the mirror. Who could be watching us?

"You like special menu?" she said, as she tucked her fingertips inside the elastic waistband of my underwear.

I needed answers. But, this was going too far.

She started making hand motions and shook a loose fist to indicate 'jerking off'. Then she moved it up near her mouth indicating 'blowjob'. Then she started removing my underwear.

I sat up. She startled back. I hopped down and started to dress. Cover be damned. I'd have no part in this poor girl's horror show.

"What wrong?" she said, pleading in her eyes. "I do nothing wrong. You happy."

I looked at her while zipping up my pants.

"I very happy. But, not tonight, okay?" I forced a smile.

She grabbed my arm.

"You stay. I do special menu."

Shirt on, I kept buttoning.

"You're very pretty. You did nothing wrong. Now just isn't the best time."

"I make you feel good. Muy bien," she said. She looked worried now, her grip tightening on my arm.

I pulled cash out of my pocket and gave it to her.

"Thank you very much," I said and bolted out of the room.

Back in the lobby, the hostess looked surprised to see me.

"You fast," she said.

"She was very, very good." I pushed out the door without waiting for an answer. The gong rang.

The air outside was cool and felt good on my face as I hustled across the street. I was relieved to be out of there. But, the girl was haunting me. I wanted to pull my skin off and wash it after being in a room with a woman who was being forced to service me. A slave. She was in the prime of her life. But, imprisoned in that pit. The last time I looked her in the eye, I saw something I hadn't seen before. A glimpse at how evil my opponents were.

24

"Well?"

"Yes."

"Yes, what? What'd you find out?"

"My girl had the same symbol branded onto her arm. And, she was Mexican."

"False advertising," DG said. He gestured to the big Buddha.

"I asked her questions. She was scared to talk. I think they were listening in," I said.

"So, nothing else?"

I was getting irritated by the questions and because I was unsettled my nerves were jittery.

"Nothing specific. It was just obvious she had been through a lot. We're dealing with very bad people."

I futzed with the air vent.

"We know they bad. What we need to know is how to get to them," said DG.

"Would you like to go in?"

"If she was too scared to talk to you, she'll be terrified to talk to me," he said.

This was true. At least DG was self-aware.

"Then what are our options?" I said. My tone was sharp.

He gave me a look.

Big breath, let it out, that's better.

"Sorry."

"Way I see it, we either wait here and see who shows up. Maybe they drop off another load of chicks."

"Or?"

"I make some calls, see who owns it. Track it from there."

"Why didn't you just do that while I was inside?"

"I'm bushed. Been a busy day of grave digging."

Sarcasm noted.

"Well, when convenient for you, please find out."

"I'd be delighted to."

He pulled out his phone and started dialing.

But, it was my phone that rang. Ilsa was calling.

"Hello?"

"Hello from Holland," she said. "What kind of trouble is my love getting into tonight?"

"Uhhh..."

I got out of the car so I wouldn't have to talk over DG.

"Sounds like quite a bit. I hope it is nothing unforgivable."

"Well..."

Damn. She really caught me off guard. And, I was half distracted watching the massage parlor.

"What's going on, Walt?" She sensed something.

"You don't want to know," I said.

"You're wrong."

"How's your mom?"

"Don't change the subject."

Shit.

Deep breath. I didn't want to give her anything else to worry about. But, I also...in the back of my mind had this fear that if I didn't tell her what was up, she'd never know what happened...if something happened to me. At least if she knew I'd gotten involved she could get some satisfaction being furious at me for being so stupid.

"I'm waiting," she said.

"Things didn't end in Jacksonville."

She knew what that meant.

"How?"

"There was a note on my table when I woke up this morning. Inside the house. It read 'Do Not Get Involved Or We Will Kill You'."

"From them?"

"From them. And, attached..." Wow, do I give her all the details? "It was attached to a dead woman."

The line went silent.

"Why was there a dead woman in the house? With a note?"

Was hoping she wouldn't ask that.

I explained the whole story to her, from seeing the truck on television to tracking down the warehouse to me sitting in the car outside the massage parlor. I braced myself for heartfelt pleading, unhinged fury, and an appeal for me to flee to Holland and hide out with her as soon as possible. Just, get out of there now!

Her silence felt eternal and damning.

"You made the correct decision," she said.

I was shocked.

She continued, "You're right. We'd never be safe. Not until we knew for sure they were forever done."

"I thought you'd be--"

She cut me off

"I am upset. I'm furious. But, not at you. At them. If they won't leave us alone then they deserve all the hell you bring them. They're lucky I'm overseas."

I couldn't believe it. I'd had to fight and plead with her to stop them last time. Now, here she was encouraging me. I straightened up with renewed life. No longer alone and desperate. She had my back and was rooting for me.

"Thank you, Ilsa," I said.

"There's only one way to thank me, Walt. Stay alive."

"I will."

A van pulled up to Ancient Delights. Two rough looking dudes, big like bouncers, got out, opened the van's side door, and walked inside. They looked like they knew the place, perhaps belonged.

I leaned down to look in the car. DG was watching the van, too.

"Ilsa, I have to go."

"Okay. Be careful. Don't do anything dumb," she said.

"I won't."

"Yes, you will."

"You're right," I said. It was reassuring knowing she knew me better than I knew myself.

"Please let me know you are safe. Soon."

"I will. I love you."

"I love you, Walt."

I hoped to hell those weren't our last words to each other.

25

"They look affiliated," DG said.

"Gang?"

"Didn't see colors. I just think they're with the guys we're looking for."

"Flunkies."

"But, can lead us to the boss," DG said.

"If they're disposable, they'll only have limited contact and info."

"I'll beat what they know out of 'em."

A flunky appeared from behind the building. He was followed by parlor girls. I counted five of them. They all looked Mexican. I couldn't see brands from here. The other flunky brought up the rear.

"Here we go," said DG. He looked at the fuel gauge. "Half a tank. Hope they ain't going too far."

The girls hurried into the van, as if they'd been trained not to delay.

"That's my girl. Second to last," I said.

"The others look too smacked out to care," DG said.

The last girl got a whap on the ass. Door closed and locked. No windows in the van.

DG shifted the car into drive.

"Are your lights off?" I said.

He nodded.

"You get a hold of anyone who knows about this place?"

He shook his head.

The van revved to life, U-turned in the parking lot, and cut east on Kennedy.

"5-4-3-2-1...and go," said DG.

73

The van veered north past the mall and accelerated onto the Veteran's expressway.

"If we lose them—"

"I'm not going to lose them," said DG. He sped up.

The van brightened as it passed under the orange streetlights. A plane swooped down and landed on the airport runway, not two hundred yards away.

It felt good to finally be getting on top of this...case, I guess you'd call it. Makes me sound like a private detective, which is weird. But, I must be doing something right if Ilsa gave me her blessing to continue this adventure. She, in her wise way, had just given me the confidence I would need to push myself further into this abyss. Most people go through life not knowing how good they really are because so few people are willing to tell them. But, encouragement makes all the difference.

Headlights in the rearview mirror. I snapped back to reality and stiffened as I glanced at the reflection of a truck. What if the van from the parlor was bait designed to draw us out?

The truck veered down the exit ramp. False alarm. But, the paranoia was good. It might keep us alive.

The van got off at the Lutz Lake Fern Road exit. Interesting choice. Not much out here. Northwest Tampa was rural and undeveloped save for a few planned communities and...

" I know where they're going," I said.

"Where? Doesn't look like much around here," said DG.

"If they turn right, turn left so they don't think we're following them."

"We gotta follow 'em. I'll drop back."

"No. It's a small two-lane road. And, they gotta be taking the girls to the country club," I said.

"How do you know that?"

I shrugged.

The van turned right.

I could sense DG's reluctance to drift into the left lane, but he did, then stopped at the cross street.

The van's red taillights grew smaller as it moved into the distant darkness.

"How bout I just follow 'em now?" DG said.

The van's lights glowed bright. Braking.

"Hold on," I said.

No turn signal from the van. But, it turned regardless. And when it did it was illuminated by lights on what I knew to be a gated entrance.

"Country club?" said DG.

"Yes. Go that way." I pointed in the direction the van had driven.

He cut the wheel and pulled out and drove towards the country club.

I pictured the gaggle of girls primping inside the van in anticipation for their upcoming appointment. Were they numb to it by now?

"Tell me where to turn," DG said.

"La Vida Estates is a very exclusive club. Football players and golfers live there."

"Big money."

"There's going to be a gated entrance. With guards. Just cruise by, check it out first."

We did. Gates and guards confirmed.

"Yamir, hey it's Walt." I looked to DG. So far, so good.

He pulled over onto the road shoulder.

"Right. Oh, great. I told you that demo would work well. Hey, listen...I know it's late, but I'm in the area and was thinking about swinging by to say 'hi' in person. You home?"

I nodded to DG. He checked his side mirror. No traffic. He u-turned and drove back to the gated entrance.

"Okay, great. I'll be there in like two minutes."

The security bar lifted and we drove into the gated community.

"Yamir is two more roads up. On Osprey," I said.

We reached the road before Osprey, Sand Crane. DG hit the brakes.

"Van," he said, pointing.

Sure enough, ten houses down. The van was parked in the drive, its profile clear in the red and green landscape lighting.

DG turned on to Sand Crane.

"Hey, we gotta go to Yamir's first," I said.

"Ain't got time for Yamir."

"It's gonna be weird if we don't show up."

DG pulled over and parked five houses down from the house where the van was parked. Lights off, car off.

"There's all kinds of weird shit happening in this neighborhood." He pointed to the van.

"I'm gonna be pissed if I lose this client," I said.

"You're gonna be dead if we don't stop these guys," said DG.

Yep.
We sat for moment, silent and watching.
The street was lined with cars. All signs pointed to a party.
"Let's get closer."
"You got a piece?"
"No."
DG looked disappointed. He reached into his boot.
"Wait." I remembered the knife I had grabbed at Groveland trucking. I pulled it out of the glove box. DG looked it over then re-sheathed the one he had started to pull out.
"Nasty enough," he said.
We got out of the car.

A huge backyard with tall oak trees and thick, Saint Augustine grass took up most of the property. There was a large pool with twinkling blue water. Through the windows I could see a celebration in progress. I moved towards the house, doing my best to stay in the shadows.

I squatted down next to a window at the back of the house. Party noise wafted out. Sounded like a rowdy affair. I stole a glance through the window and was shocked to see just how rowdy it was.

26

It was like witnessing a drunken fraternity reunion. The brothers from twenty years ago had returned and were ready to cut loose. Nearly a dozen middle-aged men mingled around the room. They had all started with business attire, straight from the office. But now, their ties were undone, shirts unbuttoned. One guy had had enough with pants.

The girls from the massage parlor had arrived and were already stripped naked and getting passed around, ogled and fondled, caressed and hugged. One party guest enthusiastically pointing out private bits to another. Most of the men had tight wedding rings digging into their fat fingers.

One guy ducked in for a kiss. The girl complied. Another fella set a girl on the couch and wasted no time parting her legs. She smiled like what a crazy man he was. Debauchery unleashed. And from what I could see, all the girls had the Kith symbol branded into their arms. Property.

But, what did it all mean? Did the Kith pimp on the side? Was this just another profit source to fund their club? Could anyone book them for parties? Or, did you have to be a member of the Kith.

That question was answered a moment later when a tall, lean chap with thinning blonde hair strolled into the room. He was wearing a robe and smoking two cigars. And, he had a Kith ring on his finger. Just like Tanjeris. This was his show. And, he was showing off.

Tanjeris had called it: Maximum Freedom. Power to do whatever one wanted, regardless of morality or legality. In fact, it was better in spite of those traditional bugaboos. Breaking the code was its own fetish. Very few people had that kind of power. It was intoxicating enough to make men do terrible things. These men.

They may not have known the collateral damage of their actions. They just ordered some girls for a good time. But, those girls knew how terrible this all was. By the looks of it, they were going to know again and again throughout the night. Mama should have spanked these boys a lot harder.

So, this was my challenge. I needed to get information. But, the person with the most information was going to be the least inclined to talk. That was Blondie. The rest of the guys looked just shy of wasted. I could probably ply information out of them. But, they weren't wearing Kith rings, so they wouldn't have the info I needed.

And, then there were the girls. I was sure they had beans to spill. But, would they? Or, would they be too scared to talk?

My phone startled me. I grabbed it fast and lowered the volume.

Yamir had texted. "Where are you?"

I knew this would happen.

Another text chimed in. "Guard said you came through the gate???"

If the gate guard started hunting around he'd find my car in just minutes and wonder why we had lied. He'd think we were burglars. Time to pick up the pace.

Another peek through the window. Blondie was talking to the crowd. I leaned close to listen.

An engine turned over in front of the house. The noise drowned out Blondie. I ducked down and looked out toward the road. The van that brought the girls to the party was leaving.

If we hurried and followed the van, it could lead us to new Kith, perhaps. We knew where this house was and could always come back. But, I had no idea where DG was or what he was up to. I hoped we didn't just lose a big lead.

Laughter came from inside the house. The men were standing around a large dining table, their eyes fogged by lust as Blondie set the last of the girls on the table.

"Hey, I'm gonna need an extra plate." hollered one creep.

Blondie smirked and replied, "Gotta use a new plate each time you go through the buffet line."

The gang howled. Lots O' Laffs.

Glass broke.

The men stopped and turned.

Blondie: "Who the hell are you?"

"The answer man. Here to get some answers."

DG was in the house.

Party guests grew uneasy and started covering their privates, pulling their clothes back on. One guy tried to hide his prick with the tip of his loosened necktie. They didn't know what was going on and they certainly knew they were up to no good. And, that made them uneasy.

"Boy, you better get outta my house right now. I'm a city commissioner. I have a direct line to the police. And, we got security in this neighborhood," Blondie said.

"We can take em, Hal," said an uppity guest. He was the most dressed.

"Man, I came here to fuck not to fight," said one guy. He was the only one that laughed at his attempted joke.

Another chap lost his balance when he accidentally stepped on the middle seam of his pants instead of through the pant leg.

Blondie put a hand out to hold the guy up. "Now, I don't know what you want. We're just having us some fun. So, if you don't beat it now, I'll call some special friends of mine. Understand?"

"Call your friends. That's exactly who I'm looking for," said DG.

Trouble. I needed to get in there before this got out of hand.

I ran to the patio screen door. It was locked. I kicked the mesh and ducked through. A girl saw me. I put a hand to my lips. Shhhh. No reaction. She didn't speak.

"Hal, we gonna get this orgy going or what? Get him outta here!" said an older, golf-course-tanned man.

I spotted a golf club in the corner. A fat driver. I grabbed it...and smashed a vase on a pedestal. It looked expensive.

Everyone jumped except DG. The men turned my way, shock in their eyes.

"Everyone in the bedroom. Now!" I yelled.

DG took the cue and grabbed Blondie by the arm, a knife to his throat.

I shoved the guy closest to me. He followed DG and Blondie. The rest of the men lined up.

"Girls stay here," I said.

We led the men down a hallway into the master bedroom.

"He comes with me," I said as I took Blondie, Hal, by the arm.

"Rest of you face down, hands out on the bed," said DG.

The party guests lined up belly-down on the bed.

"Talk to him, Walt," said DG. "I'll watch these losers." He lifted his boot and stomped the guy closest to him in the ribs. The guy yelped as

I pulled Hal down the hallway and back out into the living room. Now, we were going to get some real answers.

27

I threw Blondie/Hal down on the lingerie-covered couch. He sank in deep. I grabbed what lingerie was close by and tossed it over to the girls, who were sitting quietly, minding themselves over by the table.

"You can get dressed."

My girl from the parlor caught the lingerie. She gave me a look, but it was vague, hollow. No way to interpret it. Either she was relieved we stepped in, pissed we screwed up business, or fearful of the consequences.

"Some nice pieces of ass, aren't they? No reason you couldn't join the fun."

I turned and there was Hal, pushing back his hair, acting all relaxed. Until I swung the driver against his ribs. He wheezed and recoiled.

"I've heard that pitch before. Your buddy Doug Tanjeris tried to sell me on it," I was angry. Angry at the insult. Angry this guy was such a scumbag. Angry to be in another dicey position. Angry and scared. But, I couldn't let him know that.

A look of realization on Hal's face. "Oh wait...I heard about you."

"Was it in the club bulletin?" I said.

He shrugged. "Word gets around."

"That's right it does. Now, let me make this clear. There's a very good chance you're not going to live after tonight. But, that depends entirely on how forthright you are with me. Got it?"

He looked resigned to the prospect of interrogation but not apt to talk.

"Question One: Who are they?" I said.

"Who are who?

This prick. Swing!

Rib crack, howl, roll over wincing. He held up a hand.

I tapped the secret society ring on his finger.

"I'll talk," he said. It was more of a grunt. "I'll be happy to talk." He forced a smile as he sat up. "Doesn't matter how much information you have. You're not gonna live to do anything about it. They'll find you. You got lucky last time. So, I'll tell you everything you want to know."

I didn't reveal how much that notion scared the hell out of me. *How much time did I really have left?*

"Talk," I said.

"Your question was who are they, yes? Well, they are many and they are powerful. If you met Doug, you probably got a whiff of that," said Hal.

I nodded. "Go on."

"Let's start with me. My name is Hal. I'm on the Hillsborough City Commission. I joined the gang two years ago for all the reasons you might think, but especially Max--"

"Maximum Freedom. Yeah, I got that from Doug," I said.

He nodded, impressed I knew. Perhaps delighted by the notion.

"Well, that's all we were doing here tonight. Expressing our freedom." He laughed and gave a mocking salute.

I resisted whacking him with the golf club. Instead, I tried a verbal jab. "These girls aren't free. They're slaves. Your group traffics them. That's why they have a brand on their arms."

He glanced at the girls, like they were dents in the drywall.

"Not my department. Don't know nothing about that. Just know it's a service provided to members. For recruitment functions like this in particular," he said with a wave around the room.

"Recruitment? For what?"

"Keep the membership fresh. Increase the resources, the contacts. Good to know people in different industries."

"So, you can cover up stories about semi trucks full of dead slaves," I said matter of fact.

He pursed his lips and nodded.

"How many members are there?" I said.

"They don't really tell me. But, I can't imagine anyone turning down the invitation," he said and then glanced off. He was getting his thoughts together, like he wanted to say something important. He looked to me.

"I can't say enough how dramatically it has changed my life. It's the greatest thing that's ever happened to me."

"So?"

My response caught him off guard. Seemed to shake him out of the reverie unfolding in his mind.

"So, you should try it," he said.

"I don't want to try it. Because I don't want to be like you. Your little play group killed my friend. And, disfigured my girlfriend. And, tried to kill me. Sorry, if I don't want to hang out with your buddies."

He seemed surprised, but I couldn't tell if it was from what I had described or my rage in describing it.

"I, well...I wasn't aware any of that was going on," he said. "But, you have to understand—"

Whack!

I smashed the driver head against his neck. He howled.

A peek at the girls. They were in their own worlds. Strung out. Or simply used to nearby beatings.

"Where are they?"

Hal's pain was still resonating. "Jesus!"

"Tell me where they are. I'm going to find them and I'm going to put them out of business. Now, tell me."

"I don't know where they are," he said and sniffled as he clutched his neck.

Whack! In the ribs.

"Stop!"

"I want information, Hal. Tell me what you know. Where do you send your dues? How do you get in contact with them? Give me phone numbers. Give me addresses."

I was leaning over, yelling in his face. I had reached my breaking point. All the hassle, trouble, heartache, fear, regret, and terror they had caused...I'd had enough. I wasn't going to take it anymore. Certainly not from this country club creep. He thought he was hot stuff groping the girls earlier. King of his castle. Gloating in front of the group of men who all wished they had what he had...who showed up hoping to cross the threshold into the enchanted, anything-goes kingdom. To them, Hal held the key. And, he knew it.

Well, now he was going to use that key and unlock this mystery for me. He had every intention of talking up his beloved secret society tonight. He just didn't expect he'd be telling me about it.

"I can't."

"You can."

"No, seriously...they'll kill me if I talk."

"I'll kill you if you don't!"

"Please, no. Look. I swear."

"What do you know about the truck full of bodies?" I said.

"Nothing."

Whack! On the arm. He howled.

"How did that story get covered up?"

"I don't...know"

Whack! On the leg. He grabbed his thigh. It was already turning red and swelling.

"How did you order the girls for tonight?"

"I just...look, I can't—

Whack! Against the ear. He clutched his head and rolled off the couch, almost hitting his face on the glass coffee table.

Blood dripped onto the white carpet.

"Who are they?

Whack! I didn't wait for answers.

"Where are they?"

Whack!

"Stop." He held out a bloody hand to stop the club.

"Tell me who they are."

The crunch of the club against his hand was a clear indicator that I'd broken it. He pulled it into his chest and rolled on the floor, wailing.

"I got all night to get these answers out of you. And, if I get tired of swinging this club, my good buddy back there has more persuasive ways to open up a discussion. Ways you will not be brave enough to resist." I said.

Was he whimpering?

"I'll ask one more time. Where can I find your maximum freedom friends? The ones in charge. Tell me!"

He said something but I couldn't make it out.

"What'd you say?"

I kicked him onto his back. His face was bright red with anguish. Thin lines of blood had trickled around his chin. The side of his neck had swollen to the size of a baseball. He was in rough shape to the point where he couldn't even focus his eyes on me.

"Okay...okay...listen..." he said.

"I am."

"All contact goes through a trust company. That's all I know. The guys who...who brought the girls here tonight. Never seen 'em. Don't know who...Everything is contained. There's just the one communication channel...through the Trust. And, even then there's...layers."

This seemed like good information. Was he lying? A trust company managed the secret society. Made some sense. Trusts are used to maintain secrecy. And, that's what this group was all about.

"What's the name of the trust?" I said.

He shook his head.

"Come on, asshole, tell me."

He smirked.

"God dammit." That was it. No more. It was time to make a statement. I swung the club back ready to swing and...

Resistance.

I spun, but the club didn't and my hands slipped off it. I turned to see what—

Everything went black.

28

I couldn't see. Everything sounded muffled.

"Please no, no no!"

I blinked my eyes open. Double vision. I blinked again. Some improvement.

"You guys need me. I've got the whole Bay Area under control..."

"You talked. You failed," said a voice that played familiar. I couldn't place it.

"Please...Everything's cool. Once they go, we're back to normal. No need to over...overreact."

I knew *that* voice. The garbled one. Hal the Hillsborough City Commissioner. But, that other voice...

"Do it." Said the familiar voice I couldn't place.

Hal: "Noooo! Guys, look, what do you want? I'll give it to you. Anything!"

"We...want...secrecy," said the voice. "Know what I mean?"

Connection.

Couldn't be.

"Kill him," said the Voice.

I turned to look.

Ohio State tattoo on the leg.

'Doctor Rodrigo' from the massage parlor lobby.

He stepped back from Hal on the couch as the goons, the ones from the van, stepped up.

They left. How long was I out?

One goon pinned Hal's arms. Hal kicked and flailed. The other goon straddled his chest and choked him with a wire. Hal's face flushed red.

Blood trickled down his neck as the wire split his neck flesh. His body convulsed then went still.

My god.

What condition was I in? Where the hell was DG?

"Wow, you just killed a country club douche bag. Clap, clap, clap. Real tough."

There he is.

DG's voice came from behind me.

I spotted the dining table and chair legs nearby. A glance up revealed a quartet of parlor slaves perched atop it. The boss was back and they knew their place.

Doctor Rodrigo looked past me to DG.

"Don't worry. We'll get to you," he said. Then, he spotted me with my eyes open, "Look who's back."

He stood over and studied me like a curious predator sizing up the edibility of an unexpected prey. A look of concern grew on his face.

"Sure left the parlor early. Didn't like your girl?" he said.

I didn't know what to do yet. And, I needed time to recover from whatever had knocked me out. My head was throbbing. I stalled with some conversation. "She was fine."

"Just fine?" said the Doctor. "Ancient Delights takes pride in total customer satisfaction. Just 'fine' doesn't cut it."

He stepped out of view. One of the girls made a sound.

"Come here" said Rodrigo in a cold, soulless voice. He dragged my girl from the parlor into view. I never got her name. But, given the brand on her arm, Brandy seemed appropriate, if not in bad taste.

He looked to me, a fierce expression on his face. "What didn't she do for you? Did she refuse the special menu like I suggested?"

"I didn't ask for it."

He held her wrist and his other clutched the back of her neck like a vice. He squeezed. She winced and tried not to cry out.

"Mr. Asher was not impressed with your services, chica," said Rodrigo.

I wanted to help her. She had suffered enough. She didn't deserve this. Especially on my account.

"How come she didn't do it for you, Asher? Don't like 'em Mex? Prefer them white and trashy like your girl from the truck stop?" he said.

Son of a bitch.

"Did you put her in my house?" I said. Surging anger made me forget about the pain.

He shook his head and smiled. "No, no. We have other people for that."

The goons from the van climbed off Hal and flanked behind Doctor Rodrigo. He noticed and had them take the girl. Their grip on her was even harder. Tears were welling up in her eyes. Hal's corpse slid off the couch and onto the floor. The carpet was no longer white.

Rodrigo gestured to the girl.

"Or, maybe you did like her. Liked her so much you felt like you had to follow her here. Is that it?" he said.

I shook my head. What was DG doing? What was his situation?

"No? Oh..." Rodrigo looked off and scratched his head. "Well, I guess I'm a little confused then. Because, if you're not here for her then why are you here? I know it's not to snoop around on our secret little club. You know how I know it can't be that?"

I shook my head.

"Because we told you not to. Didn't we?" Rodrigo nodded trying to get me to nod.

I obliged.

He continued: "That's right. We told you what would happen if you kept poking your nose in our business, didn't we?"

I nodded again.

"And, you just kept poking. So, that means we gotta keep our word. And, that's why they sent me. Cause you're a little trouble maker."

I had to break this prick's momentum before he really got on a roll. And, I had a special technique just for that. Learned it in the corporate world. One of the best things I ever learned there. Basically, it's this: When an adversary accuses you of wrongdoing and is just salivating to punish you, do the very last thing they ever expected, agree with them.

I said, "You know, you're right. I really got out of line."

Rodrigo looked confused, as expected. "I'm happy to hear you say that. That way I have no qualms over what me and the boys are about to do to you."

"Well, it's more than that," I said. He was about to speak but stopped, surprised to hear me go on. "I just never gave you guys a fair shake. Granted, you didn't make a very good first impression by having my good friend killed. But, maybe that was just Tanjeris going rogue. Abusing his power."

"When you belong to our group it is impossible to abuse power. That's the whole point of the club."

Keep talking, Doctor.

"Doug mentioned that. Actually sounded quite appealing," I said. I made myself believe it so it would project as sincere.

"It's a hell of a lot more than appealing," said Rodrigo.

"See, that's where the confusion came in. Let me tell you what really happened," I said and started to sit up. He put a hand on my shoulder, stopping me. "It's hard to talk on my side. I'm just gonna sit Indian style."

I waited for him to consider it. Finally, he drew his hand back and let me sit up. I crossed my legs and acted like I needed to get the kinks out of my neck, which I did. But, I was doing it to see where DG was. He was behind me on a barstool. One of his hands was tied to a table leg with a knotted leather belt. No wonder he hadn't acted.

"Here's the deal. I was home the other night and this news report came on. Now, granted it wasn't flattering. But, I saw your logo. The one from the ring," I said and pointed to the ring now on Rodrigo's finger. It hadn't been there when he walked into the parlor earlier. "And, I thought that would be my chance to get in touch with you guys to see about joining the club. That's why I tried to talk with the reporter, Geraldique. That's why I went to the truck stop. That's why I even went out to the warehouse in Bartow."

Rodrigo looked confused by that last one. News to him. Impatience flashed across his face. "Okay, speed it up," he said.

"You get my point," I said. "I'm not out to mess with you guys. I want to...saddle up and ride with you."

That alone wasn't going to convince him. I had to give him reasons why. One of the most powerful words in sales copy is "because". Why's that? Because it gives the reason why instead of just providing a superficial statement.

"And, I wanted to join up *because* I'm tired of living my life the way it is. Working paycheck to paycheck. I mean, I do pretty well. But, I still have to work. I still have to pay taxes."

"Everyone in our group works. And, pays taxes. But, we do that essentially to keep it funded and keep up appearances. We don't want something like a tax investigation bringing the authorities around," he said.

Yes. Keep talking idiot.

"Smart," I said and pointed a finger at him like he is one special genius. "And, yes, I have more that I want to do than just not work and pay taxes. Know what I mean?" His words, my wink. To keep it between us. "Let's just say I have some exotic tastes."

He looked skeptical that a guy like me would have 'exotic tastes.'

I had to seal the deal,"...which is why she didn't exactly do it for me."
I nodded to Brandy who was still in the goons' unrelenting grip.

Rodrigo took a big breath and rubbed his eyes. It was getting late.

"That's very cute," he said. "But, that doesn't explain why you came all the way out here and started beating the shit out of our recently deceased host." He gestured to Hal's dead body.

Think.

"He wouldn't let me join," I said, so matter of fact it made it sound like it was obvious to anyone in the room that hitting Hal in the ribs with a driver was the only suitable choice.

"But, dummy...I heard all the things you said while you were hitting him," said Rodrigo.

"Yeah, and?"

"It sounded like you were trying to get to us for reasons other than joining."

"This is a recruitment party, isn't it?"

Rodrigo looked around the house, at the girls, back towards the bedroom. I presumed the guys were still there. Or, were they? Maybe they'd been sent home. I still wasn't sure how long I had been out.

"Yes, I supposed it is. Was. Party's over," he said.

I nodded to Hal's body. "Usually is when the host dies."

He looked over at Hal and I used the opportunity to stretch my arms in anticipation of action...something. I felt like this conversation was starting to fizzle out and Rodrigo would be forced to make a decision about what to do with me. The longer I kept him talking the better chance I had.

"But, here we are. And, you seem to be higher up in the organization and in greater position to, you know, bring me on the team," I said.

He studied me, almost as if he was considering that very thing.

I smiled and said, "I'll even fill out a membership application. And, pay the dues. Hal never told me how much they are."

Rodrigo sneered.

"You wanna pay some dues? Okay." He reached back and took Brandy from the thug who'd been restraining her. She looked relieved to be released and stretch out the muscles in her wrist and neck.

Rodrigo brought her up to me.

"Here's your initiation. Kill the slut then we'll talk. That way, I know you're serious."

I kept my gaze on him a beat longer to see if he was serious. He was. I looked to the girl. She knew enough English to have heard what he said. She wasn't panicking yet. But, you could see terror in her eyes. "Okay."

29

"No!"

Rodrigo squeezed her tight and wrapped a hand over her mouth. "Take her and have at it." He shoved towards me.

I stood up. My legs were off-kilter with blood rushing back into them.

"Got a weapon? I like knives," I said.

"Use your hands. It's more intimate," said Rodrigo. The gleam in his eyes revealed strangulation to be one of his "exotic tastes". "Do it over on the couch."

I nodded and took her arm. She resisted. Rodrigo gave her a chop on the neck with the side of his hand. She buckled. I grabbed her with both hands and held her up.

A last glance at Rodrigo. He sneered.

We moved towards the couch. The van goons cleared a path. Smirks. I guessed they were wondering if I had the stones to go through with it. I didn't. Something needed to change fast.

I pushed Brandy down on the couch, keeping my act up. She tried to slide away. I dropped on her, a knee between her legs. Hands on her shoulders. "Don't move," I said.

Now, it was truly kill or be killed.

"Walt, don't be dumb." It was DG.

I turned to look. Rodrigo did, too. One of the boys was already on his way over to shut DG up.

"The second you start choking her they're gonna be all over your ass, and it'll be two bloody—" The goon popped him in the mouth and shoved him off the barstool down to the floor.

Brandy screamed a shriek of death and clawed at me.

Rodrigo: "Shut them up."

A van goon started smacking the girls.

I rolled off Brandy. She jumped on the smacking van goon. She slapped and clawed. The other girls scattered off the table. They looked unsure about fighting back.

With the table no longer weighed down, DG, in a fit of rage, pulled on the belt restraining his arm and tipped it over. The belt shook loose from the table leg.

DG went nuts.

He whipped the van goon with the belt. When the guy turned his back in defense, DG jumped on him and wrapped the belt around his neck. DG's meaty, muscled arms flexed and the goon's neck snapped. He was dead and limp on the floor in seconds.

DG scrambled up.

Inspired, the girls who were lucid enough to understand what was happening attacked the other van goon who was manhandling Brandy.

DG sized up the room, belt dangling from his wrist like a whip. His gaze went to Rodrigo who was bringing a gun around from the back of his pants.

I tackled Rodrigo hard to the floor. Air 'oofed' out his lungs. I reached for the gun. His arm moved to avoid my grasp. He rolled me over, raised his arm, and elbowed me in the gut. My own air 'oofed' out. He scrambled around, straddled me, and brought the gun around to my face.

DG's boot swung in before Rodrigo could fire. The force snapped Rodrigo's arm and the yank of the break caused his finger to pull the trigger. BAM!

Girls screamed and ran. Van goon tripped over Hal's body and fell onto Brandy. Chaos reigned.

Rodrigo screamed in anguish as he looked at his snapped arm. His face flushed deep enough red to obscure the freckles that had dotted his skin. DG punched his face out of view. I felt Rodrigo's weight slide off me.

"Don't kill him!" I said.

Hal was dead. We needed Rodrigo for information. He would want help for his arm. We could get him to talk. "Stop!"

But, DG didn't listen. His was an unstoppable, careening rage. He pounded and pounded and pounded Rodrigo, then raked his face along the thick edge of the glass top coffee table. Rodrigo was alive but close to limp. His face bloody and swelling. DG leaned him against the table, his head flat on the glass. Then he stomped down with his big biker boot. The hammering force blasted Rodrigo's head right through the table. The surface shattered and cut through Rodrigo's cheeks as his body fell to the ground. He was dead.

DG was seething.

The other van goon sensed something and turned from the girl he was corralling to find DG standing behind him. Too late. DG's arm shot around his neck and yanked him around into a tight sleeper hold. The goons arms couldn't get any leverage around DG's big belly. They flailed. And, then they stopped flailing. DG didn't drop his body to the ground so much as he slammed it down.

The room fell silent save for DG's exerted breathing. Glass and blood was everywhere.

I was relieved we had won the fight. But, I was furious at DG. He'd just killed our two most valuable leads. The party guests, if they were still around, weren't members of the Kith yet and wouldn't know enough to lead us to the truck. Our only other option was...

Brandy whimpered on the couch. Her hair was a tangled mess. She sat up and spit on the van goon. She looked to us. She made a run for it. Out the slider door. I chased and caught up to her. We tumbled onto the backyard grass.

"Please, wait," I said. "We will take you someplace safe. I was never going to kill you. I promise."

She continued to struggle. I held her tight.

DG walked out.

"Come on, Walt. We gotta go. Someone's knocking at the front door. I think the neighbors called the cops."

30

We cut through yards and came out to the street several houses down. Red and blue police flashers swirled outside Hal's house. The cars belonging to the party applicants were gone. That was good. They couldn't serve as witnesses.

DG took the lead and hustled Brandy over to my car. I crept behind.

"They're not here to help you," DG said to her, fist gripped around her arm as he opened the back door and prodded her inside. Door shut. We slipped into the front seats. DG kept his eyes on the scene ahead as he started the car.

A police officer ran out of the house and over to his car. It was obvious he had just seen the fresh death inside. We waited. The officer reported to dispatch.

"Go," I said to DG. "Or, we'll never get out that gate."

His meaty paws yanked the wheel and we u-turned, gutter to gutter, and drove away from the house onto the main road out. A car turned onto the same street, towards us.

"Be cool," said DG. "Ain't a cop."

The car swerved in front of us. A hand reached out. Then, as we slowed, the car pulled up next to us.

"Where have you been? I thought you were coming to my house?" said Yamir, my client. He was visibly upset and the tone of his voice implied he was personally offended.

"I'm sorry, Yamir. We had trouble finding your place," I said.

"It's not that big of a neighborhood."

"Yeah, but the streets are kind of…It happens."

95

He gave DG a displeased look. Then he saw Brandy in the back seat. I didn't know how she looked, what condition she was in. And, I couldn't remember—was she topless?

Yamir looked to me. "Well, very strange, I must say."

"No doubt. I don't make a habit of this," I said.

He nodded, resigned. "The house is this way. Just follow me." He started to pull away.

DG gave me a look. I knew what he was thinking.

DG said, "We need to get out of here now or we ain't getting out of those gates once the squad shows up. May already be too late."

I looked over my shoulder at Yamir's car, which had slowed to a creep, waiting for us. I could see him watching us in his side mirror. He waved us to come on.

"Fuck it. I'll get a new client. Go," I said.

DG drove off. The inside of our car lit up red from Yamir's brake lights.

We turned into the exit gate. Police cars, their lights flashing, arrived at the development entrance.

"We're going. We're going," said DG. And, we went, each of us waving to the guard as the cross bar lifted up.

"Go right. Better to take country roads," I said.

To my surprise, DG listened.

We got the hell out of there.

31

The car was quiet. I was too tired to talk. Too sore. Too traumatized. Too everything.

Questions in my mind fired off faster than I could answer them— What the hell had just happened? Where were we going? What would we do with Brandy? How fucked were we?

Hal. Damn him. Damn him for that party. Damn him for not talking. Damn him for not saying Rodrigo was behind me. And, damn Rodrigo, too, for screwing everything up.

And, especially damn DG.

There we go.

That was the heart of the matter. I was pissed at Hal and Rodrigo. But, I was enraged at DG. Made no sense because he saved my life. But, he also killed a guy who had information that could wind up saving my life. Rodrigo could have told us plenty. Unlike Hal, who appeared to be a member of the secret society, Rodrigo appeared to work for it. He would know the inner workings better than any local affiliate member. He was our best lead yet. And now, Rodrigo was dead because DG's a hot head. Typical.

And, soon the police would be looking for the murderer. That made me an accessory to murder. And, fleeing made us look guiltier. Unbelievable.

I was back in the very position I never wanted to find myself again— on the run from police, being hunted by elite murderers, and desperate to find clues in time to save my life. Do it once, shame on you. Do it again, shame on me. *Way to go, Walt.*

Yes, we were in deeper trouble now. The Kith wouldn't cotton to us killing four more of their guys, driving off a group of new recruits, and releasing their sex workers.

I couldn't worry about that now. Had to think next steps. It would have been helpful to talk things through with DG. But, not now. I was sick of his obnoxious behavior. Not obnoxious. I don't know what it was. But, he was sure a pain in the ass. I wanted to punch him in the face.

My initial instinct had been to go it alone. That instinct felt right and true as we drove along the dark country road. With DG out of the way, the next steps wouldn't have to be a debate that slowed things down. And, I felt he didn't really know these guys the way I knew them. To be honest, I didn't really know them. Just that they were ruthless and relentless. So, they had to be taken serious. And, that meant not squandering any clues. Because who knew where the next one would come from? And, if it would come in time to save my life.

Brandy sniffed in the back seat. I was too tired to engage her in conversation. I told her things were going to be okay soon after we got on the road and away from the crime scene. Her response was no response. She just kind of closed in on herself. Scared, with two strangers, including me who, moments ago, had acted like I was going to strangle her. It wasn't the time for us to talk. The events at Hal's house were traumatic. We all needed a chance to absorb the trauma.

It helped to think about clues. That drew my anger away from DG. What did we have? Not we, I. I needed to extract myself from DG. Somehow. Maybe the bad feelings were momentary. Perhaps I'd get over them and he and I could work stronger together. Maybe not.

Clues, dammit!

So, what did I have to work with? I still had the invoice slips from the warehouse. That gave me eight addresses to pursue. The first address was Ancient Delights. That led to Hal's. Those addresses could be valuable. But, would they take me to the dead body truck? I needed the truck as proof.

Was Brandy a lead? She didn't speak much English. She wasn't inclined to talk. And least promising, her role in the organization had been massage parlor sex slave. How much vital information would she have been exposed to? My gut said not much. But...

The *St. Pete Times* had run stories about Clearwater's nation-leading crackdown on sex trafficking. It was riveting and disgusting to learn so many awful things were happening so close. Just a few miles from my house in some cases. The articles talked about how the sex workers would only stay in a certain area for a short period of time. 'Stay' implied they had a choice. They were moved from safe house to safe house. Making money for their owners at each stop. Maybe that was the case with Brandy. If so, she'd know of several properties within the organization. But, would she know how to get there? I wondered if the addresses on the invoice slips each belonged to a sex worker safe house. It was an avenue to pursue.

I got the chill again. The first time I felt it was several months back, when I learned people I didn't know, whom I had never met, wanted to kill me. And, they were pursuing it. The chill was recognition that there are dark forces in this world. Those dark forces had caught up with Brandy and stolen her life. I took some comfort thinking that even if those dark forces got me this time, at least I had helped her. As did DG, I suppose.

Wait a minute.

There was something else. Something Hal said. He said a trust managed the secret society. That's a clue. Thin at best. No company name. No trustee name. Nothing. I felt it all slipping away. And, that was dangerous.

The streetlight turned red and DG stopped the car. He let out a sigh. Out the corner of my eye I could see him look at me, then back at Brandy, then to me again.

"You know, a 'thank you' for saving your life would be nice," he said.

I looked to him, saw his expectant face, and ran a handful of bitter responses through my mind. What came out was, "Let's get something to eat."

He shook his head like I had some nerve.

The light turned green. He stomped on the accelerator. The tires peeled out.

32

Ranch House Restaurant. The hostess led us to our booth. I sat on one side, DG the other, Brandy next to him.

"Hi, my name is Trudy. Now, tell me whatcha drinkin,'" said the waitress.

DG and I ordered. Brandy said nothing. I ordered her water. Trudy took off. I pointed to Brandy's menu.

"Anything you want," I said. "I'll buy it."

She hesitated.

"It's okay."

She looked to DG. He nodded. She picked up the menu and watched us over the top of it for a moment, then looked down. I wasn't sure if she was perusing the menu or just hiding her eyes.

"We need to make this quick," I said. "I have a bad feeling our names and DMV photos are going to hit the wire real soon. Then, everyone will know what we've been up to."

"Just act like there ain't no problem and there won't be no problem," said DG.

Trudy brought drinks and set them around the table. "Know what you want?"

We ordered. That included Brandy who couldn't speak her order, only point to it. Made me think she hadn't been in the U.S. very long. What she must think. Trudy split.

The clinking of glasses and plates and the varied conversations from the other tables only enhanced the awkward silence at ours. As much as

I didn't want to speak with DG, we had to make a plan. The best way to get that ball rolling was give him what he wanted.

"Thank you for saving my life. Again."

He gave me a stern look. "Wasn't hard, was it?"

I had to fight the urge to unload on him. "No."

Brandy sat morose, looking down at her hands. She was wearing a jacket I had in the car that was too big for her.

He leaned in. "Did you get anything we can use?"

"Maybe," I said.

"I just got a murder rap for a 'maybe'?" DG scanned the room. He had the look of a man who had been seriously duped and didn't yet know how to extract retribution. He turned back to me and spoke with venom. "It's gotten real old saving your ass all the time. What's this, twice in the same day? And no matter how much I help, it makes it worse for me."

"I didn't tell you to ki—" I stopped and had to look around at the other patrons, make sure no one was listening. "You didn't have to kill him. We could have gotten more info from him. More than a 'maybe'."

"There wasn't time to talk. When a gun goes off in a neighborhood like that, the cops get called. We had to go."

"That's bullshit and you know it."

"Motherfucker, I don't bullshit," he said leaning in.

"Motherfucker, you do. And you don't think things through first." Had any of DG's men said that to him, they might have been killed. It was a fluke of the cosmos I could get away with saying it.

"Goddammit, Walt! You don't use half measures on these pricks. The only way is all the way. And, I am damn sick of their shit. Pull me over, try to frame me for having a dead body—*that they killed*. I'm already on their shit list. They connect two and two and me to the bloody mess we left on that cat's doorstep in Jax, they're gonna be even more pissed. No, I don't wanna hear it. We beat them all the way, finish this up, and spend the rest of our lives forgetting about it. Got it?"

"No, I don't 'got it'. If we're going to beat them all the way you gotta think just as well as punch. We're down to three possible leads and two are iffy. If those don't pan out, we're in the dark while they're sighting us in their scope. And, that should matter because you have more to lose than me."

"That's why I wish you didn't drag me into this to begin with. Shoulda just kept your mouth shut."

"That's how they win."

"That's how you die."

Standoff. Both of us took deep breaths. I moved my hands below the table because they were trembling. My heart was pounding. This was one of those sickening confrontations you have with people you love where you feel compelled to push your point but are scared of the damage it could cause. I leaned in, spoke soft.

"We've crammed two days into one. I've been in two fights and nearly died twice. We're exhausted," I said. "Let's recoup and discuss what should have happened another time."

"These guys aren't gonna give us a time out."

"I'm not saying relax..."

"Good. Let's make a plan. What are our leads?"

DG folded his hands on the table ready to listen. There was no getting through to him. My conviction from earlier stood—ditch him, solve this myself. He wouldn't like it. But, I had to put success first. Because success meant survival.

"Our options are, one, we check out the addresses on the invoice sheets." I patted the pocket that was holding them. "Two, Hal said a trust runs the group. And, it's their point of contact for all communication. If we can find the trust, it could lead to some big targets."

"Sounds like more than a maybe. That's good," said DG.

"Yeah, but we got no name, nothing."

"Anything on those papers?"

I pulled out the invoice slips, gave him a few to review, and scanned some myself. Nothing but the addresses and the name Groveland Trucking.

DG tapped my hand. "I bet you Groveland Trucking is owned by the trust. Let's start there."

"Yes. But, Hal said there are layers."

"I'll call my guy, get him on it."

I nodded. This was better than fighting.

"What else?" he said.

"Her." I thumbed to Brandy. She seemed to sense when our attention turned her way. "If she was moved around in their circuit she might have seen things, seen people in the group. She might be able to lead us there."

"Then she goddamn needs to talk." DG turned to her, "English?"

"Very little," I said. "I asked back in the parlor."

He leaned his shoulder against hers. "Por favor, tell us where they are. Where do they live?"

She looked at me, suspicious of DG.

"No se," she said and shrugged.

"Where are you from?" I said.

Nothing.

"Where did your *Jefe* find you? Get you? You know?" DG said gesturing with his arms.

She swallowed and looked nervous.

"Come on. You've been around enough English to pick up words," said DG. He was growing impatient again.

"She may not be ready yet," I said.

"We don't have time to wait," he said.

"Let me try."

He leaned back in the booth and gestured to me like, witness is yours. I made a conscious effort to look empathetic.

"It's okay. No Rodrigo, no mas," I said.

She flinched at his name. He must have been a real bastard. Yet, we couldn't have looked much better than Rodrigo and his gang. I could only imagine what was going through her mind at that moment. Stuck at dinner with two strangers, one who just beat a guy with a golf club and one who killed three men. She probably feared him less. He was bad but familiar. Add to that, she didn't know where she was and didn't speak English. She was a big, knotted ball of stress that needed careful undoing.

I continued, "We are bueno. Bueno. It's okay."

Nothing.

"We want to help you." I spoke slow just like the idiots in the movies. If she didn't understand English, it didn't matter how fast or slow I spoke. I felt foolish. "But, we can't help you unless you tell us about Rodrigo."

Another flinch.

DG noticed, too.

"Maybe I better powder my nose," he said. Good idea. I nodded and he swiveled out of the booth and disappeared around the corner.

I smiled at Brandy to let her know it would be okay. I cursed myself for not keeping up my Spanish speaking skills after high school. It would have helped mucho.

A recollection bubbled up. "De Donde?" I said. Where are you from? "Soy de Dunnellon. En El Norte."

Was that a smile?

I smiled back but contained my excitement and scrambled to come up with the next sane step. I proceeded with the caution of a man attempting to lure a killer panther off the desk in his small office.

Giving her information about me worked. I wanted to see how far that went.

"Soy write..." I gestured typing. "For television."

Another smile. This one seemed forced. She was enduring me and still only thinking about her safety. It would be a long time before she trusted me. And, even if I proved trustworthy what would she do after reaching safety? Just start a new life? No way she had any money. I could help her get started. So, could DG.

I was getting ahead of myself. What I needed to do was give her immediate reassurance.

"We are no policia," I said.

Bad move. She got spooked. Illegal status confirmed. She'd be just as scared of them as us or Rodrigo.

She took a deep breath and looked around. I didn't know what to say. That awkward moment had arrived.

Trudy the waitress brought our food.

"Alright, here you go..." She dished it out. I passed Brandy her plate.

"Looks good," I said with a smile.

Dishes served. Trudy turned to leave.

I looked over to see DG walking back to the booth.

Something flashed between him and me.

Brandy.

She shot out of the booth and ran for the exit. Once DG and I understood what was happening we ran...around tables and chairs and patrons and wait staff. Brandy had a good ten yards on us.

Her bare feet raced across the stained carpet, past the skill crane and empty lobby...right out the door.

DG pulled ahead of me. His size was enough to inspire others to leap out of the way, fast. He sprinted out the door.

I ran out of the restaurant to find DG gaining ground on Brandy at the far side of the parking lot. They flashed in and out of the streetlights.

He caught her. She screamed and turned and hit him, violent, desperate. He was big enough to handle it. With one hand around her forearm he slapped her swinging hand away. By the time I arrived, he had her subdued and tears were running down her cheeks.

"Good save," I said to DG.

He caught his breath and looked around. Something caught his eye. He looked to Brandy. She looked to him, terror in her eyes.

"Come on." DG yanked Brandy's arm and dragged her towards the street. He waited for a pair of cars to pass then marched her into the road. She was powerless to slow him down. A passing car slowed to observe this strange behavior.

"What are you doing?" I said.

"Getting answers."

DG marched Brandy through a grassy ditch and up into the parking lot of Juniper's Mexican Restaurant. *What the hell?*

I was on the street median waiting for a semi to pass. It did and I ran into the parking lot and up to the front door.

No DG, no Brandy. Where did they go?

I walked back outside. Left, no. Right, no. Where—

A scream on the far side of the building.

I hurried down the sidewalk and around the corner. A door to the kitchen was open at the back of the restaurant. I caught a glimpse of Brandy being dragged inside.

Hot steam from a dishwasher hit me right as I walked in. Kitchen staff was positioned at various stations. DG was further back and standing between Brandy, whom he still clutched, and a Mexican man who looked like one of the cooks. Tough to hear them through the clinking dishes and rattling pans. But, as I drew near I started to pick up the conversation. The cook spoke to Brandy in Spanish, and apparently under duress from DG. He spoke too fast for me to translate.

Brandy said something to the cook. He turned to DG with the translation, "She say she need help. You are holding her prisoner."

"Aw no." DG shook his head. "I just rescued her, man. I need her to tell me where to find the guys who were holding her prisoner. She was a sex slave, man."

The cook looked to Brandy and translated DG's statement. Brandy looked miserable. It was obvious she didn't want to say anything. Instead, she pulled away from DG. There was no breaking that grip.

The cook shrugged to DG.

"She doesn't want to talk now, DG," I said. "It's late, she's tired. We're all tired. Let's just get her someplace safe and we can try in the morning."

"She needs to talk!"

"She will as soon as she knows she can trust us," I said.

"We told her she could. Saved her ass. Bought her dinner. And, she ran off. We can't trust *her*," he said.

This was pointless. There was no arguing with him, not when he was this jacked up and nerve-fried. DG could be a very rational and shrewd dude. But, he wasn't showing it tonight. Getting pulled over earlier must have really un-nerved him. That reconfirmed my point about us needing rest. I tried the opposite approach.

"Give me the keys. I'll get the car," I said and held my hand out.

It was clear from the expression on his face he wasn't expecting that kind of a response. He reached into his pocket and tossed me the keys. He looked disgusted. It didn't faze me. I was over him. There was a better way to handle this whole messy situation. And it was my firm belief that was the only way we'd survive.

I tossed the keys in the air and caught them as I stepped out into the cool night.

33

Speed works wonders for DG. He sprinkled the white, powdery contents of a small wax paper packet onto his tongue, and soon he had the energy and alertness to drive us the hour plus back to his place in Dunnellon.

At first, I was hesitant. The Kith knew of my river home from a previous attack. Their first attack. Seemed like ages ago, but in reality it hadn't even been a year. No way we could go there. DG said I could stay at his place. It, too, had been attacked. Blown up, in fact. But, he'd had it re-built with extra fortification and increased the number of guards patrolling it. He also needed it for his illicit businesses. I didn't want to go there because I'd be relying on him, which I didn't want to do knowing I intended to ditch him.

Whatever. I just wanted to get someplace safe and sleep. Even hearing from DG's contact who had information on a trust company associated with Groveland Trucking wasn't enough to give me a tenth wind. I was ready to deal with it in the morning. But, he was on the line now. DG put him on speakerphone.

"This is Darrel," DG said.

"Hi," I said.

"Hey," said Darrel. "Okay, I did some digging around, looks like I found...something."

"Spill it," said DG.

"Title search for Groveland Trucking at the address on their website lists it being owned by Groveland Trust."

DG and I looked to each other, thinking about what Hal said about a trust.

"The trucking company appears to be their only asset. But, here's where it gets weird," he said.

DG and I remained silent.

"Groveland Trust lists Grove Park Trust as its trustee. And, Grove Park lists Grove Trace Trust as theirs. It's crazy, but there are, I counted, nineteen different trusts, each owning the other."

"If anyone was going to find out who really owns it, they'd have to dig very deep," I said.

"Yeah, right," said the contact. "And, that's just as far as I've gotten. However..."

I glanced at the back seat. Brandy was curled up and sleeping. She had pulled my jacket over her to keep warm.

"...it starts to circle around on itself. Grove Lake owns Grove Town, which is also listed as owning Grove Trace, which we know owns Grove Park. But, Grove Park is listed as owning Grove Lake," said the contact.

"You're losing me," said DG.

"I don't even know if this is legal. Something we might want to look into. Basically, it's a goose chase," said Darrel.

They had successfully obscured ownership for anyone looking to learn more. And whether the structure was legal or not, they had contacts in place to prevent that from becoming a problem. Depressing was the word for it. Another clue fizzled out.

"But..." Darrel's voice crackled through the cell phone reception, which was spotty on this part of the highway. "...I tried another angle."

DG and I perked up.

Darrel continued, "I did a title search on Ancient Delights, since you mentioned it."

"And?" I said before DG. Couldn't help myself.

"Same thing. Trust after trust to obscure ownership. Ancient Delights is owned by Parlor Properties Trust. Parlor Properties is owned by Parlor Time, and so on. What's different here is that the different Parlor trusts all seem to own a specific property. For instance, Parlor Time owns Ancient Pleasures, a massage parlor in Fort Pierce."

Interesting.

He continued: "Wasn't like that with the Grove Trusts. They just looped with no indication of any other assets."

"What does that mean," I said.

DG shrugged, then "They're limiting liability and discoverability. But, the pattern creates a link."

"Seems odd that parlors, which we know traffic in sex slaves, would be slightly less concerned about ownership identity than Groveland Trucking," I said.

"Oh, they're concerned," said Darrel. "They've done a lot of work obscuring things, just like Groveland. Any agency who wanted to go after them, or lawyer who wanted to sue them, would have a hell of a time just figuring out where to send the summons."

I looked again at Brandy. Even if she was a legal citizen, they'd made it impossible for her to seek retribution.

"So, are you saying we should check out these other parlors?" said DG.

"I wonder if they match the addresses on the invoice slips," I said.

"You could. But, that's not even the best part," said Darrel. "There's still a lot more to research. But, the point I'm getting at is this: I found an intersection."

"What do you mean," said DG.

"Grove Meadows Trust, which owns Grove Park Trust, also owns Parlor Ventures, which owns—"

"Another parlor," said DG before Darrel could finish.

"Right. We have a connection."

"So, it's all the same people," I said.

DG nodded. It felt like we were getting somewhere.

"So now we need to see where that intersection leads."

"Right," said Darrel. "That's gonna take more time and digging."

"We don't have time. Pop some uppers and get on it. I'll make it up to you," said DG.

"Already popped. Just wanted to give you a heads up. I'll get back to you soon."

"Alright. Thanks," said DG and hung up. He looked to me. "It's something."

"More than a maybe," I said.

But, was it enough to help? Maybe. It wasn't enough to keep me awake. I rested my head against the window and wondered how Darrel found all that out this late at night. Then I recalled that DG had so many connections around the state, from the highest reaches of government to the street level dealers who can give you the pulse of the city at any time. And, most of them were blood relatives. Best not to question how Darrel was connected. Or, how he got so much information in so little time. It was just DG's clan in action.

The car jerked hard enough to wake me up. Through bleary eyes I looked out the front window to see people, bikers, with guns, waving us away. I looked to DG.

"What's..."

A biker ran up to DG's window. "Go man! Someone is shooting at the house. Go!"

34

DG hesitated. Wasn't like him to run. But, he wasn't prepared to fight—no heavy weapons, completely caught off guard. His troops were trying to protect him by shooing him away. And, he trusted them.

DG shifted into reverse and floored it. Tall pines blurred past my window. Trail dust wafted into the headlights leaving behind a cloud of dirt.

The car shot onto a small paved highway without slowing down, jostling over the thick asphalt lip. Tires screeched and the car body shook on the shocks. DG slapped the gear into 'drive' and we raced away.

"The hell's going on?" I said.

"Safe house," said DG.

I was scared. DG looked scared. Brandy did, too. She watched out the windows with hands braced on the door and on the back of my seat.

"Damn, they move quick," said DG.

So much for avoiding collateral damage.

"They messed with the wrong hillbilly," he said. And, so much for keeping DG out of it.

"What does that involve?"

"You'll see." He waited a beat before continuing, "Usually only do it when drug gangs are trying to cut in on territory. Cats from South America and Mexico. Think it's they're god given right to run junk wherever they please. Make the mistake of thinking I'm just a dumb hick with a few guns and a bad attitude. What they never see coming...is that I got just as much money and just as much firepower as they do. But, I can be a lot meaner."

Was he telling me he's as powerful as a South American drug lord? Felt kind of slimy. But, in light of the circumstances, and considering who we were up against, maybe it would be better if we went after the bad guys together.

"Hey...yeah," DG spoke into his phone. "We're headed your way. Me, Walt, and a girl. No. Not like—just shut up and listen. Don't tell anyone we're coming there, understand? Because they can't know, got it? Shit's happening at the castle and under no circumstances can I be found. No, not a bust. Just...we'll be there in less than ten." He hung up.

"Where are we going?" I said.

"Place very few people, even in my organization know about."

He turned off the highway and cut down a gravel road that ran between two wide pastures. Didn't look like I was going to shake him anytime soon. Just had to roll with it. For now.

He turned off the main gravel road and onto another, which lead towards a massive cluster of trees.

"The Withlacoochee Forest?"

He gave me a sly nod, tongue sticking out the corner of his mouth.

The car raced into the forest. The moonlight, which had been lighting the passing fields, was extinguished. A darkness like I had never seen surrounded us. How the hell did DG have property on state protected lands? Same answer as always: Because he's DG.

DG slowed the car and switched to parking lights. They illuminated our path just enough. The road twisted and turned and then split.

The car stopped next to what looked like a supply shed for the forest rangers. DG got out without saying a word. I stayed put and watched him circle the front of the car. "Come on," he said with a wave. The keys jingled in his hand.

I looked back to Brandy. She looked to me.

"It's okay. Safe," I said.

No response. I climbed out of the car and opened her door. She hesitated and looked around. Anyone would have seen there was absolutely no place to go. And, despite being a tough woman who had endured countless horrors, it was obvious she had no desire to spend the night alone in the woods without supplies, fire, or weapon.

DG opened the shed and waved us inside. Typical enough with shovels, rakes, and whatnot. Smelled earthy. But, at the back of the shed, DG opened a hatch in the floor. Stairs. Warm light glowed below.

Brandy stopped at the threshold. Strange place, strange men, dark forest. She had to be thinking 'trap.' But, she had no choice. Her shoulders dropped in resignation. She descended into the warm light of the underground bunker

DG waved for me to go next.

"How the hell did you pull this off?" I said.

"Good, old-fashioned bribery."

"The forest rangers?"

DG smiled. "Cash plus weed, grown fresh in the forest."

That's my DG. I descended the stairs and heard the hatch door slam behind me.

35

Sleep was solid, but short. After the last two days of chaos, I needed a month to recover.

Coffee was waiting for me in the main room of the underground bunker, which, DG informed me, was built by his brother, Ronnie, who owned a construction company in Inglis, near Crystal River. Thick, dark wood beams striped the ceiling. Moroccan rugs covered the floor. I imagined DG having romantic getaways here. Also, biker drug fests. It was a multipurpose facility.

I helped myself to coffee and a biscuit and sat at the large slab of barely finished wood that served as a table. The coffee was better than expected. The moment of peace and quiet, sublime. But, it didn't last.

Flashback: What happened at DG's house last night?

Flashback: How was I going to get information out of Brandy?

Flashback: The trusts inside trusts inside...

I pulled the shipping slips out of my pocket and flattened them on the table. An address jumped out: Fort Pierce. That's where Darrel said one of the trust companies owned a business. A massage parlor. Did all of the addresses on the shipping slips belong to satellite parlors? Was Groveland trucking just the distribution network used to shuttle girls through the circuit. That made sense. And the broken down truck? Part of the fleet.

But, what about the bodies? Two possibilities: The girls either died on the truck or died before getting on the truck. If they died on the truck, how? Suffocation, heat exhaustion? Maybe. They'd have to have been in there a long time.

What if they died before getting on the truck? That would mean the truck was disposing of the bodies. Run the circuit, gather up the pretty girls who couldn't handle the party? Take out the trash. What a cold, black thought. But, it rang true.

Wait.

How many girls did the Kith go through each week if they needed a trucking system to gather up the corpses? Where were the girls dying? Parlors? How did they die at these parlors? Not die…killed. Something evil offered on the special menu? Customers come in with a penchant for pain and take it too far? Or, maybe with enough money they can indulge their darkest desires. Isn't that what Tanjeris had said it was all about? Maximum freedom.

The worst truths feel exaggerated, beyond belief. But, I could no longer discard my assumptions. I had to consider the worst possibilities, to allow the mind to travel unarmed into the horrors of men. Men whose hearts were so hollow and their souls untethered and lost that the only thing they could fill the void with was money, pain, or evil. Sometimes all three. These creeps really did belong in the same club.

I thought of the girl at the Tanjeris house. Were private residences part of the corpse collection circuit? If so, which of these shipping slip addresses were for private residences? I'd have to visit each one to find out. Scratch that. Google Earth would help speed that up. Did DG have a computer here?

I sat back and exhaled. I pulled my mind's eye back from those dark details to get a bird's eye picture of all my options.

That left Brandy and Darrel.

DG walked in. Same clothes, bags under his eyes.

"Sleep all right?" he said.

"Yeah. Could use more," I said.

He walked over and tossed a scrap of paper onto the table. A name was scribbled on it.

Dewey Lawrence, Esq.

Before I could look to DG a set of keys clanked onto the paper. They were not my keys.

"Darrel called back. He dug way deep. Found three trusts that owned all the other trusts. Those three trusts are all managed by this guy."

He pointed to the paper.

"I have soldiers down. Gotta make sure they're taken care of and secure my house. Talk to this guy and don't take any shit," he said. "I got a girl trying to get the chick to talk."

I nodded and grabbed the paper and keys. When I looked up at DG, he was holding a small gun by the barrel and offering it to me.

I took it.

36

DG was wise enough to know they'd be looking for my car. So, he hooked me up with a very middle of the road Chrysler LeBaron convertible. And, soon I was driving Highway 301 towards Zephyrhills and Tampa.

Getting the name of the trustee, Dewey Lawrence, was huge. Wind in the sails after what felt like a rough night of spinning out of control. I was anxious to make the most of it.

The name Dewey Lawrence led me to expect a small, mild-mannered guy with a vanilla life. But, the fact that he was managing the three trusts that link together a massive and massively profitable illegal enterprise meant he was deep inside the organization. He had juice. Juice made him dangerous. And, I couldn't take that for granted.

These guys were just as bad as any of the drug cartels that had snaked into the state...the Russian mob in Miami, the Italians in Tampa...DG's redneck empire? Would I ever even consider trying to take down those dangerous organizations by myself? Hell no.

Yet here I was locked in battle with a group just as powerful as those notorious criminal enterprises. I felt a new kind of scared. Not the heat of the moment, run for your life fear I'd been dealing with over the past twenty-four hours. It was the scary realization that...I didn't have much of a chance.

But, if there's one thing I know from writing infomercials, it's this: Fear is a great motivator. Fear is persuasive. Fear drives people to action. Don't believe me? If a person feels vulnerable or threatened, they'll naturally do something about it. If they think they can do something about it. Survival instinct.

Could I do something about the Kith? I had before. And, I was just an infomercial writer running for his life then. This time, I was an infomercial writer with fighting, mystery solving, and yes, killing experience. Why couldn't I do something about them again?

It was a moot point. I *had* to do something about them. And my task today was a simple one: Get answers. That's all I had to do. I didn't have to bring down the whole system. I didn't have to blow up their network. I had to drive to that lawyer's office with questions and I had to leave with answers. No matter what. All I had to do was speak to one guy. And, the guy's name was 'Dewey'.

Nice pep talk, Walt.

37

Dewey Lawrence's office was in familiar territory. West Kennedy Boulevard, straight down the road from Ancient Delights, which I drove past. The parking lot was empty, trash on the ground. No sign of working girls, their johns, or their hustlers. Of course, the hustlers wouldn't be there. They were left for dead in North Tampa not twelve hours ago.

Dewey Lawrence the Lawyer's office was in a wide, flat two-story plaza; the type that seemed designed by coked up architect "visionaries" in the late 1970's. That meant it actually had some kind of style with its angled wood accents. Whether that style was good or not could be debated. Either way, the building stood out.

As I reached the upstairs balcony, I noticed he had the whole second story to himself. There was just one glass door. It was tinted to block the sun and had small gold letters affixed to it: Dewey P. Lawrence, Esq.

I didn't have a plan. No script for this writer. But, I was ready to improvise. I had to presume Dewey would know who I was. Word had to have spread about last night's events.

A bland guy in a flashy suit was leaning over a very attractive receptionist as she sat at her desk in the lobby. She looked like a high-end porn star at the wrong gig. He was caressing her shoulder and leering down at her. She didn't seem to mind. They were into each other. So much so, they startled at hearing me clear my throat.

He recognized me.

"Stay still. Don't touch a thing." I pulled out the gun and still didn't like the feel of it in my hand.

On instinct, the receptionist started to put her hands up.

Dewey slid off her desk and stood defiant, hands on hips inside his blazer. He was short and unimposing. But, he didn't notice.

Dewey said, "I know who you are. We got no problem dealing with people like you." He pointed at me with the cell phone in his hand.

I stepped forward and waved them back from the desk. She stood up. No skirt. No panties.

Dewey scowled and started to twitch. "You're already a dead man. All I have to do is make the call and it will be official."

He did something really weird. He looked at his phone and licked the face of it. Wiped it with his fingers and licked it again. As if he missed a spot. This dude was on something. He started to dial.

I kicked the phone out of his hand. It dented an acoustic ceiling tile then dropped and tumbled across the floor. Dewey startled and staggered back. I grabbed and slammed him onto the reception desk. He 'yiped' as his back landed hard on a metal stapler. I shoved the gun in his face. The receptionist's heels clop-clopped out of the room.

"You're the dead man if you don't give me some answers," I said.

I was right in his face, gun pressed against his jawbone. My fear had turned to rage.

He sniggered. I could tell he wasn't sure what to make of this, and got the impression he was used to being in control. Blood rushed to his face.

"Who owns the trust?" I said.

He said nothing, shook his head.

"You know what I'm talking about. You know exactly what I mean. Who owns the trust? Who runs your little, secret club?"

He moved his right hand. I grabbed his wrist before he could do something cute. I saw the Kith ring on his finger. He tried to resist but wasn't very strong. I pulled his hand in front of our faces.

"This secret club. Who are they? I know you manage three trusts that run their businesses. Who owns the trust? Who runs it?"

He coughed and snorted, like he had something in his sinus passage and needed to get it out to breathe. I released his hand and smacked him hard. He gasped, inhaled deep, and started to twitch.

"I don't know what you're on. But, I have all day for you to come down. I'm not leaving without answers. Just tell me who owns the main trust and I'll split. Who runs it?"

I was getting louder and angrier. This jerk had clammed up and I needed him to talk. My life depended on it.

"Is the trust the main corporate entity behind your club?"

No answer. But, he glanced away as if trying to distract himself so he wouldn't reveal something he shouldn't.

"That's a yes."

He shook his head violently.

"Do the people who own the trust run the club?"

Another non-answer confirmation.

"Another yes."

More head shaking, more desperation. I could feel him trying to push my body off his. He was too small.

"You're going to talk or your files are going to talk, got it?"

Another head shake.

I tightened my grip on the gun and knocked it against his skull.

"Oh, Shit," he said as he grabbed his head.

That move did not work like in the movies. I hit him again, further back on his skull. He collapsed, out cold. So, that's how you do it.

I pushed myself off Dewey and got my bearings. No one outside the office, no one in the room. Where was the girl?

I hurried down the lone, long hallway leading out of the lobby. To the left was a kitchen area. No one there. To the right, copy machine alcove. Empty. At the very end of the hallway, a closed door. She had to be there. And, so did his files.

The door was locked. I looked around. Uh oh. Surveillance camera, upper corner. Red light on. Someone was seeing this.

A harder twist. The handle wouldn't budge. I stepped back and kicked the door. It was thick and sturdy. I walked back to Dewey and found keys in his pocket.

The first key worked. That never happens. I steadied my breathing, counted to three, and flung open the door. I jumped back and went flat against the wall, just in case. Nothing. I led with the gun and stepped into the room.

Dewey made serious money. I could tell by the modern Scandinavian furniture populating the room, which was pristine. Minimalistic and white. No legal certificates on the walls. The place gave the impression of wealth without revealing any details about the man who owned it. Cold. Flavorless. Heartless. Just like his colleagues.

The admin assistant wasn't in here. Where'd she go? Forget it. I needed information and a swift departure.

The desk drawers were locked. The keys worked. Only a few papers inside. I grabbed them. The bottom drawer contained an opened bottle of J&B, half drained. Dewey had work stress like the rest of us.

The wall behind the desk was glossy, white with two-foot wide columns all the way across. No knobs or handles to pull, so I pressed. Nothing.

What was I missing?

There were no other fixtures for storage. No drawers, shelves, bookcases, baskets. Strange. Nothing out of place.

Hold on.

I walked over to the corner of the room partially obscured by the office door. There was a small, white end table. It had a potted plant on it. The plant was on its side. Tipped over. A crumble of dark soil stood out against the white carpet.

I moved the office door back and forth. It didn't touch the table. It couldn't have knocked over the plant. What did?

A groan from down the hall. Dewey.

Time to move. I closed the door. No lock. At least, not one I could turn.

I moved the table. Nothing. I set the plant upright. Nothing. I knocked my knuckles against the walls. Dense, not hollow, until...

A panel just out of the corner made a hollow sound, as if there was nothing behind it. I placed my fingertips against it and pushed. Nothing. But, when I pulled my hands back, the wall drifted out like it was on some sort of slow hydraulic arm.

Bingo.

When the wall panel stopped moving I pulled it back further to reveal an entrance. I led with the gun.

Three steps later, I stood in what looked to be a private lounge. Visually, it was the exact opposite of the office I had just left, dark, comfortable, a place for relaxing and cutting loose. A montage of images played as I scanned the room: Acoustic foam padding on the walls (to keep sound out), stereo, fur rug, a bottle of clear something. Lubricant. End table with scotch in a crystal jar and lowball glasses, pigtail bolts in the wall with leather handcuffs dangling. The memory of previous Kith encounters compelled me to look from the cuffs to the floor. I expected bloodstains or discoloring, but the carpet appeared clean.

No secretary here.

There had to be another way out.

I pulled the door to the lounge shut and slid the long leather couch in front of it. Now, where?

"If you're in here, don't worry. I'm not going to hurt you," I said.

No response.

I moved further into the room. Black folders were stacked on a nearby desk. I reached over and fanned them apart. Initials had been typed on white labels and affixed to the tabs.

I opened the first folder. A black and white photo was clipped to the inside cover. It depicted a man, white. An un-groomed mustache hooked down past his upper lip. His hair was scraggly and unkempt. His smirk made me think ex-con. A homemade tattoo scribbled on the side of his neck solidified that belief.

Papers across from the picture gave a name: Ricky Aarons. Details followed:

Height 6'2"

Weight 186

Truck driver

G.T. Fleet

4 Years

Known Haunts: Frog's Bar in Daytona, The Rhondavous in Seminole, and One More Round in Lake Wales.

Lake Wales was near Bartow. Close to Groveland Trucking. G.T. Fleet. Ricky was a truck driver.

A handwritten note at the bottom of the page confirmed it.

No sign of R.A. since truck abandoned 10/14. Truck broke down. Ricky panicked and ran. Cargo left at scene tantamount to group exposure. Isolate & remove pursuant to Articles 4.16.15.

Articles? They had bylaws?

Level 3 Pursuit in progress.

Better run fast and far, Ricky.

I closed Ricky's folder and grabbed the next one. As I lifted back the cover I was greeted by a face I recognized - Hal, from the country club. I glanced at his spec sheet:

Bodeker, Hal
City Commissioner Hillsborough County Florida
Dead/Contained.
Property seized pursuant to Articles 8.2.15-6

No note at the bottom of the page. Everyone knew about Hal. That story had ended.

I pushed the folder aside and grabbed the next one, but stopped at seeing the initials: W.A.

My heart pounded faster and harder. I slid my finger under the cover and flipped it open.

There I was. Surveillance photo of me. I got spooked when I realized it had been taken outside my house. The time stamp had yesterday's date. Jesus...they had swarmed on me at the first sign of trouble.

I skimmed my stats as I was already familiar with the culprit. But, I read the full handwritten note twice.

Asher, while not our only adversary...

Wait. More people were after the Kith? Who? I needed to talk to them. A united front would be stronger.

...But he is by far the most troublesome and persistent. Following the clean break of the Tanjeris affair, we anticipated no more quarrel with Asher and were content to let things be until his guard was down.

Reading that was like a complete re-charge on my spirits. I was right to go after them when I saw the news report. They wouldn't have let me live. I had done the right thing.

Asher is on the run and under pursuit by several teams. Last seen Bodeker, Hal residence, where last night's incident occurred. Intercepts have been established in following Asher haunts: Dunnellon, Gainesville, Clearwater, Tampa.

Seeing their plan spelled out on paper was encouraging. I felt like I had been through all of this before and their approach did not seem new. Perhaps their intensity had ratcheted up. But, I believed I could handle it.

Another realization hit me: Here I was inside a Kith higher up's office. No, his secret office. And, I was reading the very dossier they had on me. I was inside. I had penetrated. Everything I was doing was working. I just had to keep it up and keep moving.

My good feeling ended with a flip of the page.

Pictures of Ilsa. Candid shots of her around Gainesville, us together...her in Europe.

They were watching her. Watching her right now. They could get her at any moment. And, I was thousands of miles away.

It was only a matter of time before they played that card. Then, what?

Click.

"Read anything good?"

38

A gun was pointed against the back of my skull. It was Dewey the trust lawyer.

"Hell, yeah. Very encouraging to see how well I'm screwing things up for you. Makes me happy," I said.

He yanked me back by my collar. I made a point to not act like it bothered me. This guy made me think I'd get a psychological advantage by never letting him see me sweat.

"Get the jokes out now because there won't be a later," he said.

"It must feel good to play tough guy after sitting around here all day waiting for orders," I said.

"You don't know what you're talking about."

"You push paper. Big whoop. So exciting, you have to fondle the help."

"Help me, Anna," he said.

The administrative assistant. Where had she been hiding? How did I not smell her perfume?

She grabbed my wrist and pulled my arm up. I yanked it down and out of her grip. Dewey shoved the gun barrel against my skull.

"Let her have it!" he said.

"Alright," I said.

I backhanded Anna right across the face. She gasped and fell to the ground. I didn't like hitting a woman. But, I also didn't like assisting people with my death.

Dewey jumped onto my back. I leaned over and let his weight pull us to the floor. He landed first. I landed on top of him. The impact knocked the gun away from my neck just before it fired.

I scrambled up and kicked the gun out of Dewey's hand and cocked my fist back to punch. A handcuff locked around my wrist. A glance over my shoulder - Anna, rubbed her jaw while revenge flickered in her eyes.

I looked from her to the cuff to the wall where the cuff was chained. Several quick tugs made it clear I wasn't going anywhere. Not good.

Dewey winced as he stood. He grabbed his ribs with his gun hand

"Nice work, babe," he said to Anna.

She looked to him and smiled.

I backhanded her face again with my free hand. She dropped hard, lights out. Couldn't have her helping him.

Dewey shoved me in the chest. "I am real tired of your act."

"You guys have been trying to kill me. How do you think I feel?"

"Ain't nothing compared to what we're gonna do to you."

"I love when you try to talk street. Sounds so tough." I smirked and kicked at him. He was fast enough to step aside. And, he was so pleased with himself that he wagged the gun.

"No no. You be good 'til the others arrive. Then, you can fight back. That'll make it more exciting."

Exciting for him, deadly for me. I searched the room for a way out of this predicament.

He leaned back on the desk, where he wouldn't have to worry about keeping clear of me. "You call it pushing paper. But, this whole operation crumbles without me," he said.

Perfect. I'd hit his pride nerve.

"I'm sure. With only about five hundred other trust lawyers in the area, they'd probably have a hell of a time replacing you," I said.

He shook his head. "I see what you're doing."

"No, you don't."

"I do."

"You don't."

He shook his head, paused a moment, then gave a most serious look. "These guys are all about running wild, indulging every fantasy, building power..."

"As I told your boy Rodrigo, I heard that rap from Tanjeris. He was real proud of it. Now, he's real dead," I said.

"That's not the point."

"There is no point, Dewey. What could possibly be the point of running slaves? Killing people? Money? You're gonna die. You can't take it with you."

"Spoken like a man who's not making the kind of money we are."

"I wouldn't want to. Not at that price."

"My point is, while they're running wild, I'm running the operation. I'm the one cleaning up the accidents."

"Like the truck on I-75?" I said.

"Yes." Irritation flared across his face.

"You sound disgruntled," I said.

"Huh?"

"A disgruntled employee. Bitching about the boss. I'll be sure to tell them when they arrive. Bet they'd love to know exactly what you think about them running wild."

"You'll shut your damn mouth. I can be disgruntled all I like. I'm an owner, not an employee," he said.

Breakthrough. I now had one of the monsters responsible in my sight. A shame I was chained to the wall.

Anna moaned on the floor and rolled onto her back.

"I guess if you were an employee, there'd probably be someone sexually harassing you, too," I said with a nod to Anna.

He waved me off. "She loves it."

"If you were an employee, maybe there'd be a dossier about you on the desk. Or maybe, there is a dossier about you on someone else's desk. Who would that be?"

Dewey appeared conflicted. But, not about what I was saying. Whatever narcotic he had taken was fighting through the anger and adrenaline coursing through his veins. Keeping the gun aimed at me was starting to take effort.

He pulled his phone from his pocket.

"I'd like a Coke, since you're ordering out," I said.

A twitch.

A sniff.

There. He did it again. A big, wet lick of his tongue across the phone's glass surface. His eyes rolled back in pleasure, like a great white sinking its teeth into the slowest harbor seal.

"You realize how many goddamn germs you just put in your mouth?"

He gave me a hazy look then seemed to remember where he was and sneered at me. He looked down at the phone and dialed. His tongue was bulging between his lips.

"I have Asher. My office. He's not going anywhere."

He hung up.

He shrugged. "With all the damage you've done, I thought you'd be some sorta action hero. Or cop. Or something."

"I'm just an infomercial writer. A very good one," I said.

Curiosity bloomed on his face.

"The things on TV?"

"Right."

He snickered. Most people do. I found peace with it years ago because it proved my theory that any business with a stigma against it stands to make a ton of money. The obvious example is pornography. But, also garbage hauling, horror movies, menstruation accessories...and infomercials.

"So...what I don't get is how that helped you fight us. Let me be clear. I don't admire you or what you did..."

"Feeling's mutual."

"But, for you to take us on and survive and even kill a few of our guys, that's kind of impressive. You were never a cop?"

"You've sifted through my entire background. Did it ever say I was a cop? Or in the military? Or, a ninja?" I said.

He shook his head. "What's your secret?"

"My secret is persuasion. I get people to do what I want."

"Unconventional weapon," he said.

"You're right. But, unlike guns I never run out of ammo."

"Not sure how that helps when the other person has a gun. Like now."

On cue, he aimed the gun at my face.

"It doesn't. What could I possibly say that would give me the advantage?"

"Nothing."

"Correct."

"So?"

"So, what? You're in control. Nothing I can do to save myself."

"That doesn't sound persuasive. You must not be very good at your job."

"From what I see, you're very good at yours. Did you practice solo before working with the group?"

He seemed to brighten at being asked to talk about himself. Everyone does.

"I did. For many years. It was okay. Security, had a family."

"Kids?"

"Yes. A boy and girl."

"I bet you were a good dad," I said.

This surprised him. "Trying to sweet talk me?"

I shook my head. "We're just talking. You had a job that provided for them. And, you're clearly dedicated to things you believe in." I nodded to the room, meaning the whole operation. "I'm sure you made the right decision to join the..."

I wanted him to fill in the blank with the name of the secret society. He didn't.

"Right," he said. "Wait, what were we discussing?"

"Your kids, previous practice and how you hooked up with the...Sorry I don't actually know the name of your group. I've been calling them the Kith."

He smirked and nodded. "Not a good name."

"I'm used to coming up with silly, catch names like Click N Shave or Fur Sure!"

"Is that the one, the thing for grooming your pet?"

"The do-it-yourself home pet grooming kit that keeps you from getting fleeced at the groomer," I said, confirming his suspicion.

He nodded, remembering it.

"That was you?"

"Guilty."

"Oh wow. You have to admit that was pretty ridiculous."

Just give me the name of the group, jerk.

"You are a thousand percent right. I also have to admit I made over two hundred grand on just that commercial. About 40 hours of work, total."

"What?" he stood up and stepped forward. "I had no idea you made that much money."

"You didn't check my bank account?"

"Well, we did, but I just never connected it to...infomercials."

"I know, right? Normally, that's lawyer type money."

"That's *good* lawyer money," he said.

"Well, hey. If I don't get outta here, they'll looking for a new writer," I followed it up with a charming smile.

He offered a curt laugh. "I should apply."

"I'm sure you could do it, but why take the pay cut?"

"I wish it was a cut," he said, oblivious to the revelation.

Time to pivot.

"You're kidding, right?" I said.

"Huh?"

"You're set up with these guys, the what's their names..."

"Don't worry about it."

"…And I make more than you?"

His eyebrows pinched and his eyes wandered. I'd hit a nerve.

"Ah, well...the base may be lower but the perks are beyond your dreams." He forced a smile to sell the notion. But, only authenticity sells.

I nodded, acting like I got it.

"Sure, but what happens when you retire?" I said.

The ghost of unconsidered consequences spooked him. He frowned and licked his lips. Almost pulled his phone up for a licking. But, the cold splash of recognizing his critical error kept him sober enough.

"Why, uh...would I ever give this up?"

I said nothing. Silence compels the last to speak to keep speaking.

"I mean," he continued, "I got it made."

"Spoken like a young man," I said.

"Thanks for the life lesson, dad. But, I manage trusts. My gig is planning for the future. I got it covered."

"Their future or yours?"

"Both."

"You have your future covered? Or they have it covered for you?"

"What are you getting at?"

"They're scary smart. You think they're gonna put all their trust in one underpaid attorney?" I wanted that one to sting.

He stepped closer and took an indignant posture.

"I guarantee you I am irreplaceable."

"The Beach Boys replaced Brian Wilson."

"I'm more important to my group than he was to his."

That was saying something. Something dumb.

"I know," I said.

"So, don't--" He stopped, unsure now what he was arguing against. Works every time.

I filled the void. "You don't have to convince me. I can see all the good you do here. You make things happen. And, they'll be reminded of it as soon as Ricky Aarons is brought in. Dead or alive."

"We'll have him by tomorrow," he said.

"Where is he?"

"Don't worry about it." Damn.

"Did you hire him?"

"I don't bring in scumbags."

"So, they make the mess..."

"Don't you worry about it."

"...But it's your neck on the line if Ricky isn't..." I recalled the words from the dossier regarding Ricky Aarons, "...isolated and removed."

"The system works."

"For some."

"For me."

"That why your wife left and took the kids?"

He punched me in the jaw. I had to shake my head to clear it. I pressed:

"Your wife knew you'd gotten yourself trapped and she didn't want to be part of it, right?"

Another punch. This time I expected it and turned away to lessen the blow.

"Things didn't work out," he said.

I stretched the sting out of my jaw before speaking. ""At least you can fill the void with your secretary."

He stepped in for his hardest punch.

And, I was ready for it.

I blocked his fist with my unchained forearm and kicked him in his belly dough. Air wheezed out his lungs. As he buckled, I reached across and ripped the gun from his hand. He went wide-eyed and wanted to chase after it. But, his lungs were still recovering. All he could manage was a small reach with clawing fingers.

I pressed the gun against the cuff chain and pulled the trigger. The bullet ricocheted across the room creating a poof of feathers as it ripped through a decorative pillow on the leather couch. I yanked my cuffed hand down, but no luck. The chain hadn't severed all the way. So, I shot it again and ducked. The chain dropped loose from the wall.

Dewey slammed me into the wall. I pounded his back with the gun and my fist, and when my two hands were closest together I transferred the gun from one hand to the other. I was a better shot with my right hand.

I pulled the trigger.

Dewey wailed and grabbed for his kidney as he crumpled to the ground.

"No…" He couldn't finish the statement.

He reached around for help. He found Anna's ankle and squeezed hard. She moaned. The pain was enough to shock her back to consciousness.

"Tell me the name of your group, Dewey, and I'll at least call the medics for you."

He said nothing and just reached for his pocket. He pulled out his phone. I swiped it from his grasp and held it high in the air. He groaned.

"Name or no phone," I said.

He shook his head.

"Make it quick."

He clutched at his lower back. "Please...it hurts!"

I heard someone call out, faint from another part of the building, "Mr. Lawrence?"

"Tell me."

"There isn't..." He took in the biggest breath he could. "Can't track...what has...no name." He smiled as blood dripped over his bottom lip. "My idea," he said.

"It was a good one," I said.

"Dewey!" said the voice down the hall, closer.

Time to go.

I dropped his phone in my pocket, leaped over Anna and Dewey, and scooped up the dossiers. I wanted Ricky Aarons' info to see if I could find him. Who knew where he could lead me?

"Wait, you can't..." The faint words came from groggy Anna calling out to me.

"Anna, call..." Dewey's pained voice rasped at her.

Anna looked his way but didn't know what to make of him.

I spotted the exit they had used to sneak up on me. It was behind the desk, another press and release wall.

"Dewey!" The voice was in Dewey's office.

I ran into the darkness behind the secret door.

39

The hidden passage led down a carpeted hallway lit by dim purple lights. At the end was a push handle door that revealed stairs, which led down to a different office.

I was in the travel agency I had seen at the end of the building. Vintage destination posters adorned all walls. Desks ran along opposite sides of the space, creating a central path on the avocado green carpet. It felt very Tampa 1970s, which I would have admired any other time.

I stood silent and still. What would the travel agency staff say seeing me run through their office?

Hold on. There was no staff. The place was deserted. A desk clock that looked decades out of place read it a little after ten a.m. Too early for lunch break. Was this place just a front?

A bang. Upstairs.

Had Dewey's visitors just slammed the door to the stairwell? If so, they'd be here in seconds.

Another bang.

No, it wasn't the door. They'd just shot Dewey and Anna.

I looked out at the plaza. At the cars. At the traffic on the street beyond. Nothing, no one. Clear? I hoped so and pushed the door. It was locked.

Another bang. *That* was the door to the stairwell. They were coming. No time to wait. I flipped the lock open and ran out amongst the parked cars then cut left and jumped through the bushes that divided Dewey's plaza from the car wash next door.

I rolled onto my belly and watched. The travel agency door swung open. A big, fit man in white from head to toe trotted out and looked around. I lowered to avoid being seen.

"Hey!"

A voice behind me.

I ignored it.

"You alright, man?" Closer now. "Hey, you."

I tried to remain still.

The man in white looked my way.

"Brother, you okay?" It was a sweaty middle-aged guy in a sopping wet car wash t-shirt. He touched my shoulder.

The man in white saw me and ran my way.

I ignored the man checking on me, got up and ran into traffic.

Tires screeched as a car braked hard. I launched off the median and hurried to the far side of the street. A glance over my shoulder revealed Mr. White running with the intensity and form of a track star. He didn't even look as he leapt from the sidewalk to the boulevard pavement.

And, that's when the F-150 creamed him.

His head smashed the glass. His leg kicked back and over as he flipped off the hood and smacked onto the pavement where the car in the next lane was unable to stop in time. It skidded onto him and stopped only after a nauseating thump-thump. The man in white was accented red.

I considered running over to him, acting like a bystander, and frisking his pockets for information.

I considered playing it cool and making my way back to Dewey's office so I could ransack the place for information.

I considered getting the hell out of there before cops showed up because drivers and pedestrians were already looking at me funny.

I chose option number three and got the hell out of there.

40

Was I being followed? I couldn't be sure. Damn, it was hot out for this time of year. No one in sight. Goddamn, Dewey.

I didn't get enough information.

But, I did have his phone in my pocket. If I could get in, I could see his contacts, who Dewey called, who called him. So much information.

Password required. Shit.

They had Ilsa. That was all that mattered now.

My mind reeled with the possibilities. They could snatch, grab, gun down, stab, strangle, or bomb Ilsa at any moment.

I shook the dark thoughts from my mind. This was the time for action, not panic. I got into this because I thought I was some kind of hero. Now, I had to prove it.

41

DG's guy Chuck met me at the Lil Champ convenience store two blocks south of Kennedy. He arrived in a rumbling Chevy Nova that looked to be in mid-rehab. Two hours later we were in Ocala watching DG pull into the Chili's parking lot. He and Chuck embraced, enacted a ritualistic handshake, and then Chuck held out a hand towards me, like 'here he is.'

DG nodded and gestured for me to get into the car. He didn't look thrilled. At best, he was wondering what happened to the LeBaron he had loaned me. At worst, things had gone bad at his house.

"How'd things go with the lawyer?" he said.

"Good enough to lose your car."

He wasn't amused. So, I pulled Dewey's cell phone from my pocket. "Here's his phone. But, it's password protected."

He took the phone and started sliding and tapping his thumb across the screen. His eyes darted between his work on the phone and the road ahead. After a moment he held the phone up to the steering wheel, pressed a combination of buttons, then released.

"Here." He handed the phone back to me. It was unlocked.

"How the hell?"

"Hang around as many criminals as I do, you pick up a few tricks," he said.

"You never cease to amaze me," I said.

"Ditto."

"They're tracking Ilsa overseas."

"So?"

"So? She's my girlfriend. Basically, my wife."

"Two of my guys were shot in the head."

Not quite the same as having your girlfriend in harm's way. "Sorry to hear that."

"We just gotta stop these fuckers fast." DG nodded to the phone. "See what you can find."

I tapped the 'Contacts' app and started scrolling. There were plenty of names that didn't mean a thing to me. And, the contacts that stood out the most were the ones that didn't seem to mean anything at all. They were just initials. Or, arbitrary words that all seemed to be named after animals: 'cow', 'pig', 'horse'.

I exited 'Contacts' and checked 'Recent Calls'. Dewey had been speaking to quite a few people over the past couple of days. Strange: not one number was repeated. I exited and checked his email.

Interesting. The same handles were applied to emails. I opened and email from 'Horse'. It read:

Keep me updated. But, handle it yourself. All my focus must be on the gathering.

Gathering? I scrolled down the email thread.

Closing in on Ricky Aarons. Found a KA who spoke with him the night after the accident. Mentioned Ormond Beach. St. Augustine has been pulled off Asher and dispatched to O.B. Other teams pursuing Asher. Attacked his KA, Donnie Gary's home. No Asher. Tightening Dunnellon/Bushnell/Brooksville triangle.

So they had a good idea where I was. But, that was before I'd shown up at Dewey's office. They'd know I had been back in Tampa. I turned to DG.

"They were tracking us between Dunnellon and Brooksville. Think they could find us in the forest?" I said.

He shook his head without giving it much thought. "No way."

"Maybe after today they'll be looking in Tampa again."

"Anything else on there?"

"They mentioned a gathering. Not sure if that's important."

There was no further communication in the email thread. No sender name, address, or contact information in the digital signature. I backtracked to the inbox and scrolled through more emails.

Much of the communication between Dewey and someone using a farm animal alias was incredibly, and I presumed deliberately, vague. Emails get hacked every day. They didn't want anyone knowing their business, period. They were smart and careful. And ruthless.

Dewey was less careful when it came to his vices—drugs and women. There were several emails regarding a deal for Ecstasy. There were email threads with a variety of women. I checked his text messages. But, they were wiped clean.

Next check: Photos.

It was a full dose of sin and sleaze in high definition. Picture after picture of Dewey's exploits revealed what really went down in the secret lounge next to his office. Orgies, drug parties, complete decadence. There were pictures of Anna the administrative assistant, on all fours and in garters and stockings. A line of cocaine sprinkled down her spine and a gaggle of partiers snorting it off of her. There were a couple guys with close-cropped hair and clean-shaven faces. They vibed white collar stiffs, married, owners of mini vans. My gut said Dewey was acting like a big shot showing them a better time than what Tampa's famous strip clubs could.

Most of the pictures on the phone were set in the secret lounge. But, the party attendees varied indicating different times, different occasions. There was a series of pictures featuring Mexican girls with brands on their arms. Perks, Dewey? Other pictures revealed more intimate affairs with just one woman in photos taken from Dewey's point of view, including a photo of Anna naked, on her knees, and drinking out of a dog bowl.

Well, Dewey...looks like you gave up a lot to go after the bright, shiny object of excess. I hope you were satisfied.

I looked out the window. The highway whipped by. It struck me as funny then sad when I considered how flippant I'd become regarding killing people. Yes, they were very bad people doing very bad things. But, I made a mental note to never take the killing lightly.

The car rocked on its axels and swerved across the pavement. A soccer mom driving two lanes over seemed not to notice or mind. But, then another car pulled up between us.

"Shit," said DG.

He stepped on the gas. The car just outside his window also accelerated as it attempted to pull even with ours. A man had a gun pointed out the window. Kith.

"DG!"

He hit the brakes. I hit the dashboard. Their car shot ahead of us. The car behind smashed into our rear bumper. I fell back into the seat.

I turned to see the car behind us. The passenger's head had cracked and bloodied the glass. The driver's arm reached out the window and aimed a pistol. DG's rear window shattered.

"Fuck this!" DG yanked the steering wheel and floored the gas, sending the car careening over the median in a sod-ripping U-turn.

Traffic on the far side of the median braked hard and scattered to make way for us. The Kith thugs followed with little consideration for collateral damage.

Once DG's 180 was complete, he floored it. The engine rumbled and the car vibrated. I grabbed the Jesus handle.

"How'd they find us?"

I shook my head. Dewey's phone slipped off my thigh and onto the floorboard.

"The phone's GPS," I said.

"So, Dewey gets killed, they don't find a phone on him, and they start tracking it. Damn, they're smart."

"We're smarter. They haven't caught us yet."

That pressed the right button. DG looked to me with pleasant surprise and a rascal's smirk.

"No, they sure haven't," he said.

He yanked the wheel and fished the car around an oblivious older driver. Highway 200 was way too crowded and lacerated with stoplights, not that DG was stopping for any of them. We needed to change streets.

And DG did, cutting a hard right down the frontage road running along I-75. Neither of us knew where it went, but that didn't matter. We needed distance from our pursuers who were still charging after us.

"Got any weapons in here?"

"Check in back," he said as he reached into his patch-covered denim vest and pulled out a pistol of his own.

There was plenty of junk on the back seat. But, I didn't see any weapons until I pushed aside a crumpled serape. Underneath was a pair of shotguns and a box of shells.

"Shotgun," I said.

"Shoot it," said DG. "Aim for the tires."

"I'll get a better shot if you slow down."

"So will they."

"Good point."

"Do your best, Walt. That seems to work these days."

I appreciated the vote of confidence.

The car swerved into the oncoming lane as DG passed a slowpoke in an old Chevette. I crawled into the back seat and grabbed the shotgun.

"Know how to use that?" said DG.

"No. But, I'll figure it out," I said.

I was on my knees leaning against the back seat. Glass from the rear window had been blasted into the car and was jabbing into my leg. The gun felt heavy in my hand. I gave it a quick once-over then broke it open. Loaded. I snapped it shut. Bullets shot out of the gun and punched a large hole in the rear driver's side door.

"Damn!" said DG startled up front.

"Sorry," I said. My ears were ringing and my hands were shaking.

More glass shattered. I ducked.

I hurried to get a handle on the gun, reached for the ammo box, extracted two shells, and plugged them into the chamber. Click and cocked.

Now, it was a matter of timing. I needed to get up and aim and fire and duck back down before they could fire back. It wasn't a recipe for precise marksmanship. Not that I was precise or a marksman. But, I needed results.

"DG, I'm ready. Tell me when to take the shot."

He glanced at the rearview mirror then the road ahead.

"Got a bend coming up. Wait 'til I make the turn. That'll give you cover to get set for when they follow around the corner."

"Okay."

My breathing was heavy. My hands, slippery. I wiped one on a pant leg. I was nervous.

When you spring into action, you don't think about what you're doing. You just do it, your body and mind react on instinct. But, when you have to wait and anticipate, it's nerve-racking.

"Here we go," said DG as he started to turn the wheel.

The tires screeched and the car shuddered. I worried about it tipping, and even had to brace the gun barrel against the door to keep from rolling over.

"Get set," he said.

I wasn't ready. I took a quick, deep breath and sat up.

No car behind us, just the fast passing road and the interstate in the distance.

I cradled the gun, got my grip, lowered my eye down to the site and aimed.

"You see 'em, blast 'em. Tires, windshield, don't matter. Just fuck 'em up," said DG.

I didn't respond. Just watched and waited...

And waited...

And wa - BLAM!

The Kith car had appeared around the corner and swerved at my shot. I missed.

No thinking.

BLAM!

Windshield glass spider webbed across the driver's side. The car veered out of control, plowed into a chain link fence then wrapped hard around a pine tree.

DG whooped. "Got him!" In his excitement he almost lost control of our car.

The other Kith car whipped right past their colleague's wreckage and gunned it for us.

Before I could get my eye to the gun site, their bullets pinged and panged into our automotive metal. I ducked. DG ducked as he yanked the wheel back and forth to make the car swerve.

I sat up and fired.

Click. No bullets.

Damn.

I dropped and reached for the shells.

Bullets shattered window glass and thumped into car seats. One missed my face by less than an inch.

The shells spilled onto the floor. I was close to panic.

"Shoot em," said DG with more urgency.

I stretched to get the shells. They rolled across the floor, evading my eager fingers.

Got one.

Then another.

I laid prone on the seat with the gun flat on the floor. An awkward angle to load.

"Say when I can get up."

"Now," DG said.

He hit the brakes hard. Tires skidded. The car shook and shuddered and, worst of all, swerved ninety degrees so that when I popped up and fired I was only shooting the side of the dirt hill that ran next to the road. And, I didn't have time to re-load before the Kith's car t-boned the side of ours.

The force of the blow knocked me against one door and then I tumbled ass-over-head into the other door. It was a surreal blur with glass flying through the scene and stinging my face. DG growled as the air was forced from his lungs. His pistol rattle across the dashboard. The crunch of metal was a sound I'd never forget.

I fell head first onto the floor, jacked my shoulder against the armrest, and felt the gun butt jam into my gut. I got nauseous.

The car stopped. Bullets peppered it. Glass flew and cushion cotton popped into the air. Smoke stung my nostrils. I couldn't catch my breath. My arms and the gun were twisted under the weight of my body.

DG fell over in the front seat and didn't move.

A door opened.

Footsteps crunched glass on the pavement.

"Promotion time," said an eager voice.

A face appeared in the window above me. The son of a bitch grinned and raised a pistol. But not before I shot DG's, which had tumbled into the back seat close to my hand.

The thug flopped back out of sight as soon as the blood splotch replaced his nose.

A moment passed. I caught my breath. I peeked out the shattered window. The man I had shot was dead on his back across the hood of the car he'd just driven into ours. His partner hadn't followed up was because he was dead in the front seat. He had been the one whose face had smashed the windshield earlier.

I sighed with relief.

DG.

I twisted and reached out for his shoulder. Just that small amount of jostling seemed to revive him. He groaned.

42

The car was jacked up and I was paranoid, shoulders to ears as I checked the rearview mirror every few seconds to see if we were being followed. And, I was in pain. Couldn't help but wonder what sort of medical ailments I'd be visiting the doctor for in the near future. If I ever had the chance.

One tough decision I had to make, and had to make alone because DG was not fully coherent, was whether or not to keep Dewey's phone. It held vital information. But, I didn't know how to disable the GPS tracking. So, I wiped our prints off and left it with the dead thugs. Before splitting, I checked their pockets and their car to see if they possessed any items that could be to our informative benefit. They didn't.

A quick stop for food and drink was enough to revive DG to where he could guide us back to the hideout; I'd never have found it on my own. Even better: we were greeted by a semi-friendly Brandy.

The main reason for the turnaround was DG's old lady, Starla. She could charm the pants off murderers and hard timers. This was a woman who had such an easy going demeanor it didn't matter what your hang ups were, there's a good time to be had, so relax baby. She got Brandy to relax.

Brandy helped DG to his room once his wounds were tended to. That left Starla to tend to me.

"You boys sure know where to find trouble," she said, smiling as she dabbed a homemade salve on the cuts across my arms. It stung, then soothed. I was grateful.

"Trouble finds us," I said.

144

"Again and again."

"I know two brothers got it, at the house. But, is everyone else alright?"

She sighed and nodded. "Yes, I suppose so," she said. "DG's ready to go to war with whoever did it. He mentioned the name but I forgot it."

"I found out they don't actually have a name."

"Not even the 'No-Names'?"

"Apparently not. They don't want to be found and they've made all kinds of moves to prevent it."

"But, you have found them." She offered a sly smile and looked into my eyes. She looked proud of me.

"I guess so."

I remembered the grainy photo of Ilsa in the dossier and how it could only mean she was in danger. "But, it's not enough. We need to..." I leaned in. "What we really need is for Brandy to help us find them. Fast."

"Have you asked her?" she said.

"She was too scared to talk."

"She's been through a lot. Not just last night, where she was basically abducted again."

"What?"

"It's true, baby. She sees you kill a couple people then she's whisked away to the woods. Can you blame her?"

"No." Then, "DG told you about that?"

"Oh, please. He tells me everything. That's what old ladies are for."

I thought again of Ilsa.

"How's your old lady?"

"Not good," I said.

"Why's that? And, how we gonna fix her? You know she's got an open invitation to stay and play down here. You know I'll show her a good time."

I couldn't help but smile.

"I'm sure she'll be ready for that when she returns. Her mother's dying, and...she's in danger." It was hard to say the words.

Starla patted my knee. "Let's go talk to Brandy."

43

Brandy was sitting on a deep-cushioned sofa running her fingers across the stitching of a patchwork blanket that covered her knees. When she heard our footsteps, she looked up and smiled. It couldn't have surprised me more.

"Ines?" said Starla.

"Si?" said Brandy in response to being called Ines. Her real name.

Starla sat on the couch next to Ines and touched her wrist. No flinch. She trusted Starla.

"¿Te sientes cómodo hablando con Walter ahora?"

I couldn't understand what Starla said. But, Ines looked me over, studying me. She nodded to Starla, who looked to me and smiled. "She says she'll speak to you now."

I smiled, first to Starla then to Ines, which was kind of weird since she saw me smile to Starla. I pulled a cushioned chair over close and sat. "I'm listening."

I assumed a posture similar to Ines, hands by my side, legs uncrossed. A proven persuasion tactic. I wanted to make her feel comfortable so she'd keep talking.

She looked at Starla, then me, then Starla again when she finally spoke. "Quiero que sepa que no soy una prostituta," and stopped. She looked to me, waiting for Starla to translate.

Starla said, "She's not a prostitute. She wants you to know that first."

I nodded. "Understood."

Starla translated my statement to Ines. For someone who looked one hundred percent Caucasian, and redneck on top of it, Starla's Spanish was remarkable.

146

"Gracias," said Ines.

Starla turned to me to translate, but I cut her off. "I know what that means," To Ines, "De Nada."

She nodded and spoke to me this time. "¿Quieres saber quiénes eran esos hombres? Eran monstruos."

Starla translated to me and I responded. "I know. And, I want to stop them. But, I can't do that unless I find them. Can you help me?"

Starla translated, and soon the conversation started to pick up momentum and provide a captivating picture into Ines' life as a sex slave.

"I cannot tell you where they are. Only some of the places I've been. But even then, I do not know the exact places. Me and the other girls were blindfolded when we were smuggled. How we were the night you rescued me. Last night. That happened often," said Ines.

"Just tell me what you can," I said in response. "I'm listening."

Ines folded her hands across her lap and began in earnest. She talked about there being too many parlors and stash houses to recall all of them. The conditions were always bad. Little food, little water. Only enough to stay alive and sexy for customers. What the men thought was sexy. She didn't feel sexy, not at all. The girls were profitable assets, after all. Yet, there were barely mattresses to sleep on. And, filth was everywhere.

I watched as her eyes squinted, looking into that past. Instead of sadness or fear, resolve and resentment appeared. And, it didn't dissipate as she waited for Starla to translate to me. Ines was lost in the moment, reliving the past. And, doing it bravely. She was, in fact, fearless in her retelling. I admired her for that.

Starla translated Ines: "Violence was used to make the girls behave. And for the troublesome girls, they hooked them on drugs. Smack. It made them listless and loyal. They would never leave and risk missing their fix," she said.

Nothing new or innovative. Hooking sex slaves was as common as executives having their secretaries order office supplies. It was so common I even knew about it from the 60's exploitation movies I enjoy from time to time. They didn't seem so entertaining now.

"Torture was also used. Beatings, almost daily. Burnings. Hot brands against skin, to mark their property. And, so much worse."

This was her most uncomfortable moment. She looked down at her lap, past the scars and scrapes on her arms, and I took it as a subconscious tick pointing her towards the location of her darkest violation. I didn't press for details. The gist was evident. Anger cooked inside me. As if I needed another reason to hate those guys.

"¿Qué más necesitas saber?"

Starla turned to me, "What else do you need to know?"

"Can she name any cities she was in? Can she give any names?"

Starla translated to Ines, who shook her head no. Starla came back with, "She says they never let her know where they were. It was impossible to tell from inside the brothels…They were stuck in their rooms sixteen hours a day, at least. Servicing clients the entire time."

"Early on, I considered asking for help. Hoping one of the men would take me out of there. Many of them would propose, but none ever saw it through. One time, I was close to asking a man who came to see me every day, but then two things happened. First, another girl in the brothel tried to escape with a man. He offered to buy her outright. Both the girl and the man were beaten by the thugs who guard the brothels. The very next day we were all moved to a new brothel. It took a long time driving, so I guessed it was from one state to another."

"You mean these guys operate out of Florida, too?" I said. Starla translated quickly, echoing my urgency and surprise.

Ines shrugged. She had no idea.

I felt like we weren't getting anywhere. Making it pointless for her to relive her tortured past. I pointed to the brand on her arm. The Kith symbol.

"Do all the girls have those?"

"Yes."

"Did you see men wearing that symbol? On a ring?"

"Yes. They were always the worst. The meanest and most violent."

I wanted to ask her again if she knew who they were. But, she'd already said she didn't. The Kith had done an excellent job of keeping their girls in the dark.

"Did you ever go to men's houses and perform?" I had Tanjeris in mind.

She nodded and said, "Yes. Often."

I racked my brain for more questions in different directions. Not much was popping up. But, then I remembered something from Dewey Lawrence's office. "What about gatherings? Did you ever attend a gathering? Like a big party, or, I don't know. Anything like that?"

Her response via Starla's translation went as such: "There was a party. It was at a large house surrounded by nothing. Just woods, trees. I could not tell where I was. It was colder than normal, but still very sunny in the time we were taken from the van into the house. I could see the light out the bottom of my blindfold. I saw palm trees out the windows."

Winter. North Florida. My guess. It was more woodsy up there, could get colder, and still have plenty of sun. Even palm trees. Of course, I could be totally wrong.

She continued: "They offered us drinks. Booze. I accepted because I knew what it meant. And, I was right. It was like a non-stop parade. Man after man. For days. By the time it was over, I felt..."

I nodded so she'd know I understood what she meant and didn't have to give more details.

"Were the men with the rings there?"

"Yes. All of them."

All of them? This was interesting.

"Dressed up. Like a formal occasion."

A formal gathering with all the Kith bigwigs. In one place, doing their worst. I had to find out where it was. I had to get there.

"Was that the only gathering you went to?"

"No, there was another. Just as bad."

"Same location?"

"Different location."

Not the answer I was hoping for. She couldn't tell me the location where the next gathering would be. I didn't really have any follow up questions.

Ines surprised Starla and me both by uttering some English, "I sorry I no help." She was unsure about the last word.

Starla patted her hand. I offered a smile.

"You did great," I said. "Thank you. I know that wasn't easy."

Starla looked to me, her hand still gently on Ines', "Why don't we let her rest up a bit."

"Good idea," I said.

I stood and walked over to the door. When I looked back, Ines was lying down on the couch. Starla was draping a blanket over her legs.

A thought hit me.

"Ines, where did they catch you?"

Starla looked down at Ines and translated the question. Ines looked to me. She told Starla and Starla told me:

"I was walking to the store in my home town and they pulled me off the street," she said.

"In Mexico?"

She shook her head and thought for a moment. I wondered how long it had been since she'd remembered home. Had the complete dousing of hope made her forget where she belonged and with whom she belonged?

"Not Mexico. Lorida."

"Florida?"

"No, Lorida," she repeated, this time directly to me, not through Starla.

"I'm not sure where that is," I said.

Starla turned to me. "Lorida's a small town off Highway 98. East of Seabring. Lorida, Florida."

"Really?"

Ines nodded.

I looked out the door, my mind racing, hope percolating. It seemed I still had a lead yet.

I turned to Ines.

"How would you like to go home tomorrow?"

Starla translated.

Ines looked at me in disbelief. Silent. Stoic.

Then she broke like a dam, crying tears of salvation.

44

Time was running out.

Options were running thin.

I had to do something.

Taking Ines home to Lorida really meant I was hoping to find a clue there that would lead me to the Kith. I also hoped she'd divulge more information about them on the drive down. Perhaps something would jostle her memory. Maybe someone in her hometown would know more and I could figure out what steps to take next. Either way, the drive would give me time to think. And, I doubted my hunters would expect me to go there. I'd never even heard of the place and couldn't be traced to it.

Unfortunately, my car was gone.

Of course, to get there I was going to need another car. How many vehicles had I gone through this week? Week? Shit. It had only be 3 days since this madness had begun. It felt like a lifetime.

I went searching for DG, but he wasn't anywhere in the bunker. When I ran into Starla coming out of Ines' room, she said DG was out taking care of business. That could have meant his typical business of assorted, and most likely, illegal activities. Or, he could have been going after Kith. She didn't know. Either way, he had taken my car.

"That was very nice of you to offer to take her home," said Starla.

"I'm gonna need some wheels," I said.

"Let me see what's available."

With that, she departed and left me to assess my situation. I didn't like where things stood. In the past twenty-four hours I had only learned that they were stepping up their hunt for me...and maybe Ilsa. That's what really worried me. She didn't even know she was being watched. I wanted to let her know. But, I didn't want to scare her. Maybe best not to say anything yet. Perhaps I could find something out in Lorida that might help first.

But, shit, shouldn't I give her some kind of warning? What if there was no new information in Lorida? *Stop worrying, start doing.* I had to keep pushing. And fast.

It occurred to me there was a difference between getting back at the guys responsible for hurting Ines and filling that truck full of dead bodies...and tearing the entire Kith system down. Even if I solved those two specific crimes, how would I be able to prevent the Kith from ever striking again? Put another way, how would I ever know for sure I'd be safe from them?

This was the same question I'd had in my mind before deciding to go against the wishes they expressed by way of Love-Mart's body. Now that I was balls deep in it, I was no closer to answering that question. Everything had become more complicated and sinister than I had anticipated.

Would I ever be safe from them? Or, had my death warrant already been signed? And, what about Ilsa and DG? Was it too late for them no matter what I accomplished in the next few days? No matter which battles I won...would the Kith still end up winning the war?

That was depressing. But, 'heroes' can't think that way, can they? I had to admit that my brash entrance into this fiasco had been because somewhere, deep in the back of my mind, I probably thought I was a hero. I had done it before. I can do it again. *Smart thinking, Walt.* Good luck getting this shit off your shoes.

If I couldn't win the war, it seemed my actions only served to achieve one goal...delaying my death.

I sighed and closed my eyes. I was growing anxious and ready to move.

Instead, I fell asleep. The clock on the wall indicated a good forty-five minutes had passed before I awoke to the sound of keys jingling. Starla had entered the room and was holding them out to me.

"Here sleepy," she said.

I yawned as I took the keys from her.

"That car you drove back from Ocala needs too much work and nothing else is available. So, take mine and I'll have the boys bring another one out for me."

Us, meaning her and DG.

Something else gnawed at my insides. Should I stay or should I go? Without DG, that was.

He was a good man and a huge help...when he wasn't killing our only source of information and being an asshole in general. But, once again, I had nearly gotten him killed. Yes, he wanted to be involved enough to kick some Kith ass. But, I still couldn't shake the thought that it was my fight, not his. My mess to clean up.

"How's he doing?" I said.

"Gonna need some rest. He doesn't like to take five. But, he hates going against my wishes even worse," she said.

That settled it. Even DG would concede there was no time to wait. I had to go without him, as I preferred.

"Then we're going to head out. Me and Ines."

"Not before you eat. I'm gonna whip up something that'll stick to your ribs."

Starla smiled and walked out of the room, and soon I heard the clang and bang of pots and pans being pulled out of their cabinets and set on the stovetop.

An hour later, Ines and I walked out of the bunker and over to Starla's Nissan 280zx. A relic of the Eighties, but still in stellar condition. It was her baby. And, she was DGs woman. And, he made sure her baby got all the TLC it needed.

Starla spoke over my shoulder. "Now, DG may let you crash, crunch, and abandon his cars. But, I expect you to bring that sweet ride back. Or, don't come back at all, understand?"

I turned to see her atop the stoop with a smile on her face, but it was clear she wasn't joking.

"I'll take great care of her," I said. "I promise."

"It's a he," she said. "I don't ride no lady."

Fair enough.

"I'll make sure he lives long enough for you to ride him again," I said.

With that, I pressed what I thought was the key fob. But, the distinct lack of a beep-beep reminded me this car was pre-fobs and I actually had to stick the key in and twist to open it up. So, I went full gentleman, walked around the car, and opened Ines' door first.

As I walked back around to my side of the car, I looked to Starla and said, "I'll take good care of him. I might need him to save my ass again."

"No doubt about that, Walt."
This time she wasn't smiling.
The car engine roared in admirable fashion as we rolled into the woods.

45

Starla's car hauled ass. Hell, yes. Slicing through traffic gave the sweet, smooth feeling of progress and achievement, at least in terms of geography. That was okay. At least I was doing something that might make a difference after the fits and starts and stops of the past several days.

And, I didn't mind ditching DG. Starla said he was out taking care of business and there wasn't time to wait around for him. He'd be mad but he'd be safer than if he were with me. I didn't feel bad.

In fact, taking Ines back to her family made me feel good. Even if I didn't stop the Kith or keep them from killing me, at least I had saved her.

The look on Ines' face when she saw her family proved that. She could barely get the word "Mama" out of her mouth before she broke down crying and running towards her mother who had been around back watering flowers. Her mother dropped the hose and hugged Ines like something she'd never allow to be lost again. Water poured across concrete and started to rise in the flowerbed.

Ines' father wasn't home. Her mother insisted we go to him right away. I offered to drive. They accepted. Tears continued to flow on the way over. As they sat in the back seat, Ines' mother proclaimed her love to Ines and said they never stopped looking for her, said they never moved from the house in case she ever came back. So much had changed and they worried she was lost forever. But, they never gave up.

I couldn't help but get choked up. The reunion was beautiful. I didn't dare say a word to interrupt.

At the Valpo Meat warehouse, located just south of Lake Jackson, all the workers stopped as Ines' mother's cries of joy echoed throughout the slaughterhouse. She ran past workers and cows and cow parts for her husband who approached from the back of a long, cold, rank-smelling corridor. He wiped his hands on a blood stained apron. He looked confused as he held his wife. But, then he saw Ines.

"Ines?" he said as he pushed his wife off him to look into her eyes. The tone of his voice was skeptical, as if he didn't dare begin to hope.

"Si!" said Ines' mother. She turned and pointed. Ines ran towards him, as she must have so many times as a toddler, arms outstretched and ready to wrap around 'Papa'.

The family clashed together in embrace. They cried. They clutched as tight as they could. I couldn't understand the Spanish they spoke. But, the love and joy and relief needed no translation.

My god, it was beautiful.

Cows received a last minute reprieve from execution as workers gathered around their friend and colleague who had just received the greatest news of his life.

All of his co-workers looked Mexican. They understood what he said. They knew what this meant. No doubt they'd heard his stories and laments, his appeals and pleadings, and his rage. To them, Ines' father's ship had at long last come in. And, you'd have to be a real son of a bitch not to love it.

This was humanity. This was life. What it was all about. This was worth fighting for. No matter what darkness or evil existed. In those few glorious moments, my life was changed. The prize had been circled and highlighted right before my eyes. This was why I had to keep fighting.

We'd won a battle today. No doubt about it. And, it tasted beyond sweet. Now, it was time for bigger risks and the ultimate reward.

In my mind, the happy faces of Ines and her parents fused with the solemn faces found on the drivers' licenses amongst the stacks of discarded clothes and belongings in the Groveland warehouse. My mind raced back to the abandoned, corpse-filled semi truck by the side of the road. Who did those corpses belong to? Where were their friends and family and loved ones and co-workers who would dance upon their return?

The rest of my life was on pause. I had one purpose now. I'd be reminded of it every time I thought of Ines and her family. What an exceptional feeling to know I was on this planet, at that very moment, only to fight. I knew what I had to do and whom I had to do it to. Now, I just needed to find them.

46

Word spread throughout the town. There had been no formal announcement. But, prior to even getting out of the car back at Ines' house, friends and neighbors anxious to see the long lost girl had started to arrive. Before long, it seemed the entire population of Lorida, at least the Mexican part, had gathered in and around the house. I hadn't been to many fiestas. But, I couldn't imagine they got more joyful than this.

There was actually a line of well-wishers running up to and through the Heraldez's front door. Soon grills and smokers and kegs and tables full of potluck dishes accumulated across the lawn. An impromptu band was soon perched on the corner and wailing through what I took to be traditional Mexican numbers. All who passed seemed to know the words.

I considered what I could have done for the other girls we'd left at Bodeker's house. Maybe I could help others, going forward. If I brought the system down.

The fiesta found its groove. People were happy. The vibes were good. I was sitting on the curb enjoying the crisp hint of a cold front that had blown in overnight when a man walked over and sat near me. He was Mexican, handsome, and looked to be in his mid-twenties.

"May I?" he said.

"Sure," I said.

I finished off my Tecate and set it and my sauce and bean soaked paper plate on the curb next to me.

"Carlos." He held his hand out and I shook it. He vibed 'good guy'. "I'm Ines' brother."

"How do you do," I said. The resemblance was there, alright. "Walt."

"Thanks to you I feel the best I ever have in my life." His smile was genuine.

I waved him off.

"Don't be humble. You have done a great thing. My family is beyond grateful to you. Anything you need, please ask. It will never be too much."

"I did what anyone should do."

"You are a good man, Walt."

I've never been comfortable with that kind of flattery. "I only brought her home. You guys have the hard work of helping restore her life."

He nodded. "A treasured opportunity we wouldn't have without your help."

"Fair enough."

A shriek of delight blared from the backyard.

I looked to Carlos. "I'm not an expert, but it's a safe bet she's going to have trauma. Lots of it."

His expression grew serious. "We will help her the best we can. Love can do many things."

A trio of kids ran into the center of the intersection and lit off fireworks. Nearby revelers applauded. Others danced to the band. The sun was dipping below the horizon beyond them, casting a spectrum across the sky, orange to pink to blue.

"They did some bad things to her. She's gonna have a hard time forgetting that," I said.

"Who did this?" Carlos said.

"I'm working on that."

I could sense him staring at me, as if further details might shake out of my ears or nose.

"How long ago did she go missing?"

He looked into the distance but didn't have to think long. "Four years and two months. It was a very cold day. She did not come home from work."

"Where'd she work?"

"For a seamstress in town. Sebring."

"What'd the police say?"

His face wrinkled with distaste for the subject. "That they'd keep looking."

Eye contact. There was much more to it than that.

"What were the circumstances? Any witnesses? Or, did she just vanish?"

Carlos swallowed and looked at the ground. He was measuring how to phrase his words. I let him take all the time he needed.

"There were rumors that Ines and one of her friends were pulled into a van."

"And, no one could identify it?"

"Si. It was very...nondescript?"

I nodded. Right word.

"The three girls had been walking home from the bus stop where Ninety-Eight and Arbuckle Creek Road meet. One of the girls, Ines' other friend, escaped by running into a swamp and waiting until the van was gone. She only caught a glimpse of the van driving off. And, she was too far away to pick out details. She did not return until the next day."

"Why so long?"

"She was scared to leave the swamp. Worried they would come back for her. And, when the sun went down, gators came out. She perched on cypress knees the entire night, terrified. Once the sun rose and the gators moved towards higher ground, she was able to leave."

"No word on Ines' friend? The other one taken."

He shook his head. "Her mother was here earlier. Said she wanted to see Ines, to believe there was still hope for her daughter."

Knowing what I knew, I figured the chances of that were slim. Ines had been exceptionally lucky I stumbled into the picture. And, I did that by blind luck.

Silence settled between us. My mind reviewed the new information to see if there was any way it could help. A nondescript van seen by a scared teenager from the back of a swamp wasn't going to do much good.

But, there was a clue.

No way the van drivers just randomly stopped and attempted a kidnapping. Whoever was inside that van had to be confident they could handle three girls at once and get away with it. Had to be more than one of them. Did they know what time the girls would be there? Maybe. If so, they had seen them before. If so, they must have been local. Not local to Lorida, otherwise they would have been spotted since. But, local to someplace nearby.

"What other towns are around here?"

Carlos leaned back, both hands on the pavement, and looked up at the stars dotting the navy blue sky.

"We are nearest to Sebring. Then Okeechobee to the southeast. Lake Placid is west. And Yeehaw Junction is on the far side of Kissimmee

Prairie Preserve. But, is not really a city. Just an intersection." He waved casually in that direction.

I had driven past the intersection where the girls were taken on my way into town, on Highway Ninety-Eight. It ran between Sebring and Okeechobee.

"Which way did they drive off on Ninety-eight?"

"Towards Okeechobee."

Something inside told me they weren't from there. If the Kith wanted poor, non-native girls to kidnap they wouldn't need to stray outside Okeechobee. Clewiston and other shanty type towns freckled that part of the state and were filled with immigrant workers who labored for little in the massive sugar fields. The drive towards Okeechobee could have been misdirection.

"Any cut off roads between here and Okeechobee?"

"County Roads 621 and 721," he said. "621 goes to Lake Placid. 721, straight south to Moore Haven then Clewiston. But, you know we check all those areas."

"Who's we?"

"Me and my father. Other men from the community."

I didn't want to make assumptions, so let's call it a guess. I guessed Carlos and his father, being of Mexican descent, knew many in the migrant communities around Okeechobee and Sebring. And, I guessed they would have a better read on illicit activities going on than even the police. Was it prejudiced of me to think that way? Who cared? I wanted to get the bad guys. Conclusion: If Carlos and his father couldn't ferret out any leads, chances were the girls were not taken South.

Unless it was very south, to Miami. There was mob aplenty down there. And, the Kith was a mob. It would be easy to make the girls disappear there.

But, Ines was in Tampa. Maybe she could tell me if her friend was shipped to Tampa, too. That might explain...

I was distracted by the sound of a plane. Carlos and I looked up. It took a moment, but then I spotted its red glowing wing lights. From what I could make out, it was small, executive. And, definitely out of place in this part of the state.

The plane flew south of us and was circling back to the northeast. It was not on its way to one of the larger metropolises like Fort Lauderdale or Miami.

"There an executive airport around here?" I said with a look to Carlos. He shrugged.

"What are the big industries down here?"

"Sugar, cattle, oranges. The standards. The big boss man for the factories. He would have a plane, maybe?"

That made sense.

Before I could ask another question, friends of Carlos gathered around. They were congratulatory. He introduced me as 'the hero,' which again I waved off. They wanted to salute me with another drink. I was ready for another salute.

Ines was still greeting visitors, friends and relatives she hadn't seen in ages. She smiled to me as I walked through the living room. For some reason it made me think of Love-Mart, whom I had not been able to save; whom I had essentially gotten killed. Very hard for me to take credit for Ines. At best, the slate was even.

Drinks flowed, but I did my best not to get too loose. I had another busy day tomorrow. I still hadn't tracked down a hotel for the night. Every time I started to look into it I was interrupted by revelers.

I was pulled into a dance circle. It would have been great fun had I not had next steps and worries on my mind. I danced with Ines, who thanked me again. Funny, not twenty-four hours ago she wanted zip to do with me. But, here she was resting her head against my chest as we swayed. I thought of Ilsa. That's who I wanted to dance with.

There was no telling if, when, how, or where the Kith were going to go after Ilsa. All I knew was the pictures in Dewey Lawrence's office were proof they were stalking her. I couldn't let them get her.

The song ended, Ines kissed my cheek, and we parted. I grabbed another plate of food, and was on my way out the kitchen when Carlos and his friend stopped me in the living room.

"Hey, this is Hector," Carlos said. "He say something maybe kind of interesting."

"What's that?" I said.

Carlos turned to Hector, "He say there is some men who come to the towns looking for day laborers. They have vans. Maybe look like the one Ines was in. But, it doesn't make no sense."

"Why's that?"

"Because is for a ranch nearby that put on big functions."

"You know, fiestas. Parties," said Hector.

"A ranch for parties? Like a vacation spot? Ranch resort type of thing?"

I had heard about a few vacation ranches in the state. People would go there to act like old Florida cracker cowboys or hunt or even do extreme mud sports. Never appealed to me.

Hector shrugged. "My cousin, he go with the one time. They make him help with catering. Said it was like a private, you know, event."

"I'm not sure what you're getting at."

Hector frowned, looking like he was trying to figure out how to say what he wanted. "There is quiet talk, you know, between los hombres, the men in the town, that not all the men they come back."

I studied their faces.

"You think these are the guys who took Ines?" I turned to Carlos. "Are you just hearing about this now?"

He nodded. "When people hear Ines return it sort of snap their mind."

"So, you haven't followed up on this?"

"I never connected the two," said Carlos.

"Would you say this ranch is one of the bigger operations around here?"

They both shrugged. "Compare to what? There is lot of money, major farms."

"I was just wondering if they'd have some sort of influence over the police." I looked to Carlos.

He brightened with a silent revelation, as if that were very much a possibility, but then darkened with skepticism.

"Why would they take Ines?"

I rubbed my eyes. It had been another long day and I was starting to feel sluggish from the alcohol.

"Something to think on. In the meantime, I need to find a place to stay."

"We can put you up," said Carlos.

I looked around. The party showed no signs of stopping. "Don't think I'll get much rest here. Any motels nearby?"

He nodded and gave me directions. We agreed to meet for breakfast and I got out of there. I looked back to the house as I walked to my car. It was warm and alive with excitement. Good for them.

47

I crashed at a modest motel on the outskirts of Sebring. Several members of the Indian family who managed, and lived at, the property went out of their way to ensure I was comfortable, despite my late arrival. They succeeded.

The next morning came quick. Despite the urgency of circumstances, I called Carlos to see if we could make breakfast a brunch, which he agreed to. I was stuck in first gear.

A couple hours later we met at a small taqueria located at the far end of Old Downtown Sebring. It wasn't fancy, but it afforded a good view of the old city. In the distance beyond, I could see the newer architecture, golden arches and all.

Plates clacked back in the kitchen. Someone said something commanding in Spanish. A moment later our waitress arrived, arms loaded with plates of food. Her smile was big and delightful, and she said "for you" with each person she served. She struck me as the type of strong woman who could take care of the smallest babies and the biggest men. Even if they were sometimes the same person.

"Have you settled on your next steps?" said Carlos.

I shook my head as I wiped my lips.

"Not yet. I wouldn't mind speaking to a few people around here. Maybe they know something that doesn't make sense unless you have the context of the Kith," I said.

"Who?"

"The people who took your sister. What I call 'em."

His face darkened and he leaned in.

"If you find them, lead me to them."

I just looked at him. Then, "We'll see."

He looked confused that I wouldn't agree.

I spoke before he could, "Know how I found your sister? I woke up a few days ago and found a truck stop prostitute carved up dead on my living room couch. They could have killed me. But, they wanted to torment me. I know you want revenge and it's deserved. But, you don't want to be on their radar. Because once you are, you don't fall off."

He appeared spooked by the story.

"I didn't know."

"You knew they were bad dudes the moment your sister went missing. And, dumb luck is the only reason she's back. I wouldn't push it."

"But, what are you going to do?"

"Stop them or die trying."

Carlos didn't know what to say. I knew he felt loyalty to me for saving his sister. But, he didn't want to risk much now that things could maybe start to get back to normal. At least, that's how the old me would have felt. Before Ken's death inspired me to take up the cause. But, once I had fully committed...once I knew there was no turning back I realized the bigger risk was doing nothing. Carlos didn't have that hopeless luxury. And, he needed to be there for his family.

"I will decide what is best for me," he said. "They are on my radar now," he said. "And, I do not forget or forgive what they did to my sister. My family."

"Fair enough," I said and leaned back in my chair.

He wasn't done. "For that matter, they are on our radar." He circled his hand in the air indicating the people around us, the Mexicans, the community. "They must fight all of us."

"And, what if they're not here?" I said. "Are you going to follow me wherever they are?"

"Absolutely."

"Really? People are going to just get up and go?" The thought of having a big group backing me up—an army to fight the Kith army— was appealing. But, there'd be no stealth and that was the only way I'd get close at this point.

"You'd be amazed what our hate can do," he said. His expression was cold. He meant it. I felt his hate. That triggered an idea.

I leaned forward, elbows on the table. "Okay, here's the deal..."

"Tell me."

"The whole reason I'm here today is because a semi-truck full of dead bodies—dead Mexican bodies—was found abandoned on the side of the road north of Tampa."

He wasn't expecting that.

"The driver of the truck is a guy named Ricky Aarons. He ran off and hasn't been tracked down. The Kith are looking for him."

"He's running from them?"

"Yes."

"Why?"

"Because he knows what they do to people who screw up. And by screw up, I mean expose the organization. The way they see it, they got a good thing going and they don't want anyone messing it up. They don't forget and they don't forgive. Not even their own people."

"And, Ricky Aarons knows that."

"Yes. He knows what they'll do. Hell, he knew he was hauling a truck full of corpses. He had to. Death is just part of their business."

"He is running scared."

"We need to find him. He knows how the organization works. Where they're located. Names, faces, addresses," I said. "If you want to do something, have your contacts try to track him down. Lake Wales, Seminole, and Daytona. Those were his known haunts, according to the information the Kith had.."

"How do you know this?" he said.

"I got close. But, not close enough."

He nodded and considered what I had just told him in silence. I watched an old man mosey down the sidewalk past our window.

"I know people in Lake Wales. Some family, too. They will turn it upside down. Daytona, a few. Plus Ormond and New Smyrna. Orlando, too."

"Check 'em all. If we can find him before they do, it could make a--"

He raised his hand to cut me off and craned his neck to see past me out the window.

"What?" I said.

"There. One of the recruiting vans for that ranch." He pointed past me.

I turned.

I stopped breathing.

It felt like my heart froze in my chest.

The van had the name of the ranch in broad green letters along its side.

Grove Lake Ranch.
And next to it, the Kith logo.

48

It was a sprinter van, long and lean. Two men stepped out. The older driver was tall and lanky with a beard and well-groomed hair, hipster style, short on the sides and long and slick on the top. I had heard that style is called a 'Fashy'. As in 'fascist'. He opened the rear cargo door. I couldn't see inside.

The younger passenger, another man with a Fashy from the Nazi barbershop, walked over to a group of Latino men gathered on the curb. They stopped talking and turned to him as he approached.

"I bet he is trying to get those men to work out at the ranch," Carlos said.

On cue: the man from the van thumbed over to the van as he spoke to the gathered men. He pulled out a roll of cash. Eyes widened.

My eyes widened.

"They take them in the van to the ranch?" I said without looking to Carlos.

"Si. Yes. Usually. That's what we hear."

We watched in silence.

The propositioned men exchanged uncertain looks. The man from the van held up the money, enticing. The other man stood patiently by the open door, like he knew the bribe would work.

Three of the men nodded and walked over to the van. The other two shook their heads and wandered off. No thanks.

Hipster hair waved the men in with a pleasant smile. They studied the recruiters one last time before climbing inside. The recruiters slammed the doors behind them.

"I hope they make it back," said Carlos.

My chair clattered against the old terrazzo floor as I ran out the door. Carlos yelled "Hey!" behind me.

The recruiters looked my way. They didn't look happy. And, they didn't look to each other; just moved to get in the van.

I ran to the passenger side. The younger recruiter leered at me over his shoulder as he dropped ass first into the van. He attempted to pull the door shut.

I grabbed the doorframe and stopped him.

"What are you doing with these men?" I asked.

He gave me a sinister look. But, it was the driver who answered. "We're hiring them, jerk. Now, move on."

I hadn't thought any of this through. Just reacted on gut instinct.

"Will you bring them back?" I said.

They looked at me like, what?

"Fuck off," said the young recruiter. He shoved me back, grabbed at the door handle, and attempted to yank it shut. I was in the way.

Carlos ran up. "It's okay. My friend is confused."

I pulled the knife out of my jacket and put it against the recruiter's ribs

"There's no confusion," I said. "You take people prisoners and make 'em do terrible things."

"We're hiring day labor for an event," said the driver.

"Walt, maybe—"

"Quiet." I pushed the knife into the young recruiter's ribs.

He winced.

"Slide over," I said.

He obeyed. I wasn't ready to cut these guys any slack.

Mumbling sounds from the men in the back of the van wafted through the metal grate behind the seats.

I pushed my way in.

"Get your car, Carlos, and follow this van. I may need a ride back." To the driver, "Come on, start it up or your friend gets ventilated." For added effect, I grabbed the back of recruiter's neck and shoved him against the driver. He glared at me as he started the van.

He didn't put it in drive.

I sensed the passenger door open behind me.

"Shut the door," I said over my shoulder.

"But, Walt, man..." said Carlos.

The driver and recruiter glanced at each other. Something had rung their bells. My name. They knew who I was.

"Don't get any ideas," I said. "I'm not giving you any chance to collect a bonus."

Driver's jaw muscles tensed. Slow and easy, he started to drop his left hand, the one furthest away from me.

"Don't do it."

He didn't listen. His hand dropped to his thigh then started sliding down the side of it, out of sight.

The recruiter slammed against me. My hand on his neck slowed him down, but my knife slipped and dug into the car seat behind him.

The driver held up a gun and pointed my way.

I propelled myself back but bumped into something, either Carlos or the door.

The driver leaned in as I was falling out. His finger was wrapped around the trigger. He shot his co-pilot. The young recruiter screamed and grabbed at his gut.

Driver looked shocked, but before he could react any further a pair of meaty hands yanked him out the driver side door.

I fell and hit the concrete and something else...Carlos' wiggling legs. He hadn't been able to get out of the way in time.

"Let me up," he said.

I rolled over and scrambled up.

A gun fired.

The recruiter was bleeding bad and trying to pull himself into the driver's seat. Beyond him the two figures swung into the frame created by the shape of the van. The driver and—

DG.

What was he doing here!?

The recruiter pulled himself up in the driver's seat, shaky and desperate as he put his foot on the brake and reached for the gearshift. His partner rolled onto the hood of the van with DG. The recruiter ripped the vehicle into gear and stomped the accelerator.

I dove in the van.

DG and the recruiter rolled off to the side.

I punched the driver in his wound. He screamed and lost control of the van. It yawed up the curb and slammed into an electric line pole.

The wounded recruiter shook off the crash and swung at me with wild desperation. I ducked, sat up, and punched him in the neck. The force was enough to crack his head against the window. I grabbed the van keys and backed out the passenger side onto the street.

DG was on top of the recruiter, punching him the face. Carlos was walking my way. And, a police car pulled around the corner and zeroed in on our commotion.

Police were only going to hold me up. But, I had to help Carlos and DG—again, what was he doing here? I couldn't let the recruiters get away. I needed to find Grove Lake Ranch.

"Freeze!" said the Sheriff's Deputy pointing his gun at me.

I put my hands up.

This was very bad.

49

DG was escorted to the jail cell by a police officer so tall and wide-shouldered there was no way someone didn't ironically refer to him as 'Tiny'. His badge read 'Murphy'. He jangled keys on a ring, slid one in, opened the cell door, and shoved DG inside. DG didn't appear to be bothered. He had spent time in jails before.

I was sore from the fight. My mind was fried from the hour-long interrogation and stress of the situation as a whole. DG would have to pardon me for not standing up to greet him. I remained seated on the hard, metal bed that had been scratched and scraped with a variety of obnoxious messages.

DG leaned on the wall across from me and stared.

"What?" I said.

"You're welcome," he said.

"Thank you?"

He shook his head.

The hell was he irritated with me for? If anything, I should be pissed at him for screwing up my confrontation with the recruiters. They were my last lead and would have been my best. Now, they were gone. Or worse, in jail. I'd have no access to them. And, while I cooled in here I was losing valuable time..

"You're the one who messed things up. What are you even doing here?" I said.

"I came to help. And, did. Again," he said. He started pacing with a disgusted look on his face. He reached the cell door and turned around fast pointing his meaty finger at me. "You know I should kick your ass for landing me in here. Last thing I needed."

171

"I didn't land you anywhere, asshole."

Too much.

DG tackled me. The metal bed rattled as we spilled off it and dropped hard against the dusty, concrete floor. Pain reverberated through my joints.

I shoved my hand under DG's chin. My finger just below the eye. He sandwiched my face between his meaty palm and the floor. I kicked him off. He reared back. I kicked again and sent him flying into the cell bars.

"Son of a bitch," he said under his breath.

He ran at me. I tried to side step, but in a cell that small I couldn't get a wide enough berth. His arm reached out, wrapped around me, and slammed me into the wall.

He clutched a fistful of my shirt. "You got my men killed, godammit!" he said.

We staggered around. He fell back when his legs bumped into the bed. I pounced and punched him right in his big, fat gut. He groaned and grew madder. His punch to the side of my face about cleaned my clock. I slid down like gelatin off a spoon. My wobbly legs cycled me back to the cell bars. He got up and charged like a bull, eventually ramming me against the steel cylinders. It's a wonder I didn't press through them and come out the other side in separate pieces.

"Enough you two!" he said. Then, he pepper sprayed us.

DG and I let go of each other and tried to get the sting and stink out of our eyes, noses, and mouths. It was beyond awful. I choked, gagged, and wanted to puke.

"Now shut the hell up," the deputy said as he walked away.

DG and I retreated to our own corners to recuperate. We coughed, hacked, and spit.

"Oh god," he said.

My eyes watered, snot ran thick out my nose. Getting a fresh breath was like trying to suck air through a blanket.

About twenty minutes later, we could see clear, breathe a little easier, and not feel the complete impact of the pepper spray's sting. I never needed to experience that again.

DG sat on the floor, back against the concrete wall, leaning into the cell bars. I sat against the back of the cell, an arm resting on the cot.

How the hell did we get here?

"I'm sorry," I said. "I appreciate you coming down to help. It's just..."

He looked at me through red, bleary eyes. "Just what?"

"It's like I said before. You've done enough. I didn't want you to get into any more hassles. After they blew up your house…" I paused simultaneously amused and disappointed. "...Again. I was hoping to pull the heat off you. Plus, I didn't have time to wait for you. Ilsa's in danger."

He let out a big breath, as if his body had just then decided to let him relax.

"Walt, I get it already. But, you need to understand I am already in this one hundred percent. They killed my brothers. I am not programmed to let that slide. That shit gets paid back in blood. It's an added bonus that I can help you, my friend, at the same time," he said.

I nodded. Good to know we were still friends.

"These fuckers need to be demolished. So they can't kill you. So they will stop blowing up my house. So they won't hurt nice girls like Ines anymore." He leaned forward to stress his next point. "Hell, I want them gone because the way they're going, they're gonna try and cut in on my action."

DG knew the risks. I made it clear I thought he should stay away. He said 'thanks but no thanks.' What could I do?

"You wanna risk your ass for me...fine," I said. "And, thank you."

He looked at me with disbelief. It was an obnoxious answer. Obnoxious enough to make him smile.

"You're welcome, asshole."

Seemed no matter how stressful things became our friendship could take it. We fought because we both wanted results. And, we didn't want either of us getting in the way of them.

"What now?" he said.

"Don't you have connections you can call to bail us out?"

He shook his head. "Very few in this part of the state."

"Shit. That's why I apologized. I was banking on that."

"You'll need to bank elsewhere."

I closed my eyes to relax for a moment.

"Ines make it home?" said DG.

I nodded. He nodded.

And then, the man with the pock-scarred face appeared. He was bigger than Murphy the deputy in every way. I knew this because Murphy was standing right beside him. And, Murphy looked intimidated.

This monster of a man, whoever he was, stood staring through the cell gate with hateful eyes. I knew he was trouble even before he zapped DG unconscious with a taser.

50

Murphy unlocked the cell. The big man pushed him aside and shoved the cell door open.

I stepped back to the wall.

He was no bullshit. The big brute's chest heaved in and out just from breathing. He stared at me like I was a goddamn pest he would tolerate no more.

And Jesus, the scars on this guy. White lashes of not-quite-healed skin spiraled around his forearms divided the black lines of tattoos and created pinkish lumps that laced over his skin. For anyone else, it would have been an embarrassment worthy of plastic surgery. For this guy, it was branding.

And then, there was his hair. Its length gave him the look of a Native American Indian. At first I thought it was grey. The wrinkles and creases from hard living mapped across his face made him look old enough. But a closer look revealed his eyebrows, too, were white and his eyes were ice blue. My next guess was albino. But, his skin wasn't close to pale. It had that deep-set tan you see on guys out in the sun all day. His bones would disintegrate before his tan faded.

So, why the white hair? The only thing I could think of was shock. He had faced and survived some sort of experience so terrifying it had shocked him to the core and bleached away pigment in every follicle on his body. He had seen the worst. Lived to tell about it. And, wasn't gonna be afraid of anything ever again.

Two large sheaths hung from his belt. Massive blade handles stuck out of each. The sheathes were covered in gangly tufts of dark hair that hung down almost to his knees

He spit and walked up to me.

I tried to step back. The wall got in my way.

He raised the taser.

He snarled.

Lights out.

51

Getting knocked out sucks. Sure, it's effortless at first. But, you get the bill as soon as you wake up. And, it's a big one. Throbbing, aching, jabbing behind the eyes. The works.

What I saw: Teal curtains, high pile teal carpet, a white fan spinning on the ceiling, the luxurious likes of which you wouldn't find at the common home improvement store. I was on a very comfortable, horribly decorated bed set in a horribly decorated room. Quite a contrast from the jail cell.

All I could see out the window was sky. It appeared to be evening. Where was I?

A glance at my wrists and ankles revealed I wasn't restrained. So, I pushed myself up. Sore, stiff, and a little woozy. Could a stun baton really knock me out that hard for that long? I doubted it. They gave me something else. A sedative. If so, how much time had passed?

My legs were weak and wobbly as I walked to the window. But, I forgot their condition once I saw the view—a sprawling vista filled with breathtaking natural scenery. Nearby, the landscaping was manufactured but attractive. In the distance, the landscape was raw and rugged. It reminded me of Payne's Prairie near Gainesville, flat and filled with scrub brush, home to an entire wild ecosystem. Amazing.

But, what a strange setting for this place. Was this a resort?

I scanned the area. Didn't see anyone outside. But, there were vehicles. Cars and...vans. White vans with the words 'Grove Lake Ranch' on them.

I'd made it. I was in the heart of the Kith operation. The thought terrified and excited me. This is what I wanted...but now what?

176

My clothes were missing. The only attire option was a jumpsuit hanging on the back of a door. It was green and white with the Kith icon stitched into the chest. Very 1970's, like something out of Logan's Run. What I'd have done to be lounging back at the river house watching that right now.

I dressed and tested the doorknob. Surprise, it was unlocked. But, I didn't open the door yet. I checked the room. Anything I could use as a weapon? No. I opened the door, and stepped back. No alarm went off. At least none I could hear.

The hallway was decorated like a well-kept, rather ostentatious home. To my right were more doors I took to be guest rooms. There was a window at the very end. To my left, a landing with a stair rail. A way down.

I checked the window. Brushing aside the sheer curtains revealed a long, winding driveway leading up to the house. This was a house out in the country with a long approach. To the right a vast garden. To the left, I could see the corner of horse stables. This was a ranch. What the hell were they doing out here?

The door next to me opened. A man, mid-fifties with a look of wealth, appeared in the doorframe.

"Whoa," he said and smiled. "How you doin'?"

All I could think to say was, "Fine."

I smiled, saluted with a single finger and walked towards the landing. I gave him enough space to reach the stair rail and turn the corner. Then, I followed. Two sets of stairs descended to a single foyer. This place was big and ritzy. I recalled the sprawl of Tanjeris' house. This place seemed exponentially bigger. I descended the stairs.

You'd think I had wandered downstairs at a bed and breakfast. But, at dinner time. There were several dining tables with people eating. The man I encountered upstairs had taken a seat across from an elderly couple, unfolding his napkin and placing it on his lap while greeting his dining companions.

There was a woman, executive type, sitting at a two-top table reading the New York Times. Another four-top had a quartet of young executive types sitting around it.

"How do you do, Mr. Asher," said the voice.

Before I saw a face, a hand took my arm and guided me down a mat covered ramp that led to a pair of French doors. My guide was a man who looked dressed for golf wearing a powder blue polo shirt tucked into plaid shorts with a silver clunky Brighton belt. He smiled as we made eye contact. His face was red from too much sun, hair salt-and-pepper grey and black, male pattern baldness. He fit the stuffy Republican mold.

"I'm so glad you're up and we finally have the chance to talk," he said.

"What about?"

"A tremendous opportunity. Trust me. I think you're really going to like it. Right this way..."

We weren't three steps outside when a golf cart brandishing the Grove Lake Ranch logo—a.k.a. the Kith logo—pulled up. At the wheel was a woman I took to be in her mid-sixties. She was a stunning testament to money's beauty benefits.

"Hello, gentlemen," she said with a wave. She was all sunshine.

My escort gestured for me to get in the cart. I slid to the middle spot, next to the woman. He sat down on my opposite side.

"Hang on, fellas," she said with a giggle.

The evening was cool and the wind felt good on my face. Our cart scooted swiftly down a winding cement path.

"You'd probably like to know who we are, wouldn't you?" said the man.

"It would help," I said.

He chuckled. "Of course. I'm Rogers Aufderheide. This is my wife, Kay. And yes, we know who you are."

"That Rogers with a 's' at the end?"

"Indeed."

I nodded. "Don't hear that often."

"Not many men like Rogers," said Kay. "That's why I let him scoop me up."

Save the love story, I thought. What the hell did they want?

"This is our stable. Well, one of them," Rogers said.

He gestured to a vast wooden compound that appeared as we cruised over the crest of a hill. It was the largest stable I had ever seen. And, it was packed with cattle.

"Quite a spread," I said.

"It's proof that hard work really does pay off."

"Seriously, Walter, you couldn't imagine a better business...or a smarter businessman than Rogers. He made it all happen."

"From scratch?" I said.

"Well, mostly. My father, his father, and his father before that, my great grandfather, were all Florida cracker cattle ranchers. It's been the family business for over a century. But, it was a small operation when I took over."

"Rogers made Grove Lake the largest cattle company in the state," said Kay.

"That answers the immortal question—where's the beef?" I threw in a smile for kicks.

They just laughed and laughed. Kay slapped my knee.

"We have a lively one here."

"That's good!" Rogers said, coming across genuinely enthused.

I sat up and folded my arms. "Well, Rogers...since you are such a good businessman, what say we get down to business? You know, the meat of the matter," I said with a gesture to the passing cattle. Cow dung stung my nostrils. They were amused by my terrible pun but knew it was no longer a time to laugh.

"Why am I here?"

He shifted in his seat to face me. Without humor, "But for the grace of God."

"And, by 'God', he means himself," said Kay with the plucky side note.

"Oh, how's that?"

Rogers kicked his foot up onto the golf cart dash and hung his hand from the plastic roof. "It's simple, Walter. We could have killed you. Most in the organization wanted to. But, I vouched for you."

I never expected him to be that direct, or casual, about it.

"Why?" I said.

He just smiled. And, it was creepy as hell.

52

We were sitting around a feast-covered table, looking out at the unbelievable vista of the prairie. It might have been the best view in the state.

"We like to come down here about once a week for supper. Usually candlelight," said Kay.

She said 'supper', not 'dinner'. Midwest roots?

"Meat's fresh off the ranch." Rogers pointed at the steak on my plate. "You'll never taste better."

"I don't know. I sold a Sous Vide cooker that makes steak better than most restaurants."

"This isn't most restaurants."

"Fair enough." My steak was gone five minutes later.

Rogers prattled on about the cattle business. How Rogers found ways to work deals that greatly expanded his reach. The problem with some of the current regulations. I didn't care. I was here for two things, to learn and destroy.

"So, why did you vouch for me?" I said.

Rogers dabbed his lips with his napkin, set it on the table, and leaned forward. Was he trying to match my posture? I noted and made a point to resist the subliminal coaxing.

"Because you're a remarkable man," he said.

Flattery. More persuasion science.

"I mean, look...there have been a number of, well, people in your shoes who didn't last a day," he said.

So, I wasn't the first. I hoped to be the last. I shrugged.

"So, it's as natural as grass growing under the sun. Why wouldn't we want you on our team? Hell, that's what this is. An invitation, fella. We'd like to draft you."

"For what position, coach?" I said, sticking with the athletic euphemisms.

Rogers chuckled. Kay smiled.

"I do like me some college ball," he said. "But in this scenario, I think you'd be great at just about everything you do. You've proven yourself at subversion. And hell, you're one goddamn good salesman."

"Watch your language, Rogers," said Kay with a pat on his arm.

"What's wrong with the word 'salesman'?" I said.

Roger roared.

Choke on the charm, asshole. It goes past eleven.

"We've seen your work. Both on and off the TV. You can get people to do what you want. And, we need someone like that."

"I wasn't aware cults had marketing divisions."

Rogers frowned. "Now, that's neither fair nor nice."

Was this debate really happening?

Kay said, "You're missing the point, Walter."

I hadn't been called 'Walter' since my mom last had to discipline me. That was a good twenty-five years ago.

"What's the name of this club you're inviting me to join?"

"You mean like Skull & Bones at Yale? Walter, please. We are just a network for friends and colleagues with a similar worldview. It's no more than a social club. No need for fancy names," said Rogers.

"We don't even have official stationary," said Kay, giggling.

"Are you the trustees?" I said. My tone was serious. I wanted answers.

"I am," said Rogers. "I took over as trustee for my father's business. Then, there's the charitable trust, which does all sorts of wonderful things."

"They build houses for migrant families," Kay chimed in. "Purchasing land for environmental protection..."

"We're big on the environment," said Rogers.

That was a surprise. But, I guessed they needed a healthy environment for their cattle.

And, burying bodies.

Whoa. My sarcasm just sparked an epiphany. Were the trucks full of bodies brought to the ranch and buried?

"I'm talking about the trust that runs the other businesses. Ancient Delights. The massage parlors. The trucking company. The exploited girl delivery service."

I watched close. A not quite imperceptible shell of denial hardened their faces.

Kay leaned in. "The real question is why wouldn't you want to join us? I mean, frankly, it seems crazy to me."

That was a whopper. And, I took their answer pivot to mean, 'yes.' He ran those other businesses.

"I don't think you recognize crazy anymore, Kay," I said.

"Walter, would you just relax for once," she said. "We're not bad people. We just see the world a different way."

"No kidding."

She frowned, disappointed. I considered each crease in her face a small victory.

"Listen…we only get one chance at life. Why would you squander it with worries and niceties and, and…why let other people, people you don't even know, dictate your life?"

I did not want to get into some absurd philosophical discussion with them. Time was running out.

"Kay, you kill people."

"I do not!" She put a hand across her heart. Perish the thought.

"Fine, your friends, your club members, your servants do. How can you justify that?"

"I'm not justifying anything."

"To feel the need to justify would imply a sense of guilt. We don't feel guilty about anything. And, that's the beauty of it," said Rogers. "That's the beauty of maximum freedom. It's permission to live without any guilt at all."

They looked harmless. But, what a pair of creeps.

"Life is so much easier when you don't have to worry about all those other…things," said Kay, a bit of venom on the last word.

"Look Walter. I understand why you're concerned. But, trust me when I tell you…"

"I never trust a man who says trust me. That's why I never write that phrase in any of my shows," I said.

"Fair enough. But, I am one hundred percent sincere when I tell you this is a genuine invitation. No tricks, no deception. If you accept, you get to be one of us. And, you will be safe. Safer than you've ever been your entire life. You and your loved ones."

He meant Ilsa. Now, I was pissed.

"More importantly, you'll live the best life you could ever possibly live. That's what we've been doing."

It was surreal to sit before these two and discuss recruitment in what had to be the most sinister social club ever. "You guys kill me."

"Well, we tried," said Rogers clarifying the joke with a smile.

It wasn't funny.

"Sorry, bad timing."

"Bad joke."

"Suppose so," he said.

"You killed one of my best friends for no other reason than he was married to the woman one of your members wanted to be with. It was cheap and it was bullshit and...Tell me what man worth his salt wouldn't try to figure out a friend's shady death, huh? None. Especially, if the victim is a good man like Ken Kerenz. That's why we're talking today. I tried to find out who killed Ken in the prime of his life. You think I want to be here dealing with you two? Do you really think I want to spend every day running and fighting? I don't. But apparently, I have to because you and your little fun club don't like to have your hands slapped for bad behavior. You don't want to play by the rules because someone convinced you you're above them. That's deranged thinking."

"Walter, now..."

"Just stop. You're being dumb. You're lying to all of us. Maybe if you'd stop killing people, stop pimping innocent women, stop leaving your trucks full of dead bodies on the side of the highway, you wouldn't have to worry about people like me. Seems pretty easy to avoid it. Just don't be heartless assholes."

They looked to be growing impatient. I didn't care.

"I know there's no getting through to you. You're like Jesus freaks, rotten with conviction. So, how do we end this? Hmm? How do we say enough, I leave you alone, you leave me alone? No more chasing, no more spying, no more leaving dead girls in my living room. If you believe in maximum freedom, why don't you give me some freedom from your bullshit? Yes, I'm sorry I followed up on the truck. I think my curiosity was reasonable. And really, I didn't do anything to you guys. You jumped first with your little living room trick."

I stopped talking and looked at Rogers and Kay. They looked befuddled, like they didn't know what to make of it. After a long moment, Rogers cleared his throat and said, "The only way to end it is to join us. Otherwise, you'll never leave here. Not alive."

53

The sour scent of manure stung my nose. Loose dirt soiled the tops of my shoes. When I looked up I saw a barn door being opened by the huge man with the white hair. The albino Indian. His glare was lethal.

Inside, Rogers and Kay were silhouetted before an intense light. White Hair bolted the barn door shut behind me. I didn't like this. It felt like a trap. Rogers and Kay stepped into another room within the barn, where the source of the intense light was housed. I stopped walking. Kay beckoned me with a wave.

I stepped forward and looked into the room. All I saw was Rogers. He was looking off-screen, where I couldn't see.

White Hair stepped up behind me.

"Stand by, Opae," Kay said past me. Opae. White Hair.

"Come on, Walter. We want you to see something," she said.

Her hand was soft and cool on my wrist. It amplified the chill up my spine and neck.

Given the shabby surroundings, dirt on the floor, I didn't expect to inhale a friendly aroma. Gardenia, one of my favorites. There was a woman. She was stunning. Voluptuous, with sun-kissed skin, ample bosom, and a look that said 'yes' to everything. She was naked except for garters and stockings. Under any other circumstance, she'd be appealing as hell. But, now? No. Their cheap trick was as insulting as the woman was beautiful.

"Another one of your sex slaves? Sorry, but I couldn't live with myself. And frankly, I expected a better pitch," I said looking between Rogers and Kay.

Rogers waved me off and smiled. "Shucks, I am not surprised at all. I knew you had more integrity than that. Although you should know, she absolutely is all yours."

"Whenever you like. However you like," said Kay.

"Thanks. I'll pass."

"Well, then how about this?" said Rogers as he stepped over to a door at the back of the room and opened it. He waved us over. Kay led, I followed. The naked woman gave me a smile soaked in sin. I didn't smile back.

In the next room sat a man between two bright clip lamps. The bright light washed against his face, revealing sparkling drops of sweat and face creases deepened by frustration and fear. He was tied to the chair. What startled me was that he looked most scared when he saw me.

Then I recognized him.

This was the man I had seen managing Ancient Delights. The one who was rough with the hostess. Gone was the arrogant swagger and dominant presence of being boss to a bunch of battered and drugged up women. Now, he was the meek one. But, why freak at seeing me?

Rogers said, "I believe you've met Mr. Muncy. He used to run the Ancient Delights parlor."

I gave Rogers a look. He held up his hands. "Doesn't mean I own it." He smiled. Then..."Doesn't mean I don't."

His expression grew sinister. As if he was getting tired of maintaining a veil of pleasantry. Things were getting serious. And, so was he.

"You're not happy with this man, are you Walter?" said Kay.

"Never did anything to me," I said.

"But, he did plenty to Ines. And, he was quite rude at the parlor."

Flashback: The closed-circuit camera in the parlor waiting room. They saw it happen. Reviewed the tapes.

I shrugged.

"Did you know, Walter," said Rogers, "that this is the very man who helped kidnap Ines right off the street. If it weren't for him, her family would have no reason to celebrate last night."

Jesus. These guys were everywhere.

"Am I supposed to shake his hand?"

Roger shook his head. "Of course not. It's your chance to kill him. For Ines."

Muncy whimpered and looked past me, terrified.

I followed his gaze, and at the same time heard metal rattling. Opae the brute was rolled over a small cart. It looked vintage, like something from a garage sale.

And, it was covered with killing devices.

A gun, blades of assorted menace, a drill, and something that vibed medieval torture.

Opae released the cart, stepped back and folded his arms.

So, that was it. That was them. All they did was dirty work. What did the CIA spooks call it? Wet work? Sure, they were inviting me in...to solve their problems. And, this is how I would be solved if I ever became a problem.

"No thanks," I said. I kicked the leg of the cart, rolling it away from me. It only went two feet.

A glance at Muncy. He looked relieved.

A nod from Rogers.

Opae nodded.

The big brute's white hair wafted behind him as he grabbed a blade from his belt, clutched Muncy's tight, curly hair, and scalped that perm right off the top of his head. Blood dripped from the loose curls.

Muncy's scream echoed in my ears. Blood drizzled his face red as his mouth muttered and his body convulsed with shock.

Rogers and Kay just stood there. It was like they'd just watched a pro golfer sink a long putt. My god...they were impressed!

Opae held the scalp up, admired it like a trophy then tossed it at my feet. I jumped back, grossed the hell out. My heart pounded double time. The tension in the room was constricting.

"We're all about solving problems," Rogers said.

"Wouldn't you rather be part of the solution? And, not the problem?" said Kay.

"What kind of solution is that?"

"A swift one," said Rogers.

"A sick one," I said.

He shrugged and looked to Kay. "He's not very receptive."

Muncy whimpered.

Opae grabbed the other blade off his belt and slammed it into Muncy's chest. He stopped shaking, stopped living.

Kay wrapped an arm inside the crook of Rogers' elbow and leaned her head on his shoulder. Like a long, wonderful date night was coming to an end. "I was worried he wouldn't be."

"What say we give him one more chance?"

They locked eyes in what looked like some kind of silent renewal of faith in the pursuit of their goals, their dreams.

Would have been a good time to run. I was closest to the door and I suspected swifter than Opae. But, Rogers turned to me just as I was about to take the first step.

"Not yet, Walter. You're all about the pitch. I got one more for you."

He didn't wait for me to respond, just walked over pulled something out of his pocket.

A smart phone.

His face illuminated cool blue as he slid his finger across the screen.

I knew where this was going. He was going to show me pictures of Ilsa. I steeled my nerves, not against shock, but against that grim reality. It'd be the worst thing I could see. I couldn't panic. I couldn't wilt. I just had to take action.

"Care to see a familiar face?" said Rogers.

Son of a bitch. I was going to kill him. Where was Opae? How far was the gun...the knife...the drill? Who do I take out first? Opae. He'd be the most trouble. I could probably take Rogers. Kay would only require a punch. Then, what? I'd have to get off the ranch, find Ilsa...I needed to stop them.

Rogers held the phone out to me. I hated the look on his face. I reached carefully for the phone. I didn't want him to see my hands shaking. Show no fear.

The phone's plastic presence revealed the clamminess of my hands. I clutched harder to prevent dropping it.

The light of the screen washed across my face.

My eyes focused on its content.

Video.

Movement.

"That's right here at the ranch," said Kay.

What was right here at the ranch? Ilsa? Good! Kill them, save her, run, and hide forever. Australia? South America? A deserted island?

I looked at the screen with renewed vigor. I wanted it to be Ilsa. I wanted to know she was within reach.

It was a familiar face.

It was shocking.

It was something I never expected.

It was something that, in a flash, made me consider accepting their offer and doing what I, without ever having verbalized it in my mind or out loud, swore I'd never do.

Join them.
Become a killing, torturing, slave pimping Kith creep.
Because it wasn't Ilsa.
Somehow, some way...it was so much worse.
I went numb.
"Ain't they just the dickens?" said Rogers.
"Adorable, I'd say," said Kay.
The phone revealed two children playing in a room.
It was Ken's kids, Kory and Kelvin.

54

"Now, those are some happy kids," said Rogers. The son of a bitch even smiled at me.

Kelvin and Kory wrapped around my waist, thrilled to see me. "What are you doing here?" said Kory.

We were in the next stable over.

"Did you hear that bang? Sounded like a gun shot," said Kelvin.

Keep it together, Walt...

"I just stopped by for a visit with the, uh, ranch boss," I said with a nod towards Rogers.

"They have a pool. We can go swimming again!" said Kelvin.

"Terrific." I figured the quick lie was better than any hint of what was really going on.

The boys ran over to the television where they had been playing video games when I walked in. They dropped to their knees and grabbed the controllers. "Hey, that's my controller..."

Kay said, "I must admit I wish we'd been able to have some of our own. Not that Opae isn't the apple of my eye."

The big dude?

Rogers looked to me. "You'd never know by the looks of him now, but he was just a tot that fit right in the crook of my arm when we adopted him." He offered a fond, reminiscing smile.

And, that proved just how insane these people were; daydreaming and celebrating the joy of children as they showed off their ability to kidnap them. And, just after the apple of their eye had scalped a man. I wanted to puke so bad I couldn't even speak.

189

Did I really have a choice anymore? As disgusting a thought as joining their sick club was, I was more disgusted by how they had plucked away all my options. They were too good. It was going to take hurricane force delusion to accept this world. I looked to Rogers.

"So, am I in?"

He looked pleasantly surprised.

"You are if you accept our invitation."

I didn't have the words. But, finally...I nodded.

"Well, that is wonderful!" Kay clapped her hands together then opened her arms and hugged me more than I hugged her. I wanted to break her back. I was stunned. It was like I had gone through the looking glass...of a crack pipe.

"Is there a hazing?" I said, unsure exactly where that notion had come from.

Rogers reached out to shake my hand. I took his hand and willies of disgust about paralyzed me. I'm surprised I didn't lose my bowels.

"No, ha ha, no hazing. But, of course, we'll keep an eye on you for a while. You know, like a ninety-day probation at a new job."

"Okay. Any health benefits?" I said. My mouth was making up conversation while my brain tried to process that which could not be processed.

"Would be nice, but no," Rogers said. "Plenty of member privileges, but you're on your own with the health care. Although, we do have many doctors in the club who will treat other members...and be discreet."

His look said *Know what I mean?*

I nodded.

An idea hit me. A good one. It was time to milk him for info. There was time to wait.

"You've convinced me," I said. "I'm not going to lie and say I approve of all your methods. But, I'm starting to understand."

"That's good," said Kay. "Although, you can't blame us for remaining a touch skeptical of your enthusiastic turnaround. That's what the probation period is for."

"Let's be clear. I'm not enthusiastic. But, I've stopped resisting. My mind is open," I said. "You have...persuaded me."

"We know how much you appreciate the art of persuasion," said Rogers.

"True. But, I also appreciate a good bonus to go with the deal."

"Mr. Infomercial."

"That's me."

"What would you like? The girl back in the room?" said Kay.

"No. The only woman I want is Ilsa. You don't touch her. You tell your people to leave her alone and stop watching her. Immediately."

Kay and Rogers looked to each other and agreed with a silent nod. To me:

"I think we can make that happen," said Rogers. "Anything else?"

"Whoever you have to ask. Do it."

Kay turned to Rogers. "I'll speak to Razook."

"Who's Razook?" I said.

They turned to me. Hesitant. They didn't want to say.

"He's part of the management."

"Are you part of the management?"

More hesitation.

"We're deeply involved with the group," said Kay.

That was my opening.

"Tell me about the group. I want to know more about the club I'm joining," I said. "Do you run it?"

"Well...no," said Rogers. I could tell by the expression on his face he was distressed at losing control of the conversation. "You'll learn all that in due time. Are we finished with the bonuses?"

So, even though Grove-this and Grove-that was all over the trusts, the businesses, and even the truck full of dead bodies...it seemed Rogers and Kay didn't have sole control of this insane operation.

It went higher up.

"Not yet," I said. "Who's the brass? I wanna make sure I don't accidentally insult them in the lunchroom."

Kay flashed a cold, almost bitter expression, but then caught herself and smiled.

"Walter, there's no need to worry. You'll get along with everyone here. We're more like a family in that way."

"Then doesn't it make sense to know who my brothers and sisters are? Anyone I know?"

Rogers threw me a bone. "Your friend, Yamir."

What!?

"The same Yamir I saw the other night?" My shock was genuine.

Rogers nodded. "We spoke to him afterwards. Frankly, no one moves into that neighborhood without being affiliated with us."

He raised his chin, his confidence returned. He had the information. And, the information was the upper hand.

"Yamir is Razook?" I said.

Rogers waved me off. "No, he's not. And, I think we're done with the bonuses." He looked over my shoulder. "Opae, why don't you make Walter here comfortable," said Rogers.

Before I could react, Opae's massive, vice-like hand squeezed around my neck.

"Hey! What's--This is how you treat new members?"

"Too many questions, Walter. Should have played your hand better."

"What are you--I said I'm on board!"

Opae was dragging me a way.

"We've come to doubt your commitment," said Kay.

"One more bonus and I'm done. No more questions."

Rogers and Kay looked to each other, ignoring me.

Opae almost had me out the door, to where, who knew?

"The kids...you have to let the kids go. That's my only other request."

Rogers looked to me.

"You've squandered your requests. But, you'll be happy to know the kids won't be harmed. They weren't even kidnapped. Their family belongs to the club, too."

BOMBSHELL.

"They were never going to be harmed," said Kay.

Who? What?

Karen was in the league. But, wasn't that just because she was having an affair with Tanjeris?

Who else?

Wait...

Opae dragged me out of the room...out of the barn. It was dark out. Humid. I was sweating. My struggles were impotent. My heels dragged grooves into the dirt as Opae pulled me along. As we passed the rough-cut stable fence, I heard a familiar voice, "Evening, Mr. Asher."

Who...?

I looked.

Gale was perched on the wooden fence like a patient vulture. The nanny from West Palm Beach. The one studying International Finance. The one who'd been watching Kelvin and Kory. The one who brought the kids to the ranch. Who would help them now?

55

Don't give up, Walt.

Gale hoped off the fence and pranced towards the stable.

Opae grunted. He was dragging me over to a small, metal shed. The door was open. He pulled me inside and threw me down on a chair. I pushed off the chair and made a run for the door. The soft sand neutered my launch and I wasn't able to escape Opae's reach. His fingers dug through my shirt and into my back and he pulled me by the skin.

This time, no chair. He lifted me, one-handed, and tucked a hook under my right arm.

A meat hook.

Then, the same with the left arm. Next, he grabbed my ankle and tightened a leather strap around it. The strap was bolted into the wall. What the hell did they normally do in here? He grabbed my right ankle. Same result—strapped.

Even though my hands were free, there was little I could do. The hooks held me up but my arms couldn't reach a thing. The ankle straps prevented me from swinging my legs. I was stuck, suspended in air, as if they'd tied me up mid-jumping jack.

Opae walked around and faced me. There was something terrifying in his eyes. Revenge, perhaps. Like he had been waiting ages to catch and punish me.

And, there was his fist. It smashed my gut good, enough to knock my wind out.

Worry and wonder flashed through my mind. Was he going to torture me? Kill me? What about the kids? Saving them was vital. That meant saving my own ass had become even more necessary. I couldn't succumb to those 'just kill me already' feelings.

Metal on metal clanged behind me. I tightened, anticipating a strike.

A low humming noise purred to life. Before I could decipher it, Opae walked into view. He stood close and studied my face. He looked to my forehead and ran a thumb across my hairline. Oh, no…

He nodded, as if I had passed inspection. Then, without a word, he walked out and slammed the door shut.

Now what?

Sweat drizzled down the sides of my face. It was hot, getting hotter.

I connected the dots. That hum. That metal screech. That lever he'd pulled. It clicked: Cattle ranch, hot box—dehydrator.

I'd sold several of them through television. But, nothing room-sized. This was different. The Kith were going to sweat me to death. Turn me into human jerky. I had to get out now.

Two-Part Question: How? And, if I do get out, how the hell am I going to get the kids and stop them.

Answer: Forget Part Two. Just get out. Improvise later.

I wiggled. Nothing. My legs pulled the straps. It was enough to make the sheet metal walls wobble, but no break.

Sweat stung my eye. It took a moment to blink it away. My jumpsuit was sticking to my skin. That made it tougher to kick.

I tried to raise my arms and slide out but my jumpsuit fabric caught on the hook. I twisted and turned. The fabric wouldn't rip. Not enough leverage to push off in any direction and break something loose.

An idea: The hook had created a hole in the jumpsuit. Could I slide my arm out of the sleeve? I raised my arm over my head and worked my shoulder out a few inches. But, with nothing holding the cuff the fabric just moved with my arm instead of shedding off. I was getting more twisted up.

Damn.

The more I moved around the more the air started to feel like dusty carpet lining my lungs. Breathing was a limited-time offer.

I yanked my arm hard. Harder. Do it!

Nothing.

I scanned the room for any other way. The zipper on my jumpsuit stood out. I was able to reach that and pull it down. But, the air that rushed in seemed hotter than the air that had built up inside.

I contracted my arms and legs to give my restraints a full body yank. *Come on!*

Nothing.

The other arm.

Pull. Pull. PULLLLL!!!

Crack!

The wood beam running across the top of the shed cracked. The hook under my left arm was hanging from it. Its chain was near the crack. I reached up, grabbed the chain, and slid it off the wood beam. The chain dropped to the ground. I had the hook in my hand.

One arm free. And, I had a tool to work with. Maybe.

Another glance around—There!

A small loop in the leather strap holding my left leg. If I could swing the hook into it and pull with both my arm and leg, I might be able to get free.

First swing—not even close.

Second swing—close, but no hook.

Third swing...

I lost count. But, it was at least forty swings later that I finally snagged the loop. I was running out of energy. And, my right arm was numb. Not much time.

I pulled the chain, which pulled the hook. I lifted my leg to pull on the leather. It stretched, but didn't break. Nor would it. You can't snap leather. But, maybe I could snap the two-by-four it was connected to.

My hands were sweaty. I tried to tighten my grip, but the metal chain links weren't budging. I coiled the chain around my wrist until there was no slack.

How many more chances did I have? What if they came back while I was trying to get out? I had to make this one count. I pulled with all my strength. *Break, goddammit!*

No.

Again.

The strap leather creaked, but wasn't close to snapping.

Again.

No.

Again.

No!

Again.

NO!

A big sigh. Breath was fleeting. My lungs felt cramped. My biceps and thigh muscles felt weak and jellified.

I dangled in the air. I started to swing and twist my body. It was easier than pulling. And, it built momentum. With each swivel of my hips there was a small tug on the leather straps. I encouraged it, twisting and turning...but staying with the rhythm of it. Building, swelling.

The straps rubbed the insides of my ankles raw. No time for pain. Mind over matter.

I kept twisting. Left, right, left, right...

A micro boom. The sheet metal warbled to my left, then my right. The straps weren't close to snapping. But, they pulled the two-by-fours to which they were attached. And, the two-by-fours pulled the sheet metal.

A small boom. Left, right, left...moving back and forth.

I twisted my hips with more force. More than what the length of the straps would allow. But, that difference is what generated the pressure. I stopped watching for results and stared ahead at the door. Tunnel vision was setting in. I twisted and twisted, this way, that way. Boom, boom. The momentum built. Soon, I was riding it more than propelling it.

Boom. Boom.

The chain from which I dangled started to creak against the wood beams above.

Boom. Boom.

More. Twist. Swivel. Sway.

Left. Right. Left Right.

Creak.

Boom.

Twist.

Creak.

Boom.

Twist.

Creak.

Boom.

Twist.

BOOM!

A thunderous clang shook the room as my left leg dropped. A panel of sheet metal had been yanked off the wall and was now on the ground below my foot. Fresh, Florida air blew in through the hole in the wall. It wasn't overly cool. But, it was a hell of a lot better than the heated air I'd been sucking in. I inhaled massive gusts. Heaven.

But, I was still stuck. One arm, one leg still chained. And, it hurt. Looking up, I figured my best chance was to snap the beam above. That's how the first chain broke free, why not the second? I put two hands on the chain. Only one hand could get a decent grip. Then, I contracted my leg, using it to pull the leather strap still attached to the wall. Nothing doing.

A new idea: I grabbed the loose meat hook, swung it towards the wall. It hooked around a two-by-four. I pulled on it as hard as I could. My arm felt ready to burst. I pulled harder. Sheet metal started to bend. The chain creaked on the stud above. No luck.

The fresh air had revitalized my senses. But, it did little to renew my strength. My arms were weak and ropey. I pulled again. With a loud warble another panel of sheet metal ripped off the wall. Why couldn't they have made this tin box a little more rickety?

Bingo.

Instead of trying to break the beam from which I hung, I looked to bring the whole house down. So, I started to swing. Left, right, left. Finally, with enough momentum, I was able to touch the side of the hot box with my foot. I kicked off and swung faster to the other side. With each swing, my foot landed harder and harder on the sides of the building.

The walls started to rock. The place heaved and creaked each time I hit the walls. I pulled the chain above. It bent the ceiling stud it was wrapped around. My foot slammed into the side of the hut and loosened some vertical supports. The place was rocking.

I had the disappointing realization that if I did manage to knock down an entire wall, the whole thing could--

BAM!

One wall fell. The other wall folded in, slamming hard against my body as the ceiling collapsed. I crashed down. Soil swirled up my nose and into my mouth. The hut roof fell on me.

Son of a bitch, I did it. And, I wasn't dead.

I waited for the dust to settle before I started to crawl out of the wreckage. The meat hook held me back. I twisted my numb arm around. Once loose, I crawled as fast as I could out of the wreckage.

Uppity voices barked in the distance. The sound of footsteps followed. In almost no time, several ranch hands had arrived. Opae was right behind them.

"Find him!" he yelled. "Pull that up!"

It was the first I'd heard him speak. His voice was deep and gravelly in a way that sounded like he'd swallowed bleach as a kid. It wasn't right.

The ranch hands stormed the wreckage and hoisted up planks of wood and sheets of metal. When they finally had a clear view inside the wreckage they were shocked to find I wasn't there. At least, that's how I interpreted their body language. The discovery triggered a mad scramble in all directions at the behest of Opae, who was waving his arms in wild fury.

They didn't spot me in the patch of prairie scrub some twenty feet away. But, I knew it wouldn't be long before they searched it. I had to go.

But, which direction?

The kids were still in the house. I should get them.

The information I needed to stop the Kith was here at the ranch. I should find it.

This monument of maliciousness and murder was still standing. I should burn the whole damn place down.

But, I couldn't.

The thugs who protected it were swarming. And, I was in no condition to raise hell. I only had the strength to try to survive. Maybe not enough.

56

I ran for the prairie.

The woods would have been the obvious place to run. Opae and his men seemed to agree. They were already charging that way with torches, guns, and a pair of Polaris off-road buggies. That gave me a clear route to run, along the far west side of the stables as they drifted towards the east.

The other reason to run for the prairie was simple. If map memory served me, that was the direction closest to town. Although town could be at one latitude and the ranch at the other. Who knew where I would end up? It was still the best bet.

Cows mooed as I ran along the pasture. The donkey used to keep the cows calm stuck his snout through the stable fence for a closer whiff. No time for petting.

A quick survey of my path ahead: A long, flat-roofed stable to the right. Further away, parked tractors and large farming equipment. At the end of the run stood what looked to be a junkyard of old vehicles. Beyond that, stars twinkled over the prairie landscape.

Time to run.

But, I didn't get far.

What I hadn't seen when I surveyed my route was a small wooden alcove attached to the far side of the stable. The shower nozzle, pipe, and garden hose indicated it was used for cleaning up after a dirty day dealing with the herd. But, that's not what was happening now. The only liquid dripping here was blood.

"DG!"

He was tied to the stable and looked half beaten to death.

"Can you hear me?"

He mumbled.

It's a strange kind of heartbreak when those big, mighty men in your life—the ones who look like they could never be stopped and would live forever—take a fall. Typically, it's a father. But sometimes, a friend. And, DG, my friend, looked the meekest I'd ever seen.

I hurried to untie his ankles, then wrists.

His arms dropped and he fell forward. I caught him, let him down easy, and set his back against the wall so he wouldn't tip over.

The hose worked. The water was cool. I spritzed his face then opened his mouth to get him to drink. Most of the water spilled out. But, it was enough to get his body stirring out of the daze. I tossed the hose down and got face to face.

"Hey man. I know you feel like shit. But, the guys who did this to you are hunting for us and we only have a few moments to get out of here. Can you move?"

He just looked at me for a moment. Then...

He nodded.

"Help me up." His voice was barely a whisper.

I scooped under his arms and lifted. Heavier than I expected. We almost spilled over. But, he caught his hand on the wall and pushed himself up the rest of the way. He looked to me with a dark, unhappy expression. Busted blood vessels webbed across his pinked eyeballs. Laceration shreds along the side of his neck were still blood moist.

"Get me outta here," he said.

He forced himself off the wall as I took hold of his arm. We hurried towards the prairie. It was obvious his entire body was in pain. It was more obvious he didn't care. He knew the deal. Run or die.

We almost got caught.

In fact, they should have seen us. But, as I watched a pair of Kith workers from behind a dilapidated water trough, it was apparent they were focused on fulfilling their immediate mission, which appeared to involve grabbing supplies, maybe some netting, and running off towards the woods where the rest of the posse had gone. Once they did, we split.

"What's the plan?" said DG between winded grunts.

"They're looking for us in the woods. So, we're running straight ahead, towards the prairie," I said.

"We're going out there at night?"

"Got a better plan?"

"No." He caught his breath. Talking winded him. "All kinds of something out there."

"Something?"

A panorama of Florida ecology played through my brain—panthers, gators, bears—were bears this far south in the state? Does it matter if there are also panthers and gators? But, I thought panthers were going extinct. Even so, there were still gators.

What choice did we have? None.

"Town's on the other side of the prairie. If we've made it this far, I think we can make it one night on the prairie. Two tough sons of bitches that we are."

He shook his head. "Wild boar. They kill you fast."

Shit, now there were boars.

57

We could still hear commotion in the distance. But, by this point we pretty much had the place to ourselves. We passed the lot of parked farm vehicles. Trucks, tractors, even some king-size crop sprinklers. I spotted a water spigot jutting up from the ground. We stopped, knelt down, and drank. The water was warm, but refreshing.

I surveyed the land. Twenty feet away was the start of the junkyard. It looked filled with vehicles similar to those we squatted next to. But, the older, put out to pasture versions.

"Look," said DG. He pointed past me.

Parked off to the side of the junkyard was a Polaris. It had a tow trailer connected to the back of it.

"Think that'll work on the prairie?" I said.

"Beats the hell out of walking."

"That trailer."

"Come on." DG took the lead, his energy renewed by hope of a faster escape.

"Thing's gonna be loud," I said.

He shrugged. "Probably just blend in with the other noise. If not, we'll still have a hell of a jump on them."

We could be five hundred miles ahead of them and I'd still be uneasy knowing they were looking for me.

DG detached the trailer and set its hitch on the ground. "Know how to drive these things?" he said.

"I can figure it out," I said while hopping into the driver's seat. I pressed the gas pedal.

Nothing.

"Turn it on first," said DG. Good to know he was lucid enough to be a smart ass.

I twisted the key, which thankfully, was in the ignition slot. The Polaris rumbled to life. I bristled. It was too loud for my liking. Too late now. I pressed the gas. It revved. It rolled. I got the feel, twisted the wheel, and accelerated. The Polaris chugged past tractors and around the school bus.

I hit the brakes.

"Look!" I said and pointed, like a kid finally spotting a comet shooting across the black night sky. Before DG could react, I was up, out, and running ahead of the Polaris. I didn't expect it. And, I sure couldn't believe it. After all this time. After all the battles...

I finally found the semi truck and trailer with the Kith logo on it.

"The hell you doing?" I heard DG call from twenty feet back.

It was filthy, massive...and unlocked. And, it was proof I wasn't crazy. I had seen what I thought I had seen on that television.

The trailer door groaned and creaked and cried for grease as I swung it open. The smell hit me hard. I buckled and vomited.

When I had found Ken's body by the river he had been freshly killed. This was my first experience with decomposing flesh. And, it was awful. Worse than what you imagine the detectives smell in movies.

DG said something, but I couldn't make it out. All I heard was myself retching.

I held my nose and staggered back. Flies buzzed and swarmed in and out of the trailer. But, I couldn't see inside. Not until DG pivoted the Polaris so its headlights illuminated all the way to the back of the trailer.

Inside, pushed to the very back of the trailer was a small pile of dead, rotten bodies. My friends from the television. The shed skins of the souls for whom I had searched.

Not all of them had been taken off the truck at the crime scene. That meant the police business by the side of the interstate had been quashed before it could finish. By the powers that be. The deep connections of the Kith. Word must have come down as soon as the newscast aired. *Get that camera outta here and pack it up boys.*

Was no one else on the force wondering what happened to this monument of evidence? Were they too scared to do something about it?

A million thoughts raced through my head.

I found you.

Brown skin. Black hair. Mexicans. Like Ines. Helpless and hopeless. In a silent transfer of good will, I wished them well on the next leg of their journey. I didn't get a return blessing.

But, I had THE TRUCK. I had proof. Rogers and Kay owned the Grove businesses, the trucking, the parlor. All of it. They had been involved with quashing the news story. They hid the bodies. Poorly. And, they'd been involved with the trafficking. They knew Dewey. They killed Love-Mart. They sent people to kill me. And, Ilsa...

We got the hell out of there.

58

The first sign of trouble was when the man on horseback stopped and turned to watch us after we had passed and waved. He looked like a typical Florida scrub cowboy. But, then it looked like he put a phone to his ear and made a call, all the while watching us navigate around palmetto clusters.

"He's following us," said DG.

"What? On a horse?" I said.

DG grunted in affirmation.

On instinct, my foot pressed the gas pedal to the floor. Despite the urgency to escape, we hadn't been racing away at full speed for fear of hitting unseen road hazards. The biggest hazard, of course, was that there was no road.

"If he follows us across the prairie, we'll just have to lose him in town. Should be easy with him on a horse."

DG closed his eyes and leaned his head back.

"What happens then?"

"How do you mean?"

"In town? What's our next step?"

I thought for a moment. "We know where they are now. We have a target."

"Can't call the cops," he said. "I bet they have every police department locked up for at least a two-hundred mile radius."

I had no idea what we would do. Part of me felt it was a mistake to even leave the ranch. While they were out looking for me I could have been looking for the kids. I could have been destroying the ranch...gathering evidence...burning it all down.

Why the hell didn't I? Should we turn back?

It had been survival instinct. Not all the Kith members had chased after me into the forest. Some were still on the property. I was in no condition to fight them. Not now. And, DG was even worse off.

I heard a bang. I felt the steering wheel go rigid. The Polaris fishtailed, the engine whined. DG grabbed hold of the dash to steady himself. Too late. The Polaris flew out of control.

"Walt!"

The Polaris slid perpendicular to a sinkhole, tipped over sideways, and dumped in. My leap out the side was no match for our momentum. It only delayed my landing hard and ribs-first on top of the vehicles' roll cage. The bend of my body swung me down and I flopped atop DG who'd already been catapulted into the sand.

He groaned. I groaned. He spit sand from his mouth. "Off."

I rolled off him.

The Polaris' wheels slowed and stopped.

Shit.

"You okay?" I said to DG.

"Fuck, man..." he said.

I rolled onto my side and took a moment to blink vision back into my eyes. Wreckage to my right, DG straight ahead, the dark prairie to my left. DG looked to me.

"Sounded like a tire popped," DG said. A veil of sand was dusted across his face.

Sand exploded at the lip of the sinkhole.

Gun shot.

We scrambled rolled over to the sinkhole rim.

"Who the hell is that?" said DG.

I gave him the quiet sign. Somehow I knew it was the man on the horse we had passed. Had to be.

The ridge of the sinkhole was our only cover save for the tipped-over Polaris and a palmetto cluster roughly ten feet to my left and ten feet out. It wouldn't do much.

"Check for a weapon," I said to DG while thumbing at the Polaris. He crawled to the wreckage.

I didn't know how close the shooter was. If he was still on his horse, he'd have a higher vantage point to see into the sinkhole, which wasn't that deep to begin with. Maybe about six feet at its lowest point. But, the ridge under which we leaned was almost a straight drop, enough to hide us until he walked right up to the edge. Our other advantage: It was dark. We'd be harder to spot.

"Nothing," said DG. He had the bench seat opened to reveal the on-board storage beneath. Nothing in there but--

"Give me those," I said.

He held up the jumper cables. These?

I gave a curt nod and crawled over, careful not to raise my head above the ridge, careful not to kick up dust. DG handed me the cables but I let them drop, and worked my way to the front of the Polaris. The hood had been janked open in the crash. But, not far enough. I pulled it open another six inches. The front corner dug into the sand and wasn't going to budge either way.

I spotted the cart's battery and reached in for it. It jostled a few inches out of its frame, but wouldn't come loose. It was secured by wing nuts. I tried to loosen them, but they were on tight and I couldn't get leverage.

"See anyone?" I said to DG.

"No," he said. "Fucker's probably sneaking up."

I changed my body English for a better angle. The first wing nut twisted off and dropped in the sand. Wing nut two was still stuck.

"You have a multi-tool?"

"They took it," said DG.

Damn. I looked around. A small rock jutted half way out the wall of soil forming the vertical portion of the sinkhole. I dug it out, quick to glance up, anticipating a horse, a face...a gun.

The rock spilled out. I grabbed it and reached back into the Polaris' innards.

One hit: Little budge. Loud. Screw it. That guy knew where we were. I smashed the rock down. It slipped before really impacting. I recovered fast and smashed again. The wing nut spun loose. My fingers finished the job. I yanked out the battery.

It was too heavy to support at such an odd angle and I had to let it drop to the sand.

"Gimme those cables."

DG looked at me, the cables, grabbed 'em, "Here." He leaned forward and tossed them to me then fell back against the edge of the sinkhole.

Cable one, attached.

Cable two, attached.

"Don't move," said a voice from above.

Too late.

There was the man who had been riding the horse. He was standing on the edge of the sinkhole. His shotgun was pointed at the back of DG's head.

DG looked angry, not scared.

"Whatever you're doing in there just leave it be."

I dropped the cables.

"Up."

I nodded, rose, but hung one of the jumper cables from my back pants pocket, which he wouldn't be able to see behind the Polaris hood. I even raised my hands for added effect.

"Did you already call for help?" I said.

"Don't you worry 'bout that," he said. He looked flustered, like he'd been in the middle of something really important and our shenanigans had interrupted.

"Want me to walk up there?"

He nodded but said, "No. Stay there." It was like me offering that idea made him immediately hate it.

And, that's just what I wanted. If I could get him to come to my way, I'd be in business.

"Stay still." The gunman tensed.

But, I just kept lowering myself back down behind the Polaris hood.

"I'm gonna blow his head off," he said.

I didn't stop.

"Walt. I think this guy's serious," said DG.

I didn't stop.

The man with the gun was rigid with anticipation to strike. He leaned in. He stepped forward.

I looked him in the eyes and said, "I'm just getting something."

"God dammit!"

He pivoted the shotgun from DG to me.

I ducked fast and he fired.

The first blast shot the Polaris. The next did the same. But, the engine blocked the bullet's hot metal from hitting me.

A yelp. A grunt. A scream. And, it wasn't DG's voice.

I peeked around the Polaris. Just as I had hoped. Taunting the man forced him to step forward and he fell off the sinkhole ridge.

DG jumped him. And now, they were battling each other on the ground, each trying to control the gun without getting shot first.

I grabbed the jumper cable off my pocket and leapt over the wreckage. My knees hit the sand first and I fell forward. With a squeeze, I opened the cable jaws and released them onto the gunman's neck.

He screamed. The jagged, copper teeth ripped through his neck skin and blood spurted out. The jaws snapped off. Red flesh was caught between the vice.

DG grabbed a handful of sand and slammed it into the open wound. The gunman squealed to high hell and grabbed his neck with both hands. DG grabbed the shotgun, staggered up, and aimed it at the guy's head.

"No!" I said. My face was inches from the gunman's. Half my face would have gotten blown off, too.

DG twisted at the hips, aimed the gun, and blasted the man's kneecap.

His scream echoed across the prairie and turned into anguished murmurs. His shaking fingers reached around, feeling his new disfigurement.

DG looked to me. I looked to him. Message communicated: Gotta go.

DG tossed the spent weapon.

I scrambled up and peeked with caution over the sinkhole ridge. No cavalry in the distance. But, there was something.

I looked to DG. "Can you ride a horse?"

59

Even on sand, the horse's hooves made that clip-clop sound. The night critters were operating at full volume. It was so loud, in fact, that I had to project for DG to hear me talk, even though he was right behind me, slumped against my back, arms around my waist.

He was just about out of it. The ordeal with the horseman had zapped most of his remaining energy. He even needed me to lift him onto the horse, which had been tied to a palm tree nearly a hundred yards from the sinkhole. By the time we rode back past the sinkhole the horseman was dead, bled out on the ground.

So now, there I was on a stranger's horse on a wild prairie in the dark. Exhausted, beat up, hungry, and thirsty. I felt the windows of both opportunity and survival closing. We just had to move on and try to reach safe civilization as soon as possible. Clip-clopping right into town would be great. I'd settle for simply finding the highway and hitching a ride. But, we'd have to be careful. I was sure the Kith were swarming the area.

Where did things stand?

I knew where their base was. At least one of them. I knew Rogers and Kay Aufderheide were running it. And some guy named Razook was running them. Those two bits alone were major breakthroughs. But, I didn't know what to do with the information. If you squeeze a fist full of sand too hard, it slips out your fingers. I had to pull my focus back and let the answers come at me. Think about something else...

Urgent matters. Ilsa, how was she? Still being watched? Presume yes. Was she safe? Until they decided otherwise. Did my actions back at the ranch make her less safe? *Think action, Walt. Think next steps.*

Ken's kids were in danger. That's the new big question. How did they get there? Answer: Gale. Did she dupe Ken's father, Oren? Or was he in on it? *Focus, Walt.*

The trust bubbled up in my mind. Sounded like Kay and Rogers owned it. Regret flushed through me when I thought about how I should have questioned them longer. I could have gotten more information. Like what about the gathering I'd read about in Dewey's phone? That sounded big and important. A big Kith gathering? A cult ritual? That plus the kids plus Razook plus needing more information plus revenge...

I had to get back to that ranch. At that very moment, the one thing I needed more than information was speed. I had to get to town as soon as possible.

The horse's gait drew my attention. I remembered all of the cowboys I'd seen in movies. I envisioned the old cracker cowboys who crossed this very land year after year moving herds of cattle. So, I did what I thought they would do. I kicked the horses ribs with my heels.

Nothing.

I kicked again.

Nothing.

It was going to be a long, anxious night.

60

DG was right. Wild boars were out here. And, one had just charged out of the palmetto scrub. It startled the horse, which reared back and threw us to the ground. Before I could wrangle it, the horse ran off into the night.

Now, I was scared. Real, non-Disney Florida is a wild and dangerous place. Especially at night.

"I hope you got your rest because we need to keep walking," I said to DG. He was dusting himself off from the fall.

"I got enough," he said. "Which way?"

I pointed to what I thought was west, the way the horse had been heading.

The moon was white and bright and lit our trail enough to keep us from wandering shins first into razor sharp palmetto scrub. Between mosquito slaps, I updated DG on who I had met at the Ranch, what I had learned, and the connections I'd made with the new information.

"You're right. We have to get back to that ranch."

"Last place they'd look for us."

"I can call my boys down," said DG.

I liked the sound of that. "How fast can they get here?"

"Five hours? Soon as I make the call."

"How many?"

"At least twenty."

"Seems light."

"They pack heavy." He made a gun with his hand. "I might could call some satellite gangs in South Florida."

"If we go in guns blazing, that's going to attract a lot of heat. More than they could cover up," I said.

"Isn't that what you want?"

I had to think about it.

"Yes, as long as we're not caught. I don't want to go to jail again. Especially not here."

"I want that big, white hair son of a bitch for myself. Gave me a bad working over."

"His name is Opae."

"Good to know."

We walked on.

Had to be about two hours later. Cloud cover had spread across the prairie and our guiding moonlight was gone.

My feet were killing me. Calf, thigh, lower back, upper back all fought for my attention with pain. I wanted to sit and rest. There was no time.

"I gotta sit," said DG.

We were gonna make the time.

He found a clearing and sat on a thick palmetto root arcing out of the ground. I sat on the other half. It wasn't comfortable, But, it was sweet relief. Everything throbbed.

I was glazed in sweat and cold at the same time. Winter-ish in Florida. Cool, but humid. And, we were filthy. A sarcastic thought: I'd join the Kith for a shower at this point.

"How far to town you think?" said DG.

"Too far the way my feet are feeling." By that point I'd removed my shoes and was rubbing the arch of my foot.

We'd made some tracks on the Polaris. Let's say five to ten miles. We'd gotten maybe two miles on horseback. And, we'd been walking for three hours, perhaps a mile every half hour given our crippled pace.

"Eighteen miles max, I'd guess."

"Semi-precise guess."

I shrugged.

"How many more you think?"

I had seen this part of the state on a map. Knew its size in relation to the state borders. But, had no idea on the mileage.

"Seven maybe?"

DG looked disappointed. "Not sure I can make it that far, Walt."

"What's your other option?"

He didn't know. Just looked out into the night.

I slipped on my shoes. "Come on, let's go," I said with a pat on his back. I stood, held my hand out. He took it and rose.

But, before either of us took a step something crunched.

Something very dangerous.

A rare Florida panther had emerged from behind a large palmetto fan, which was still pressed against its tight, golden fur.

A marvelous and terrifying creature.

Its eyes reflected in the night.

It looked right at us.

61

Something to consider if moving to Florida: Be wary of the alligators. Something else to consider: Be very wary of the animals that eat alligators. Like Panthers.

The wild beast swayed side-to-side as its thick, furry paws padded across the dirt until it stopped just a few feet from us. Its nose twitched, sniffing the air, the scents we were putting out. We had been bleeding. We were vulnerable. Is that what brought him here? Or, was it just dumb luck? Didn't matter now.

The panther gave a low growl as it moved closer.

Man, was I ready to run, sore feet be damned. But, I was terrified and petrified. What about DG? If the cat jumps DG do I attack it? What's the best place to strike a panther? It would all be futile.

No. It's never futile.

On the upside, Rogers, Kay, Opae, nor any of the Kith killers would ever find me if this killer cat took us out.

But, neither would Ilsa.

DG and I stole glances at each other. We had no answers to share.

The panther stood within two feet of us. Even on all fours, it came up to just below our waists. One pounce and it could have driven us both into the ground.

It put its nose against DG's bloody pants and licked his leg. For the first time since I've known him, I was able to picture DG as a scared, young boy. It didn't bolster my conf—

The panther sniffed my leg. Knee to hip. Then, across my belly. I could feel its hot breath steaming through my shirt.

It licked its chops.

215

Please don't kill me. My body is filled with fear and stress and anguish...that can't taste good.

The panther pulled its snout off me and looked past both of us. It snarled, reveling large fangs. A dark stripe of hair bristled along its back. It crouched.

We heard a splash.

Then, a croak.

DG looked to me.

I looked at him.

We knew that croak.

A fat, wet gator crawled out of a body of water we did not know was there.

The panther sprung.

The beasts collided in a flash of violence, thrashing and crashing through the tall grass, splashing and kicking into the water.

I ran.

DG ran.

We hauled ass so fast we didn't feel the prickle of palmetto leaves or the mosquitos or the sand trying to slow us down. It was all reaction, pure adrenaline.

DG pulled ahead of me, as if he knew exactly where he wanted to go. But if that had been the case, he would have seen the river in front of him and not spilled into it. I was paying so much attention to him I didn't see the water either.

DG's arms chopped and splashed as he swam further out.

I hesitated. Lots of water, lots of gators. And, I wasn't quite sure I could make out land on the other side. But, what was my other option? Turn back to land I knew contained at least one gator and one panther? No.

What would the Seminole Indians have done? I wasn't a scholar on the exploits of the only Indian tribe to remain unconquered by the white man—something you learn without fail growing up in Florida. But, I knew enough to know Coacoochee, Osceola, and the rest of the tribe wouldn't have gotten themselves in this dumb, deadly situation. And if they had, they'd get their asses out double time.

So, I paddled and kicked and paddled. Irrational fear got me. I panicked imagining gators were closing in behind me. My chest heaved. My body tightened with fear.

DG's splashing figure pulled away from me and closer to—

Land!

Yes.

It was in sight. All I had to do was swim. I ignored the fatigue in my arms and dropped under the water to swim with less resistance.

When I popped up for air the land was close. And DG, with his wet-slopping clothes sliding off his portly figure was staggering up the shore.

I went under and swam.

Something underwater bumped me.

I shot up from the water, gasping.

Through watery eyes I could see DG waving me on. He was saying something I couldn't understand.

Another bump.

I couldn't look back.

That's what they do in the movies.

Just get out of the water.

Paddle. Kick. Splash. Breathe. Paddle. Kick. Shore. Scramble. Hurry. Sand. Crawl. Get up. Slip. Crawl. Turn over. Look back at the water.

Two gators bumped into each other as they broke through the black water's surface. White froth splashed into the air as the beasts lurched forward.

Something under my arms.

DG's hands. He pulled me from the water. I kicked at the gators.

The gators chomped at each other. That created enough room to twist over, get up, and run off into the night.

62

This vast prairie, which captivated from the highway, was close to eating us alive. Add to that the torture, stress, fighting, beatings, and heartache of the past how many days? It was amazing we didn't crumble into dust.

My suburban upbringing hadn't prepared me for this type of ordeal. My writing profession—where I work with words in the air-conditioned battle zone of my home—hadn't prepared me. Even my last battle with the Kith hadn't prepared me for the sheer physical and mental strain this was putting on me.

How much more could I take?

I'd find out, wouldn't I? Because there really was no choice in the matter. I had kids to save. I had Ilsa to save. I had all the people the Kith was torturing, enslaving, and killing to save. And, the only way I could save them is if I first saved myself.

Debate over. All I could do was walk. No matter how winded I felt. No matter how much my wet clothes weighed me down or how frigid the night air chilled. No matter how much I had to prod DG along. Staggering and limping was still moving. So, was crawling.

Over hills and through sinkholes. Around scrub and amongst livestock. Through veils of gnats and under attack from mosquitos. At my demand and to my relief, we kept moving.

That sun was going to come up. And, it would get hot. Hot enough to scorch, even in winter. The sun was going to help the killers in off road vehicles and boats and helicopters find us. We'd survived gators and panthers. We'd survived hunger and shivers. We'd survived fear and dread.

We would survived…

We could survive…
We survived.

The white plastic fence running along the back of the sprawling suburban housing development was proof. It was designed to keep the wildlife out while still affording a top-dollar view of one of Florida's few majestic untamed wildernesses.

Hi, I'm Walt and this is DG. We're the wildlife. Could we have a drink of your swimming pool?

63

The last thing I remembered before blacking out was a plane juxtaposed against the faint blue sky. The sun hadn't fully come up. Warm orange light was bleeding into the deeper blue of night. But even against that, the white body of the executive jet stood out. It was flying east.

That's what woke me up. The thought that that jet might be flying to the ranch. The Kith had said today was a big day. Perhaps the guests were starting to arrive...by plane.

Wait.

What day was today? Where was I? Not the ranch again. Please.

I looked around the room. Blue striped walls, white sheers over the windows. Thick carpet. A very comfortable bed. Looking across the room I saw a dresser topped with trophies. Kids...no. This was a teenager's room. Say what?

Sitting up hurt to the max. Every muscle ached. Buddhist teachings I had read once advised concentrating on the pain, naming it, and mentally allowing it to pass. I did that. I envisioned simultaneously untwisting the tightest knots in my muscles. Results showed I needed more meditation practice.

The house belonged to Maria and Denny Kapikolis. They lived on the Northeast side of Sebring. And, they had seen us staggering out of the wilderness. To their credit, they let us in, cleaned us up, and did not call the cops.

Over a robust breakfast, I gave them a generic version of what had happened. We were sportsmen out at the ranch, got lost, our Polaris broke down, couple close calls, and so on. They were amazed and enthralled by our tale. Denny couldn't help smiling with amazement during the dangerous parts.

At mention of DG, they said he was asleep in the guest room. And, it was their unprofessional opinion that we should get him to a doctor. I said we would, but there was one place I needed to go first. That struck them as curious. I didn't feel the need to explain, just asked for a ride as I cleared my plate.

Denny's convertible Chrysler Lebaron pulled up to Ines' house. He studied it with the prejudiced eye of a white man from the white part of town.

"This is it?" he said.

"It is. Don't wait for me. I'll get a ride back to your place and get DG soon," I said. The look on his face expressed wonder at who exactly would be giving me a ride back and did he really want them driving whatever it is they would drive into his Eagle Glen development?

Carlos appeared in the doorway.

"Walt?" hurried over and hugged me. It was a surprise, but I welcomed it.

"My god," he said. "We had no idea what happened to you. I tried to talk to you at the jail. They wouldn't let me. And, when I returned with el abogado they said you were gone."

"Where did they say I went?"

"Only that you were transferred."

Creative.

"Where did you go?"

"Get me a soda and I'll tell you."

I guzzled half a Coke in one go. Now, I was ready to talk. Carlos and his father, mother, and Ines were ready to listen. I couldn't help but notice how much healthier Ines looked. The burden over her life to date had been lifted and she was starting to bounce back. Made me feel good.

"Carlos, there is a ranch just on the other side of the prairie," I said.

"The one written on the side of the van?"

"Yes. I don't know if it's the whole operation, but a hell of a lot is going on there. And, they're planning something big. A gathering. Happening as soon as today."

"It's Friday. Maybe over the weekend," said Ines' father.

I nodded. "I'm pretty sure most of the top people in the organization are going to be there."

"Must be why so many planes have been flying over. You know the small ones, not the big passenger planes," said Ines.

Dots connected in my mind. I bet Rogers and Kay would have loved showing me off to all their guests and boasting how they finally captured this troublemaker.

"We need to nail them," said Carlos.

"Exactly." I took another pull off the Coke. "Remember the semi truck I was telling you about?"

They nodded.

"I found it. It's sitting abandoned, bodies still in it, on the other side of that prairie."

They were repulsed and didn't know what to say.

"DG's hurting. They took his phone, so I can't call his people for help. And, I can't do it alone."

Carlos sat up straight as pride rippled through him.

"We will help you."

"The three of you?"

He shook his head. "All of us. The community."

I was doing it again. Getting others involved. But, you know…that was okay. Because they had as much reason to hate the Kith as me. Probably more. Ines had lost years of her life. Her parents had lived in pure misery. Her brother in anguish. And, the community? One could guess many others had experienced the same Kith misery. Perhaps they had loved ones buried in the hot metal of that truck. So, who was I to say no? I couldn't. And, I shouldn't. They were in the battle before me.

I'd been looking at things all wrong since the beginning. It wasn't about who should or shouldn't be involved. It was about saving the kids. Protecting Ilsa. Who cared who was helping? The only thing that mattered was stopping the Kith.

I snapped out of my thought bubble and looked to Carlos.

"Sure you want to do that? Doesn't seem like you guys get a fair shake around here as it is," I said.

His father answered: "Then what is there to lose?" He had fire burning in his eyes. Pride.

"Good point," I said. "But, we need a plan. And, we need weapons. And look…you know that people can get hurt, right?"

"If we have our way, many people will get hurt," said the father.

I nodded and finished my drink. Ines took the empty can.

"Mind if I make a phone call?" I said.

Carlos gestured to a phone sitting on a TV tray next to a recliner.

"Thanks," I said.

The soft recliner felt like heaven under my aching body. If I wasn't careful, I'd fall asleep for a year. I dialed Ilsa's number. It had been too long since we had spoken. There was much to share.

"Hello?" she said.

"Ilsa."

"Walt?"

"Yes. How are you? How's your mom?"

A pause.

"She passed. Two nights ago," she said.

The weight of her lament seemed to sink me deeper into the plush chair.

"I'm sorry, love. She was a good woman."

"Walt," she said. Her tone threw me off. It was as if the topic of her mother was of little concern. "I'm back in the States."

"You are? At home?"

"Hello, Walter," said a voice. A familiar voice.

"It's your dear friend Rogers."

No.

"Why don't you come and visit us out at the ranch? I'm sure you two would like to get reacquainted, huh? You'll be here just in time for the big party. Kay has really outdone herself on the food this time."

The phone went dead.

64

We had to get the hell out of the house.

The Kith could get the number I called from off Ilsa's phone and trace it back here. Despite coaxing me out to the ranch, I couldn't trust those bastards not to strike here first.

Ines helped her father and mother pack. Carlos phoned to rally some friends to pick up DG and take him to a hospital. But, not just any hospital. He said they had an under the radar hospital the community used. DG would be safe there. Sounded like a brilliant plan. In particular, because I figured Sebring and Lorida and all the surrounding areas were already crawling with Kith killers. We had to avoid the police, too.

I made a silent wish for Ilsa to stay safe and unharmed. I wished for Rogers and Kay to treat her with the same welcoming charm they had afforded me. Perhaps that would buy me enough time to get to the ranch and save her.

Carlos interrupted my thoughts. "We are ready to leave."

"Where are Ines and your parents going?"

"We have relatives up north. In the panhandle."

We hurried out to the garage. As the big door opened, I could see Ines' father pulling away in his Ford pickup truck, his wife in the middle, Ines in the passenger seat. She waved and blew me a kiss. I waved back.

"Get in," said Carlos.

Carlos' old Ranchero was revamped with a custom paint job and the rumble of the engine was enough to shake the house to its foundation. He backed out to the street and we drove off.

"Do I have time to see DG?" I said looking to Carlos.

He nodded. "On our way now."

It wasn't five minutes later that we pulled onto a farm on the southeast side of Lake Istokpoga. A private property fenced off with a long dirt road leading up to what looked like your typical ranch style home. About one hundred yards away from the house stood a barn in need of a paint job.

You couldn't see it from the road. But, there was a steep ridge just beyond the house. Part of a massive sinkhole with a lake in the middle of it. As we drove over the peak, I saw that the house was actually three stories built into the ridge. And, there was an additional wing built off its east side.

Carlos stopped the Ranchero in front of the building. "The hospital," he said pointing to a door on a porch. It looked like the front of an old shotgun shack.

Didn't look like a hospital inside either. Just like a house. But, with many, many rooms and hallways that stretched beyond my view.

However, each room did have real hospital beds. And, DG was lying in one, hooked up to an IV and monitors. His eyes were closed. He looked serene. The muscles in his face were relaxed. Creases, wrinkles, and the visible signs of aging appeared diminished. I've used that line a million times in infomercials. Never expected to need it in real life.

It was super strange to see DG out of his standard biker denim. The teal and white cotton smock made him look like any old patient. Sort of.

I looked to the nurse who had escorted us in. "Can I wake him?"

"I'm up," said DG. One eye, then the other, popped open and looked my way.

Carlos gestured to the nurse to give us a moment alone.

"Beats the hell out of the prairie," I said.

"I need to get one of these beds for the house. They're righteous," he said.

"I take it you're feeling okay."

"Yes, if 'okay' means rotten. That ordeal took something out of me. Physically."

"And, mentally?"

"I'm ready to spit fire in their faces." His body tensed as he said it. But, something inside, something painful, forced him to calm down and relax.

"Better take it easy."

"Easy, shit."

"That guy who came in with me? That's Carlos. Ines' brother. He's a good guy. We're lining everything up to go back to the ranch. This time, we're packing."

"I don't have the patience to stay here more than a couple days. Should be out by the time you're ready to roll," he said.

"We're leaving this afternoon," I said.

"Why so quick?" The angry, scowling DG I knew best had returned.

"They have Ilsa."

DG's expression softened. "Those fuckers would do that, wouldn't they?"

"I finally screwed it up for everybody," I said.

"I'm aware."

"I wish we could wait for you. Could use you."

DG waved me off. "Would you stop being dumb? Just go out and kick their asses. Better yet, kill 'em. For me. Especially that white hair scab."

"I'll do my best."

"Make it a goddamn work of art," he said with force.

His hands clutched the sheets and his blood pressure monitor elevated the reading.

"I'll make you happy," I said.

"Make him dead," said DG. "And, get your old lady back. She's too good a woman."

Didn't I know it.

DG held out his hand. I shook it.

"Go. Before I rip these tubes out and follow," he said.

He released my hand and I was out of there.

65

Cars were parked haphazardly up and down both sides of the street. The warehouse stood tall beyond and created a large shadow. The sign read Tavares Air Conditioning. Carlos and I stepped through a side door that had been wedged open.

The space was lit by beams of light bursting through the half-opened transom windows that ran along the top edge of the warehouse and the slow churning ventilation fan. It was hot and humid. No A/C at the A/C place.

We wandered through a maze of metal racks filled with air conditioning parts. They were dusty and many of the boxes were discolored. Like they were past their 'use by' date. Beyond the racks was a workspace that featured tables and tools and air conditioners torn open to expose the coils, compressors, and other guts. A group of men stood around. All looked Hispanic. All looked surly. All looked at me.

They weren't the biggest or strongest looking group of guys. But, something in their expressions, their posture, their vibe was very reassuring. In that split second I had the presence of mind to consider what their struggle to get here must have been like. I'd heard stories— long treks, being smuggled, getting ripped off by smugglers, forced labor, shit work. And, they persisted. They had chips on their shoulders and scars on their skin to prove it. These guys were tough. I was glad they were on my side.

"Come," said Carlos.

I recognized a few of the men from the Ines reunion fiesta. I nodded. They nodded. I got a pat on the back. But, no smiles. They weren't here to socialize.

Carlos spoke Spanish to a man. I gathered his name was Eber. He was taller, hair slicked back, tattoos running up both arms. Twisted roses inked to look like their thorns were keeping his skin pinned to his muscles. He exuded certainty in his response then led Carlos over to a workbench at the far side of the room. It had a large air conditioner on it.

Carlos gave me a look that said 'follow.' I did.

Eber stepped up to the air conditioner, found a latch, and pulled open its metal body.

Wow.

There was an arsenal of weapons inside. Nothing too big or menacing. But, plenty of pistols, rifles, machetes, even bows and arrows.

Most impressive were the knives. They looked handcrafted and spit polished. They were like fetish items to worship with intricate gold and pearl inlay and carved wood handles.

Eber selected a gorgeous blade and slid it into the tattered leather sheath on his belt. He nodded to the other men who went for the weapons like a family digging in on a platter of chicken wings during a Super Bowl party.

"Walt." Carlos waved me over to the weapons table. I stepped up and became as enraptured as the other men had when faced with this slaying smorgasbord. What to choose? The viciousness of the gun and blasting Kith members away was very appealing. But, blades don't run out of bullets. You can use them without giving your location away. And yes...I had enough hate in my heart to want to get in close and feel the life being carved out of them. The sons of bitches had earned it.

But, I was only so good with a knife. So, I took one of each—a pistol and what I guessed to be a six-inch buck knife. Full tang. Sharp blade. The name 'Elvita' had been carved into the handle. The grip was worn smooth and the carvings stained dark from years of use. I had sold plenty of knives through infomercials. And, you have to know the features of a product to sell it. I knew I'd picked a winner. Elvita.

I grabbed a scabbard off the table. It had the image of a mountain range tooled into the leather. Didn't take but a moment to undo my belt, slip it on, and sheath the knife. I caught myself puffing up with courage.

Carlos put a hand on my shoulder.

"You are leading, so you should say something to them," he said.

Quick glances to the men. They were gathered around in a semicircle expecting words.

"Do they speak English?"

"Si," said Carlos. He followed it with a devilish smile.

I looked down at the dusty, dirty concrete floor and took a moment to collect my thoughts. Then, I looked to the men.

"Hey look," I said. "I want to thank you in advance for participating in this...expedition." A quick read of the crowd made me think they wanted something more inspiring.

"We're going up against some very bad guys. They don't just kill. They enjoy it. You need to know they have tremendous resources at their disposal. Weapons, vehicles, and access to more men they can call if they get in a pinch. We can't let them do that. We need to strike fast and leverage surprise. Follow me?"

They nodded.

"I don't know what your particular interests are in helping me fight these guys. Maybe you're friends of Carlos and his sister, Ines. Maybe you've been knocked around by these guys. Seen some of the rotten things they do. Maybe you're just looking for revenge...for something worse. I hope not. But, if so, this is your chance to pay them back in full."

A man to my left pumped his fist, happy to hear that. He was sweating, anticipating the moment I said 'go'. Blood lust was in his eyes.

"I hope you get what you're looking for. I can tell you what I'm looking for. A woman named Ilsa. She's pretty much my wife. They kidnapped her. I don't have to tell you what they do to women they kidnap."

Oh yeah, they knew. You could see it on their grave faces.

"I'm also looking for two kids. Two boys. They belong to a friend of mine. These people killed their father. My number one goal is to get Ilsa and the two boys back. But, that won't be enough."

My speaking-in-front-of-a-crowd jitters melted away. I was preaching my new gospel. Knew it by heart and felt its urgency. I wanted these men to feel it, too.

"Our mission is not successful unless we stop the people who run that ranch. We are not successful unless we tear that place to the ground."

A few of the men shifted weight between their feet, getting anxious.

"But, before we do that, I need to get as much information about these guys as I can. Once we have them immobilized, once we've taken control, I need computers, papers, files...anything you come across that could tell us more about them. Truth is, they could exist beyond that ranch. And, if we don't get all the information we can, they'll continue to torment and kill elsewhere. Maybe even come after us. And, your families."

Postures straightened, hands gripped weapons, a man frowned and spat on the ground. They were being infected with duty. And, it was inspiring.

"I was at that ranch yesterday. You might see some terrible things. Things you won't be able to forget. Be horrified. Be appalled. Become enraged. Let that motivate you. Understand?"

Most of them nodded. One said, "Comprende."

66

The mission was almost over before it started. As soon as we stepped into the sunlight, two police cars rolled up. I recognized the two officers who had arrested me the day before. These cops were Kith. Maybe not official members. But loyal, for sure.

"Not sure what all you Rodriguezes had in mind, but it's time to cancel those plans," said an officer I hadn't seen previously. He was tall and thick with a potbelly that appeared to torture the buttons of his shirt. His gun was on display.

No one said a word.

I looked to Carlos, he to me, then to another guy who looked to a man standing behind the officers. They had flanked out and circled behind as the cars rolled in.

Carlos nodded. His buddy knocked a cop to the ground. The other cops turned to see what happened. Our guys jumped the cops. It took about thirty seconds to sandwich them all in the back of the police cruiser. The man who slammed the last door shut jumped into the driver's seat and drove them out of there.

As the police cruiser drove off, Carlos waved the men over to a trio of jeeps. They looked rugged in their outfitting. And, that's when I knew we wouldn't be taking the highway. It was back through the prairie swamps for me.

The breeze was crisp and cool on my face. I sat up front next to Carlos. Sun had set. We were deep into the prairie. I thought I recognized a cluster of palm trees DG and I had passed the previous night.

"How much longer?" I said to Carlos.

"An hour. Then we walk," he said. "We don't want them to hear us approach."

"Amen, brother," I said.

I ran the plan through my mind. Carlos would lead one team of men and charge the front of the ranch. That would keep that route clear for us in the event we needed a quick escape.

I was to lead a team of men straight into the ranch house. We had to find Ilsa, the kids, and information. Revenge was secondary.

But, I couldn't leave before stopping Rodgers, Kay, and the Kith for good. Kill the weed at the root. If this ranch died, the satellite massage parlors, strip clubs, and slave services would wither away, too.

We also had a third group of men. They were designated as second wave. Not my idea, but I liked it. Sounded like one of the men back in town had served in the military. He recommended not sending everyone in at once. That way, they couldn't surround and trap us.

The jeep jostled over the pocked land. Some kind of bird flapped out of a bush just in time.

What if the Kith had heavy artillery? What if we were outnumbered? What if...*Don't sweat those details, Walt.* We needed to charge in there and raise hell. We had the upper hand.

Feature: Surprise was on our side.
Benefit: We could strike first. And, if we strike hard enough, they'd never recover.

Feature: I had been there already.
Benefit: I knew where most things were. Enough to get a jump on our target locations.

Feature: Some of my compadres had been there, too, while working.
Benefit: They knew of places I hadn't even seen. They also suspected they knew people still working out there who would be sympathetic to our cause. They would even look for friends they had lost. That'd be a huge help.

Feature: We were pissed.
Benefit: Never underestimate the power of fury.

It felt good to think things through.

But, as soon as the jeeps rolled to a stop and cut out their low projection amber headlights, and I heard the chatter of creatures on the prairie, I got nervous again. The adrenaline flowed.
I heard the whoosh of an executive plane overhead. It was flying low, coming in for a landing. I couldn't help think the big boys were arriving for the party. We were getting there just in time.

67

The teams divided up before reaching the ranch perimeter. By the time I could see the ranch house I was traveling with just three men—Raul, Emeliano, and Santiago. I told them I'd probably get their names wrong in the heat of it all.

Raul said, "No problem, Willie." They laughed. Good icebreaker.

We watched from the palmetto scrub. The Ranch looked deserted and dark, save for pockets of light thrown by fixtures attached to the sides of the buildings. We heard a commotion in the distance. Music played. It sounded like music for people who hated music. The low hum of arriving planes cut through the night. All private, executive jets.

"Looks clear," I said. "We need to get in that main house." I pointed to it. "But, I want to check these stables first. Could be girls in there."

The men nodded. Emiliano the tallest of the bunch, yet still shorter than me, gestured to himself and Santiago. They'd check the stables to the left. Raul and I would check the stables to the right. We pulled out our weapons.

A ranch hand in a check-patterned shirt walked in the direction beyond the house, where I suspected a party was being held.

"What do we do with any captives we find?" said Raul.

"Take them back to the jeep."

He agreed.

"Ready?" I looked each of them in the eye.

The men nodded. Their eyes glared, their jaw muscles flexed. Their expressions said, "Bring it."

It was happening.

Santiago grabbed Emiliano's arm before he touched the barbed wire. He pointed to a nearby metal box. The shit was electrified.

Santiago got on his hands and knees then waved us up. One by one me, Raul, and Emiliano used Santiago's prone back to launch ourselves over the wire. We all cleared the hurdle. But, it wasn't clear how Santiago was going to get over. He backed up five large strides took three deep breaths and he ran for the wire. Step, step, step, spring...and he launched himself into a straight up high jump-style Fosbury Flop. Over he went, landing hard on his back, then rolling to cushion the impact. Raul and Emiliano each grabbed an arm to help him up. Santiago wiped himself off and smiled. More than impressive. I liked these guys. They made me feel better about our chances. We crouched and ran.

Raul tried the first door. Locked. I moved past him to the next. The wood around the doorframe had started to rot. I tugged hard on the door. It opened enough for us to step through.

Not a single animal inside the stable. But, the work of animals was abundant: Each of the wooden stalls had chains with metal cuffs hanging off the walls. Water buckets and hay on the floor. In the middle of the room was what looked like a gymnastics pommel horse. Only it was topped sandpaper, not soft padding. Connected to it was a wooden stock with holes for a head and wrists. People got beat here. The crimson stain across the ground proved it.

A moan.

I crouched into a fighting stance and looked to Raul. He pointed to a shadowy stall beyond him where we found a young woman coiled in a fetal position. Tattered rags for clothes. Shaking, shivering, crying, bleeding.

I knelt beside her.

"Shhh," I said.

She startled. I steadied her with a hand on the shoulder.

"It's okay. We're getting you out of here."

"No...no...NO!"

Raul slapped his meaty hand over her mouth. The girl's eyes grew wide with panic. I gestured for her to be quiet and then for Raul to remove his hand. He did with some reluctance.

The girl didn't scream. Just looked at us in bloody terror.

"Hablas ingles?" I said.

"No trabajamos aquí. Sólo ayudamos a las chicas como tú a escapar," said Raul.

She looked to him mystified. Then, nodded. She understood.

We stepped back. She got on her hands and knees. We helped her up. She leaned into Raul and he escorted her towards the open door.

The rest of the stalls were empty.

"Ask if there are other girls," I said to Raul.

He looked to the frightened girl. "¿Hay más chicas por aquí que podemos ayudar?"

She clutched his shoulder enough to get him to glance at it. Then, she looked to me. "Están siendo vendidos como esclavos. Por favor, sácame de aquí antes de que regresen por mí. Son horribles!"

Santiago and Emiliano arrived. "Nada."

Raul looked spooked. "She says they're being…sold." He looked to her. "¿Dónde? ¿Aquí?" He gestured to the property at large.

She nodded.

Son of a bitch. It was the twenty-first century in the United States. In sunny, tropical Florida. And, we were at a goddamn Kith slave auction.

68

Emiliano and Santiago ran off towards the runway. Raul took the girl, Rosa, back to the jeep. I waited for him to return. We moved towards the ranch house. It was bigger than I remembered.

A group of Kith members, four of 'em, walked out. They were dressed in suits, a look reminiscent of the President's Secret Service detail. We ducked back in shadows to let them pass.

We entered the house through a side door that led into a busy kitchen and cut through it into a hallway just off the main lobby/living room area. Gale hurried past without seeing us. She stopped a female server: "Did Rogers and Kay already head out to the pool deck?"

"I believe so, Ms. Williams," said the server.

"Would you mind taking this out to them?" Gale held out a bag.

It was full of rings.

"They're for tonight's initiations," she said.

The server reached for it. But, Gale pulled it back against her chest. "Know what? Forget it. I'll just run it out there myself. See how everything's going."

"Very well," said the server. She wiped her hands on her apron and dashed off to tend to some other matter.

Raul hit my shoulder.

"What?"

He was looking at something else.

Someone else.

One of the staff. Jumpsuit, white rag hanging from his belt. He was Mexican and looking right at us.

"How are you, my friend? You mind to help us out?" said Raul.

The servant looked unsure. He glanced in both directions. He saw the gun on Raul's hip. Raul held up his hands like everything's fine. You have nothing to worry about.

"Will you help us?" he said. "We can help you leave if you help us."

Another glance in both directions. The servant knew he could get in trouble. But, he wasn't racing to blow the whistle on us. He nodded.

Raul nodded back. "Gracias." Then, "Where are their offices? We need information. Where do they keep the important items?"

The servant pointed upstairs.

"Everything is upstairs?" said Raul.

The man nodded.

"Have you seen what they are doing out there?"

The man nodded.

"Do you approve?"

The man shook his head. "They are selling our sisters like cattle."

Raul nodded solemnly then put a finger over his lips. Don't tell. The servant turned back to cleaning a vase, as if he hadn't seen us.

"Stairs are that way," I said and led the way.

The place was quieter now. I guessed the last of the hurried preparations had been made and whisked out to the pool deck, as Gale had mentioned. It felt like there were fewer people around. That would help.

We took two stairs at a time. Careful steps, keep the feet light. No ankle twisting on this deep, green country club carpet. On the second floor, we dashed over to a small alcove off the side of the landing. Standing close together, we caught our breath and looked around. No activity. Two hallways. We split up.

The first door was locked. Next, locked. Shit. Third –

Open.

I ran in to find it was a bedroom, but got spooked at the thought someone might still be in there. I stopped, watched, and listened. Nothing. Clothes on the bed. Just like an occupied hotel room. So, who was staying there? I checked for a wallet. I found a suitcase. Name tag: Earl Belcher, Pensacola, Florida.

The name meant nothing. Nothing suspicious in the suitcase. Time to move on.

I looked before stepping out of the room. The hallway was empty in both directions. No Raul in sight. I moved down the hall.

A door opened behind me.

I turned to face a guest room door that was locked and fiddled around as if trying to find the key in my pocket. A peripheral peak revealed it to be Raul. Nothing in his hands. He checked more doors.

The door to my left opened fast. A man stepped out and turned to shut his door. He was black, salt in pepper hair, and a look of refinement and wealth.

"Hi, how ya do--" He stopped.

Something made him suspicious. Recognition?

No time.

I charged at him.

69

He ran back into his room. I jumped through the doorway and tackled him. A punch to the face, a punch to the gut. As I swung, I caught sight of the open door behind me. Couldn't have that. I kicked it closed.

"Get off!"

He was big. He looked strong. But, he fought for shit. And, I'm no pugilist.

I grabbed the back of the chair at the desk and brought it down. The hard, heavy wood smashed across his nose. He yelped and grabbed his face with both hands, surrendering his defense. Blood oozed up through his fingers and over his gold wedding band.

I showed him my pistol, barrel first.

"My face," he spoke in mumble-ese.

"Quiet," I said as I stood and backed up. The gun was trained on his chest. Once he saw it through his watering eyes, he settled down a bit.

"Did you recognize me?" I said.

A pause. "Yes."

"If you know who I am then you know what I've done and what I can do to you. So, don't be dumb."

"Yes, yes. Okay.'

I let my hand find the chain on the door and locked it.

He sniffled blood.

I stepped over him into the heart of the room and gave it a quick toss. "My gun is still on you."

He didn't move.

"Any weapons in here?"

He shook his head.

"How did you know who I was?"

240

He mumbled something. It took me a moment.

"Bulletin? Like at a country club? They circulate news?"

He shrugged and nodded.

"On your phone?" I said.

Nod.

"Everyone gets it?"

Another nod.

So, they had an entire communications system that connected all members. At least as far as important messages were concerned. It was like their own little Amber Alert. Caution: Pissed off infomercial writer is on a rampage.

I kind of liked that.

No name tags on the luggage. No wallet on the desk. It had to be in his pocket. I knelt down and put the gun to his nose.

"Wallet, please." I said.

He rolled onto his side never taking his bloody hands from his face.

I extracted his wallet, tossed it on the desk, and flipped through it. Identification: Shelton Ainsley, Maryland driver's License. Maryland?

"You guys national?"

No comment.

I kicked him in the shoulder, which shook his face, hands. It cause pain and he screamed.

"Tell me."

"I don't know. Shit." He pulled his hand from his face just long enough to spit out blood that had pooled in his mouth.

My fingers flipped through his wallet. Lots of cash. Thousands. A few receipts. Picture of his wife and kids.

"Your wife know you're here?"

No shrug. He rolled his head away.

"Apparently not."

Health insurance card, credit cards—platinum and black—health club ID, what's this? A card with his picture and the Kith symbol on it. Say what??

"Membership has its privileges," I said.

He looked over. I flashed him the card. He said nothing. I leaned on the desk, gun pointed his way.

"You fly in on your own or did they fly you in?"

"They did," he said.

"Nice service. They do that for all their customers?"

He yelled as best he could. Blood gargled in his mouth.

I got low to the ground, gun in his face again. I doubted anyone heard him, but he pissed me off.

"Shut your goddamn mouth and only open it when I tell you or I'll blow those fingers through the back of your head."

A nod.

"I don't give a good goddamn how much freedom you think you're entitled to. I'm the one with the gun. You're the one bloody on the floor at a ranch you've traveled to without telling your family, and you're here to what, have sex? Buy slaves? Both?"

He gave me that aww c'mon man look people give when they're busted.

"Seriously? You of all people are buying slaves?"

He kicked in a fit. I slammed the gun butt down on his hand. It stunned him and he fell still.

"I'm gonna leave but I just have a couple more questions. Where did you get the club ID?"

"Mail," he said.

"Good. Who sent it?

"No contact. All online."

Interesting.

"Through this site?" I held the card up to him. A URL address was printed on the back. Instead of a dotcom address, it was a series of numbers and periods.

"What's your password?"

He sighed.

"Come on. You want to tell me because you don't want to die. But, you're worried if you do tell me, they'll kill you, right?"

He nodded and looked away, ashamed.

"You're in a tough spot. But look, I'll never tell them it was you who gave it to me. I'll just log on, look around, and that's that. They won't know the difference."

He looked at me, gauging if I was serious.

"Peppermint," he said.

"That's the password?"

"Named after my dog."

"Cute. I'll test it first computer I find. And trust me that will be before I leave. So, if you lied, I'll be back to make it all hurt so much worse."

"I understand," he said. He was more composed now, but still in pain.

"Does that ID get you in to all club properties? Like the massage parlors?"

He nodded.

"We're almost done and I'll be out of your hair. Tell me, what's going on out at the pool?"

"You know."

"Slaves, yes. But, who all is there? Everyone? All the brass? All the members."

"Most."

"Were you here to buy a slave? For your pleasure?" I tacked on a lascivious smile. It turned his screws and he turned away. "Dirty boy, Shelton. But, I guess that's just you being free. Free to be pervy Shelton."

I couldn't tell if the look on his face was anger or embarrassment or a mix. Both were dangerous. I needed to be careful.

"Have you seen the European woman? Ilsa. Or, a pair of boys?," I said.

"Nah, man."

I watched his face. He watched mine. Standoff. He vibed honest.

"How high up are Rogers and Kay?"

He looked to me and looked confused.

"In the organization? How close to the top?"

"Pretty high up," he said.

"Is this the headquarter? This ranch?"

"One of 'em."

Damn. I worried this nightmare wouldn't end today.

"Is this like a big annual event. The big slave auction?"

"My first one. They have 'em quarterly."

Jesus. Sickos.

"Who is above Rogers and Kay?"

"Man, I don't know. We just meet some of the other members as we go along. It's a club, but they don't let us know much about the running of it."

"Who is Razook?"

He seemed to freeze at hearing the name.

"You know don't you?"

Despite the gun and violence and the threat of telling his wife he was buying a sex slave, mention of Razook's name was the most scared he'd looked.

"Don't clam up now," I said. "Tell me who he is and I'll be on my way."

"He's the top. Th-the number one. That's all I know." His expression turned pained, like he'd really just screwed himself over.

"What does he look like?"

"Don't know. This is my first time here."

"He's going to be here?"

He shrugged.

I aimed the gun at his eye.

"Thank you," I said.

He exhaled and his body seemed to wilt into the carpet.

"Give me your phone," I said.

He pulled the bloody hand away from his face and dug into his pocket. Blood smeared on his pants. He offered me the phone.

"Drop it."

He did, on his chest.

I scooped up his shirt and wiped the phone as clean as I could. Then opened it, no password.

"What's your wife's name?"

"Loni," he said.

"Good woman?"

He nodded and tears welled in his eyes.

I flipped through the phones contacts, found Loni, and forwarded the contact to DG with a text that I read out as I typed: This is the contact info for the wife of a Club Member named Shelton. She doesn't know he is here buying sex slaves. Please let her know if you don't hear from me in five hours.

Shelton looked shattered. I looked back to the phone and typed: Make that three hours.

Shelton cringed.

"I need you to keep your yap shut. Best you just stay here out of the way. Things are going to get crazy down there."

He nodded.

"Don't open that goddamn door once I leave. I might just be standing outside. And, I'm trigger happy."

He nodded again and curled onto his side.

I tucked the ID in my pocket, stepped over Shelton, and stopped at the door. A look back showed him to be a broken man. He wasn't going anywhere.

There were two more rooms on my wing of the floor. Both were locked. At the end of the hallway was a large window that looked out onto a winding path that led to a pool and a large, office type building in the distance. The man we saw downstairs was wrong. The important information wasn't up here. It had to be in that building.

70

The announcement came over the loudspeaker: "Freedom Enthusiasts, bidding begins in ten minutes, poolside. Ten minutes poolside."

A tubby Kith member accelerated his waddle. This was good. The guests were all focused on their purpose for visiting the ranch instead of looking for me. And the hosts had a show to put on. We'd have room to maneuver.

The walking path was lit by glowing rock lights. It set an enchanting ambiance. But, we played it safe and cut behind nearby bushes. A slower route, but less exposed.

We had been on the property too long. I had hoped for a quick strike. But, that was unrealistic given everything we wanted to achieve.

I recalled the Branch Davidians in Waco, Texas. That battle went on for days and they were a small handful of cultists with a stash of weapons. Who knew what these freaks had stashed away? That would be something to look for, too. Either as a way for us to build our arsenal or something to destroy so the Kith couldn't use it.

Listen to me. Talking about arsenals and strategy and battle. I needed to think in much simpler terms befitting my amateur status: Destroy everything. If it was valuable to the Kith, blast it to bits, period.

The path sloped past the pool area. I could hear chitchat and music building behind me. Sounded like it was going to be one hell of a party. Raul stepped carefully across a loose assortment of rocks, stopped, ducked, and watched.

I followed suit and almost knocked him over. He held me back and gestured up the path. Two armed Kith walked past, scanning the area. It was the first time we'd seen weapons that weren't ours. I connected it to bigwigs in attendance. We got flat in the darkness.

And, I smiled. This was what I had been fighting for; the chance to destroy the important Kith.

The guards passed. We got up and ran to the bottom of the slope, which ended at the cusp of the runway. It was long, wide, and covered in green grass minus the dead patches where plane tires had flattened the sod.

Raul said, "Look," and pointed.

What a sight. At least fifty private planes and executive jets were lined up along the sides of the runway. Their stairs were folded down to the ground and awaiting important people.

Raul seemed to read my mind. "They're going to buy our girls and take them away forever," he said.

"That's not gonna happen," I said.

A plane broke through the clouds. Its wing lights winked. We watched it land on the grass tarmac. Rather than pull next to the last plane in line, it taxied all the way up to the ranch property, not far from us. The door opened, gates dropped, and three men walked out; two handlers and a VIP I didn't recognize.

A Kith member walked into view and greeted the VIP. All four men walked up the pathway and past us. I didn't recognize any of them. We were losing time.

We took a chance. Raul and I mimicked like we were discussing logistics for the event as we walked past the plane attendants on our way to the tree-lined berm behind the executive jets. It worked. "We have to be getting close to that other building," I said.

Noise. A purr. A buzz.

We hopped behind bushes. *Don't move. Don't even breathe.*

The sound increased. A golf cart appeared from the direction we were headed. Tough to see who was driving as it whisked through the shadows. Males. Two of them. Kith staff. And, there was something on the back platform of the cart.

It moved. It murmured. But, it wasn't free. It was restrained. It was a person tied up. A prisoner. *These guys.*

I couldn't tell who it was before the cart disappeared around the bend. And, I didn't sweat it because the coast was clear.

One hundred winding, bush-lined, pebble-surfaced meters further and there it was—the building I hoped had everything I sought inside. It was lit by an array of colored landscape lights, red, green, and blue, like a lush, tropical fantasia.

"This?" said Raul.

"Feels right," I said.

There were no overt signs indicating it was an administrative building. But, the brass door handle was worn bright and shiny from heavy use. And, a few of the windows were lit up, two downstairs, one upstairs.

Applause rose in the distance behind us. Showtime. Could be perfect timing to keep our work undisturbed. What were Carlos and our other guys were doing? Would they cause a commotion and send people scrambling this way? We still had to hurry.

Raul's elbow jabbed my side. "Mira!"

He was pointing up to the building.

There was little Kelvin waving to me through the window.

I smiled and waved.

He smiled then looked over his shoulder and said something to someone I could not see. Little Kory appeared, saw me, and waved.

What a relief. Ken's kids were safe.

71

Gale appeared in the window behind the boys. Her demeanor looked pleasant-ish, like she'd grown tired of watching them and had hours to go. Or, perhaps she was resentful for having to miss all the poolside fun. Maybe little Gale wanted to buy her own slaves.

She saw me and got spooked.

"Come on!"

Gale ran from the window.

We ran to the building entrance. Two staircases inside. I took the one closest to me. Raul took the other.

Second level landing. The floor was dark. Offices filled with desks and computers. No sign of life. A closed office at the far end of the floor caught my eye. Solid information had to be in there.

Kids first!

I dashed up to the third level. Gale crashed into me on her way down the stairs. I grabbed the handrail as she stumbled past, letting the boys go in the process. She rolled down the steps and hit the mid-stair landing hard.

She grunted and looked up at me through evil eyes. It was shocking. The juxtaposition of that look with her freewheeling summer girl nature was all kinds of wrong. The words hissed out of her mouth: "Give me those boys."

"Never," I said.

I could see her mind racing. She looked at the boys then back to me. What shocked me most was the fact that she was as loyal to this demented group as all the others I had encountered. And, she was so young.

"Where's Ilsa?"

Gale dashed off down the stairs.

"What's wrong with Miss Gale?" said Kory behind me.

"She said you were here to hurt us," said Kelvin.

"No way," I said. "I'm here to take you someplace safe."

"We're not safe?" said Kory.

"How about I tell you all about it in a little while?"

Raul appeared around the corner, startled at seeing us.

"Is you," he said.

I nodded.

"Boys, this is Raul. He's a very good man. He'll take you to our truck."

They weren't so sure.

Raul, ever the father, leaned down. He pulled two engraved pocketknives from his jeans and flipped out the blades. "It will be like an adventure."

The boys brightened with excitement as they took hold of the knives.

"He'll take you across enemy lines," I said.

They looked to Raul. He saluted.

"Come on," he said, his hands outstretched. The boys each took a hand

Raul looked to me and said, "We see you soon."

"Ilsa first," I said.

"Find her fast," he said.

He and the boys ran down the dark staircase. Something told me he'd keep them safe.

I was on my own now. My three objectives had been reduced to two: Ilsa and information.

A quick look around revealed kids' toys on the floor, a cocktail cart with both adult and non-adult beverages, two open sodas, and a peeled wrapper of crackers. It was more lounge than office.

I moved through the dark corridor from which Raul had appeared. The walls were lined with shelves and books. Titles by de Sade, de Laclos, Perrin, some guy named Claude Prosper Jolyot de Crébillon. Not to be outdone, John Wilmot had a book called *Sodom, or the Quintessence of Debauchery*. Lovely. And, stored behind glass in this lending library for letches.

A slender volume caught my eye. *You the God*. Son of a bitch. It was written by Razook.

Disappointment hit. You mean all this came about because some self-help guru wrote a book and people were dumb enough to believe it?

I pulled the book off the shelf and flipped to the author picture. It was just a silhouette of the man. Waist up shot. He was looking out a window, his back to the camera. His eccentric attire included a Nehru collar (fine) and waist sash (the hell?). I flipped to the front of the book. Other suggested reading by Razook included *Living With Permission*, *What Padre Taught*, *Libertine Sunrise*, *The Final Blessing*, and the ambiguous *Sinless: Anything Goes*. Give me a break. I clapped the book shut.

I'm all for having some fun. But, this guy was like the Jerry Falwell of sex fiends. But, no doubt smarter than the average yanker.

Time was running out.

I hurried down to the next level. This felt like 'the office.' I walked fast past desks. All the papers were stacked neat on top. Who does that?

There. Groveland trucking documents. They were less important now that I'd tracked down the mother ship.

There. A clipboard with a list of names. Guests? I scanned it quick. None of the names were familiar.

Noise outside. Yelling.

A glance out the window revealed Kith guards flooding in from three different directions. They were dressed in slacks and tennis-white polo shirts with embroidered Kith logos. And, they had clubs and guns.

Out of time.

There. A light in the office at the end of the hallway. Two men in the window. Late night meeting? One raised a glass. I bumped into a metal desk. The sound drew their attention.

Didn't know the blonde. But, I knew the other one.

Oren.

He recognized that I recognized him. He waved me over, like a father welcoming his son home.

I was too stunned to hear the guards' footsteps behind me.

They grabbed my arms.

72

I was dragged into the office. Oren pointed to a nearby chair. The guards pushed me down into it.

"Hello, Walt. Good to see you." said Oren. He greeted me the same way the other day.

I looked to the other guy. He was leaning against the desk. He looked wealthy and mildly curious.

"You gotta be kidding," I said.

"About what?" said Oren.

"This." I waved my arm in a flippant gesture.

Oren looked around the room, looked back to me, and shrugged.

"You're the prick behind all this? You had your own son-in-law killed?"

"We're getting ahead of ourselves, Walt."

"Oh, are we? I figured you'd be anxious to get back to your slave auction."

A guard tightened his grip on my shoulder.

"He is feisty." It was the other guy. He looked to Oren with a sly, amused smile as he said it.

"I told you," said Oren, keeping his eyes on me.

It was a blow knowing these guys weren't worried in the least about me.

"Who's he?" I nodded to the guy leaning on the desk.

"That's Rance. Gale's father."

Of course he was. Oren had told me he knew Gale's father from the club. I never would have thought it was this club. That seemed naïve on my part now.

"So, that explains why Gale's here. And, the boys," I said.

"The boys are fine," said Oren. "Gale's a great nanny. And they're not here under duress, despite what the Aufderheides may have led you to believe."

"But, Ilsa is."

Rance nodded. Oren shrugged.

"So, save the nice guy act."

"Easy enough." It was Rance.

He lifted off the desk and stood before me. "Walt, we're going to kill you. And, your girlfriend. And, then we're going to go about doing all the things you've been trying to stop us from doing. Things we enjoy doing, regardless of consequences. And, we're going to do them all without guilt or remorse or regret. We're going to enjoy every bit of it."

He stared me in the eye, daring me to challenge his conviction. Oren had the same look. I was intimidated.

"Is this what those books in the hall teach you?" I said.

"They present ideas. We've learned through experience," said Rance.

"We're tired of you being in our business," said Oren.

A cold statement coming from someone who had been kind.

"You guys started this when you killed Ken."

"You continued it when you started looking for the truck," said Oren.

"You were going to come after me anyway. Weren't you? For Karen."

"Probably," Oren said with a laugh.

At least I could take comfort in knowing I'd followed the only possible path. They'd never have let me live.

"We're ending it today," said Rance. He looked to Oren. "He's not worth the trouble anymore. And, we have guests."

"I agree," said Oren. He grabbed his keys off the desk and dropped them in his pocket. "You'd have been a great libertine but you decided to be a hero."

Oren and Rance walked to the door. Rance stepped out first. Oren looked back in and tapped a finger to his chest. "Take him to Opae. Tell him I get the scalp."

The guards yanked me out of the chair.

73

The guards pulled me onto the back of a golf cart and held me in place. Their grip was so hard I could feel the blood tightening in my forearms and my fingers starting to tingle. The cart started rolling.

A golf cart was following us. Even if I was able to wiggle free and jump off, there was a good chance I'd get run over.

But then, the cavalry arrived.

Carlos and his team leapt from the bushes and dove onto and into the golf carts. They shoved the passengers out and the driver into the passenger's seat. Carlos yanked the wheel. The cart spun into the high rocks lining the pebble path. The front wheels got caught up and the cart flipped. The two goons gripping my arms went flying.

I was airborne enough to land at the bottom of a grass slope; a good twenty feet clear of the wreckage and the men, who were all now fighting each other. They could handle it. I ran off into the dark. Thanks, Carlos.

Mosquitos nipped my arms as I cut through the night. My legs were killing me. It had been a relentless and brutal several days. The good news was that no matter what happened over the next hour, two hours, however long...by the end of tonight, it'd all be over. Either the Kith would be no more. Or, I'd be dead.

Ilsa and information. I needed both. Her more than the other. And, I wouldn't mind taking a crack at Oren and Rance. Especially, Rance. I couldn't believe I didn't get any information out of them. They said I'd make a great libertine. And, they had a wall full of books on the matter. Including Razook's. That might be all the information I needed. Plus, I had Earl Belcher's member ID and access to the Kith website. That would have to do for now. I needed to find Ilsa fast.

I almost ran too far, right into the crowd of guests.

I stopped short and willed myself back into the darkness of shadows...and watched.

Tuxedoed men and ladies in expensive gowns laughed, drank, and mingled around the pool. Teeth gleamed. Rings clinked on champagne flutes. Music played. Who the hell DJs a slave auction?

It was unbelievable. In this day, this age, at this very place people were gathered to buy slaves as if they were at a charity event put on by the local professional baseball team. But, all the proceeds went to degenerates. This scene, this abomination, ran against every definition and example of what I knew to be right. This couldn't be happening. But, there...being led up the steps was the first offer of the night.

An older man, who looked like a partner in a law firm and had skin that gleamed from the good life, cheeks rosy from alcohol, misbehavior in his eyes…he was the one who tugged the chain which was attached to the collar around the young woman's neck. He pulled her on stage and into the spotlight. Yes, there was a spotlight! And, it seemed to blind her. Was it to prevent her from seeing the monsters and their sequin-adorned wives sizing her up like market meat?

She was barely dressed. And, barely there. She looked dead inside. Whether she'd had her will broken or she was drugged up didn't matter. Something was done to make her accept her role in this nightmare.

In the dark behind the dais stood more girls to be featured. All chained. All next to what looked like plastic plaques. Details, bidding info. Odds were the guests got to inspect the merchandise up close before the bidding.

I watched the guests. Most were holding programs and bidding paddles.

An unseen emcee spoke: "Item number MX9901, starting bid is ten-thousand dollars."

Ten K was a lot of money. But, not for a person. You couldn't put a reasonable amount on this girl, this daughter. Her poor parents.

Paddles started popping up. They were bright neon green, and stood out in the dark poolside environment.

Sometimes I am struck with an unexpected clarity that provides generous insight. In this instance, it had to do with the item numbers, MX9901. I broke it down - 'MX' and she looked Mexican. '99' and she looked older teen, post high school. If she was born in 1999, that put her at eighteen years old. That felt right, looked right. '01'? She was the first on the auction block. Or, maybe the first Mexican? Would they have other nationalities? I could stay and find out. But, I needed to hustle and make sure none of these girls were taken away. At least not by these rich creeps.

"Going once...going twice...gone! Item MX9901 goes for $35,000!" the emcee announced.

A man turned to his wife. They smiled excited, as if they'd just gotten a steal of a deal.

Before the first girl left the stage, the next girl was already on her way up.

"Item number HA9701. Starting bid is twelve thousand dollars," said the emcee.

She was darker skinned. And, she looked older. 'HA' had to stand for Haitian. Plenty of Haitians in South Florida. They were brought over to work in the sugar cane fields around Clewiston. Not far from here. '97' put her at 20 years old. Other than the last two digits, I had figured out their auction code. Not that it meant much. But, maybe they weren't as sophisticated as I gave them credit for.

Footsteps, bated breath.

I ducked down.

A guard ran past. Something was happening. He looked to be in pursuit. That meant they were distracted.

Time to work.

"Going once...going twice...gone. Item number HA9701 goes for $24,000!" came the emcee's announcement. Interesting. Were Haitians less valuable to this group? Try telling that to the father of the girl now being led off the stage in a zombie-like stupor.

The crowd clapped. Wine glasses clinked. Some guy yelled, "Gonna have a good time tonight!"

Gross.

What kind of mayhem could I cause? It had to be big, bad, and bold. And, it had to scare the shit out of these bastards. Guards were stationed around the pool. I could start shooting, but they'd be on me in seconds.

The emcee's voice cut the air. "Up next, a special treat."

The spotlight ballyhooed across the heads of the crowd. I found its operator standing on a section of scaffolding at the far side of the pool. On the ground below him was just one guy running the audio and lighting board. Simple audio-visual set up. Not much more than you'd find at a hotel convention.

There we go.

My best weapon was surprise. First kill the lighting board. Then, kill the spotlight. I could do plenty in darkness. I worked my way to the back of the pool.

The lighting guy was just a few feet away, on the other side of the bushes. The crowd and pool sprawled out beyond him. Everyone was watching the stage, even the guards.

I stepped through the bushes. The board op couldn't hear me because he was monitoring the audio through headphones. He was absorbed in the process. Cables ran from the control board to outlets attached to pipes sticking out of the ground. Evidence the place was built for this very type of function.

The emcee said, "Ladies and gentlemen, a special low opening bid to get everyone involved."

Re-run the plan: Board op. Spotlight power yank. Lighting board power yank. Darkness. That's the plan.

The emcee announced, "Item number NE6509."

I broke down the auction code as I approached the board op. 'NE'? Nebraskan was my first thought. But, that's not a nationality or ethnicity.

Netherlands.

'65' seemed a high birth year for what these people were buying.

'09' still didn't know what the last digits in the codes meant.

Brain snap.

09/65.

Hey, that's the same birthday as--

I stopped short of the board op and looked to the stage.

Ilsa.

On stage.

In chains.

74

The same goddam chain puller had dragged her into the spotlight. I felt ready to fracture and crumble. I could only watch.

It was my beautiful Ilsa. But, it wasn't. Something was missing. Emotion. She was zombified like the others.

"Help you?"

It was the lighting board operator. He looked at me strange. He saw the knife in my hand. He pivoted and took a swing at me. I dropped back. He missed. I turned and shoved him into a scaffold leg. The scaffolding swayed above.

The spot op spoke down in a hushed, irritated voice - "Hey! Careful down there."

"Ten thousand dollars. Do we have fifteen? Fifteen thousand dollars? We have fifteen! How about twenty? You'll have a good time with this gal. Direct from Europe where they're experienced in the art of loving and serving."

I pounced on the board op as he scrambled to get up. My weight shoved him down. I wrapped a power cable that had been taped to the ground around his neck. He bucked and kicked. I pressed the tape against his face, over his mouth. I yanked the cable noose tighter.

He sunk into stillness. Dead? No. Unconscious.

The on-stage handler raised the chain connected to Ilsa's neck as the emcee announced, "...Gone! The winning bid is forty-two thousand dollars."

They bought her. No more games. And, forget the plan.

I ran to the lighting board and slid all the faders down. The place went dark except for the spotlight. The crowd started to murmur, sensing something was not right. The spotlight hit the slave handler and Ilsa. He was trying to find his way down the exit steps in the dark.

I ran over to the power distribution box and ripped the cables out. Now the place was fully dark except for the blue glow of the pool light.

A woman screamed.

"Get those lights on," came an urgent order.

I ran past the pool, blending right in with the commotion. I bumped shoulders. I plowed through guests.

Head's up—Guards were running my way.

I dashed down one of the seat aisles. A man said, "Aww. Just when it was getting fun."

"No need for everyone to get crazy. Just turn the lights on and bring back the pretty girls," said his female companion.

The guards passed. I hurried towards the stage.

Where was Ilsa? The handler? People were scattering in all directions around me.

Emcee over the loudspeaker: "There we go. We'll have the lights on in a second."

I couldn't be right in front of the stage when the lights came on. So, screw it. "Ilsa! Ilsa!"

No response.

I broke stage right. No Ilsa anywhere.

"There!"

A glance over my shoulder and there was Opae, blade gleaming in the moonlight. He charged at me. I ran through a break in the bushes, out of the pool area.

On the other side were three lighted paths. People were gathered around the lights like moths. No Ilsa. No time to wait. I took the middle path, cutting past the party guests. One lady said, "Where's a waiter? I'm losing my buzz?"

Opae appeared through the same break in the bushes. He scanned the land like a hawk sizing prey from above.

The lady whose buzz was fading waved to Opae. "Looking for someone?" He nodded. She pointed my way. "Some guy just ran that way."

Goddammit.

Opae looked my way. His eyes squinted, peering into the shadows. Stay still? Run?

He approached.

My back was against a rock wall.

Opae passed the revelers. "Good luck, handsome," she said as she caressed his shoulder. He ignored it.

I ran.

Opae sliced at me. I felt the air of the blade but evaded the metal.

I launched myself off the path at full speed.

Where was Ilsa? And, what was going on with Carlos and--

A massive explosion rocked the compound. The concussive force pushed me sideways. I had to stop to steady myself. A huge fireball unfolded into the night sky, beyond the bushes and trees. I couldn't see ground zero. But, it had to be the main ranch house.

It caught Opae's attention, too. The blaze illuminated his face to reveal a deeper distress. I got the impression he was responsible for keeping things in order on the ranch. And, that wasn't happening.

He scowled and looked my way. I ran into the darkness.

75

Where could Ilsa have gone?

I hadn't been more than five beats behind her. But, she and her handler had eluded me. Where would they have taken the girls? They'd have to protect the merchandise, right?

The stables didn't seem right.

Could she have been in the ranch house?

No. Please, no. They couldn't have reached it that fast. I mind-mapped the property, trying to recall what had been where. Pool, ranch house, stables, entrance, runway...

Runway. There was a building next to the grass airstrip.

Not a building. A control tower. That felt right. Closer to the planes, easier to ship out the girls. The airport was south and west of my location. I ran.

Guns fired. More guns returned fire. Screams indicated the guests were no longer partying.

Victory #1—Inside information on the Kith.

Victory #2—Slave auction disrupted.

How 'bout we round that out by getting the girl, okay Walt?

My body tightened as my limbs worked faster—arms swinging, feet running. Both burned with effort as my mind sizzled with anxiety. *Faster, faster, Mr. Asher!*

Bush branches cut my legs. Leaves smacked my face. The humid air pumped heavy into my lungs. I ran past a ramshackle storage bay made of stacked field stones and a tin roof. Maintenance vehicles were stored inside. I tripped on a rock they forgot to clear away.

The planes were lining up on the runway like cars leaving the stadium after a game. Wing lights flashed, headlights beamed, blue lights defined the take off route.

The planes that weren't moving seemed to have people hurrying towards them. Elite beating feet. Ladies grabbed their gowns and held their high heels in hand. Husbands/lovers whisked them along the grass. Ranch staff guided patrons to their planes at the nearest part of the runway.

A plane pulled up and stopped in front of the control tower. Its stairs dropped. On cue, the slave handler stepped out from under the lighted portico. He led a slave by her arm over to the plane and up the stairs. Slave in, handler out, steps up. Traffic controllers on the ground wearing reflective vests swung orange-coned lights, giving the plane clearance to take off. And, it did.

The next plane pulled up to the control tower. A sleek executive jet. Out walked Ilsa.

76

She was still chained by the neck. The handler gave her a mean tug out from under the portico. She didn't fight. They waited for the plane stairs to drop.

So, this was my gauntlet: a runaway full of moving planes, armed guards, and a cult of maniacs ready to kill me. Running right through the middle of it was the only way I would reach Ilsa before she was loaded onto the plane. And, if that happened I could damn well lose her forever.

Time to risk it all.

I ran.

I ran.

I ran.

The grass was slick from nighttime dew. My feet slipped. But, I kept moving forward and avoided falling on my ass. My gait stabilized as I reached flat land. Plane headlights blasted my eyes as I ran across the runway. Tough to see. And, the moving planes made it like walking through a house with all the walls turning. You knew you could get through but you didn't know when you'd end up smack against something hard and vertical, like landing gear.

I ducked under a rotating jet. Its wheels swung in a tighter arc than I anticipated and it almost knocked me down. I dove clear, but scrambled back up before my knees hit the turf.

I could see Ilsa's legs take the first stairs into the plane. No time to run around. I dropped to my knees and slid across the wet grass beneath the plane. I grabbed the stairs, used them to twist myself around, and start climbing.

Ilsa stepped inside the plane.

The handler saw me charging.

"Hey!" was all he could say before I slammed him against the mahogany interior. He dropped, unconscious for the moment.

"The stairs," someone shouted.

The stairs started to close up and in.

The plane began to move.

We were going to be trapped on this plane with the handler and...who else?

Wait a minute. We could escape this way. I'd have to hope for the best for the others. And, I wouldn't get the deep information I needed on the Kith. But, maybe this was best.

The plane picked up speed.

I felt my weight sink to the floor as the aircraft lifted off the ground. Bracing myself against a white leather seat with a crest embroidered into the headrest, I reached down to turn her over.

But, there was one big problem.

It wasn't Ilsa.

Something not meant for heads slammed against the back of mine.

77

I came to with an ugly son of a bitch standing over me. Kinky, red hair parted down the middle, a dopey mustache, and a neck full of scars. His slick grey suit completed a look that would have been right at home in an 80's Cannon Films action movie. Gleaming across his fingers were the brass knuckles he had just employed.

Cannon Films put out a lot of Charles Bronson movies. And, CB reminded me of Ilsa because we have a mutual appreciation for his work.

Where was Ilsa?

I looked up at the girl in the chair. Still not Ilsa. Pretty sure this was the Mexican girl that kicked off the auction.

Whose plane was I on?

And, how the hell was I going to get back to the ranch?

This was bad.

"No free rides, fuck nuts," said the ginger enforcer. "Soon as we get clear, we're dropping you off. And, that don't mean we're gonna land."

My head was killing me. But, his jokes were murder. I had to size things up and figure my pitch.

Feature: I was in a plane flying over Florida.
Benefit: I escaped the ranch.

Feature: It was just me and Redhead Richard Simmons. And, the handler, but he was out cold.
Benefit: Decent odds.

Feature: There was a closed door behind this goon.

Benefit: Whoever was in there might have more information on the Kith.

Feature: I still had my knife. Freshly sharpened, full tang, and with an ergonomic grip.
Benefit: It slid fast and easy into Rusty's ankle.

He screamed.
I kicked.
He grabbed his leg.
I grabbed the length of chain still dangling from the zonked out girl, ran it through the metal chair leg and one, two, three...wrapped it around his neck until there was no slack.
I pressed the knife to Ginger's neck. He relaxed his arms and watched me through wide, worried eyes. A quick reach inside his coat revealed a gun. I slipped the brass off his hand. They were heavy in mine. I was impressed. I slipped them on. Then returned the favor. Lights out, Ginger.

Seismic pain rippled through my head. It was either a change in cabin pressure, a concussion from getting whapped by the brass knuckles, or both. A decanter caught my eye. I poured a glass and enjoyed the bourbon's mellow sting.
There were closed doors in both directions of the cabin, the pilot's and the rear chamber.
I went towards the rear cabin and knocked.
Almost.
A provocative thought stopped me short—the thing I needed to do most was get Ilsa. She was back at the ranch. And, the only way I was going to get there was to engage the pilot. Who knew where to or how far he was flying? The farther away from the ranch this plane went, the lower my chances of saving her.
But, who was in the back room? And, what could they tell me about the Kith? There was no interference. I could pump a ton of information out of them. If I didn't talk to them now, I wouldn't be able to once we get back to the ranch.
This could be my one chance to finally destroy the Kith.
How many lives would that save...including my own?
My arm and wrist tensed, ready to knock.
No.

Destroying the Kith didn't mean anything if I couldn't save Ilsa.

But, how the hell was I going to get this pilot to turn around and fly back to the ranch? Why, persuasion, of course.

78

I opened the cabin door.

The pilot was focused on the path ahead, two hands on the yoke.

"Who are you?" he said.

"The new stew."

He gave me the once over. His eyes stopped at the knife in my hand.

"This ain't the friendly skies, so do what you're told."

He glanced out the cabin door.

"Orphan Annie's out cold back there. And, I just had a talk with the old man." I held up the knife to make sure he saw the blood on it. Ankle blood looks the same as old man blood.

The pilot spooked. He looked out the windshield and re-gripped the yoke. Palms getting sweaty?

"All you need to do to is turn around and fly back to the ranch. You flew there before, you can do it again," I said.

He nodded. But, didn't turn.

"You have to actually make the turn," I said.

He glanced at me. But, he didn't turn the plane.

He reached to check a dial.

"Don't," I said.

My words stopped him short. He drew his hand back.

"Turn the plane around."

Without looking at me he said, "Better to land in Winter Haven at this point. I can set down there."

"I didn't say 'go to Winter Haven'. I said go back to the ranch."

"But, we're much closer to Winter Haven."

"Turn the fucking plane around," I said. "Now."

I put the knife to his throat. But, the gesture played hollow. What was I going to do, kill the pilot? That'd be suicide. And, he knew it. I needed a reason to make him set the plane down.

"Know what I do for a living? I write infomercials," I said.

He looked at me like I was some kind of creeper. To be expected, I guess.

"It's a good gig. And, I learn a lot about many different topics."

"So?" he said.

"I did a show once. About a supplement that improves circulation. While I was writing it, I learned about arteries."

I slashed the knife through his slacks and cut into the meat of his thigh, pressing the blade in deep.

Blood spurted across the dashboard.

The pilot screamed and grabbed his leg. The plane started to drop. He reached fast to steady the yoke with his now bloody hand.

"The hell you do that for?" he said. He was sweating now.

"When I wrote that show I learned about the femoral artery. It's the main large artery in your right leg. Lotta blood flows through there," I said. "Fast way to bleed out, brother."

He looked worried.

"We haven't been in the air very long. I suggest you turn around and get back to that ranch. I'm certain they have a medical staff that could help," I said.

He nodded, with an anxious look on his face. And, then he turned the plane.

It was a long, slow arc. But, the plane re-directed 180-degrees. And, it wasn't long before I could see the ranch's blue light runway in the distance.

I watched the pilot do his thing. His face had blanched white. His expression reflected great uncertainty about his future.

"Planes are still taking off. I don't think I'll be able to land," he said.

"Call the control tower. Tell 'em you're coming in with a medical emergency."

He tried to reach for the radio with the hand controlling the yoke. The plane shook and he re-grabbed the yoke quick. I reached forward and handed him the mic.

"Control tower, this is Flight 809RZ requesting clearance for landing," he said.

A beat, no response. Then...

"Flight 809RZ, you do not have permission to land. Runway is departure only at this time," said the man in the control tower.

"Tower, this is a medical emergency. Landing is imperative. Requesting immediate clearance."

The pilot and I had the same goal now. He, as much as me, needed to land that plane at the ranch without fail.

"Flight 809RZ, repeat you do not have permission to land. Please change course."

The pilot groaned, anxious and worried.

"Come in Flight 809RZ. Do you copy? You are not cleared to land."

The pilot said nothing. He pushed the yoke forward. The plane started its descent.

The call came from the control tower, "You are not cleared to land, understand? You are flying directly into the departing flight pattern. Change course immediately. Do you copy?" Their desperation cut through the static of the transmission.

"You're doing fine," I said. But, the situation was getting dicey.

Our plane continued descending.

The pilot clutched his leg and whimpered, trying not to freak out.

A plane took off from the runway below...and looked to be flying straight towards us.

"809 abort descent now! Do you copy? Abort course now!" said the control tower.

"Shit," said the pilot.

Now, that he was returning to the ranch I did him a solid by grabbing a jacket that had been left on the co-pilot's seat and wrapped it around his leg as a makeshift tourniquet. I pulled it tight to staunch the bleeding.

"There. Now, bring us in safely," I said.

He nodded. Beads of sweat rolled from his forehead to his cheek.

The ascending plane was still tracking towards us.

"Tell that plane to change course," said the pilot into the radio.

"809 abort your descent. You're going to hit the plane!" The control tower sounded beyond panicked.

I sat down in the co-pilot's chair and steadied myself.

"If he doesn't move, he's gonna nail us," said the pilot. "No way to survive that."

What could I say?

I scanned the land to see if there was another flat patch nearby. Someplace else to land. The terrain looked too choppy.

"Can you flash your lights?"

He shook his head.

"809 you must change course now!" said the man in the control tower. He forgot to cut off his mic and we heard him say "We're about to have a big mess on our hands." Another voice in the background, tougher to hear, said, "We don't want that kind of attention here."

The other plane approached fast.

The pilot gripped the wheel. "If I go up to get out of his way I'm gonna overshoot the runway."

And, they'd never let him circle back for a second chance. If I hoped to get Ilsa, we needed to land now. Which meant he couldn't change course. He couldn't be the chicken.

"Keep it steady," I said.

"He's gonna crash right into us!"

"Just focus on the runway."

"He's not moving."

"Control tower hasn't called back. Means they're talking to him," I said.

The pilot had no response. He looked from the plane to his leg and back to the plane.

I tightened my grip on the seat. I hoped I was right.

The other plane lifted towards us.

"Oh, god," said the pilot. His voice went up in terror. "He's gonna hit us!"

79

The other plane moved first. It made a sharp twist, which shot it just out of our path.

The bleeding pilot kept the plane steady. "Holy shit!"

My heart pounded. I let out a deep breath.

"Good job," I said. "Now, land before they launch another one. Otherwise your leg's gonna do you in."

The pilot looked down at his bleeding leg, saw the blood-soaked jacket and started to worry again. But, that led to renewed focus that hunched him forward and set him about doing the standard plane landing protocol. He was a pro.

The control tower transmitted a message, "Flight 809 you are now...cleared for landing." They sounded exasperated.

The pilot smiled, ready to do this.

There was plenty of activity below—planes pulled off the runway to clear a path for us...the house fire still blazing...people still scattering down the walking paths. It was complete chaos. Wish I had time to relish it.

The pilot reached for his radio and spoke, "Thank you for clearance. Please have medical personnel standing b-by. Copy?"

"Copy."

I presumed they'd also send thugs for me.

Looking back in the cabin I saw that the girl, the handler, and the ginger had missed all the excitement. I had a gun, a knife, and brass knuckles. But, there was just one way off the plane. I needed to get out that door before the response team arrived. Otherwise, they'd have me trapped.

"Better brace yourself," said the pilot. It was an unexpected courtesy given what I'd done to him.

"Our angle's not perfect," he said. "But, I think we'll have enough runway."

"You think?"

He nodded without looking at me. That was all I was going to get out of him.

Time seemed to accelerate. My nerves tingled more with every hundred yards we closed in. I heard the landing gear come out, felt my gut start to float, and my ears pop.

"Where do you expect we'll come to a stop?" I said.

"Right at the end of the runway. Won't be able to slow down in time to pull into a gate."

That meant we'd end up right near the walking paths. The steps were on my side of the plane. That was good. I could hop out and run. But, where would Ilsa be? Still at the control tower? Did I really stand a chance of getting in and out of there alive?

The plane swooped low across the dark Florida landscape. Creatures of the night dashed into darkness.

The ranch neared.

Tall palm trees whipped past.

I'm coming Ilsa.

I perked up at seeing a couple of our trucks driving across the prairie and away from the ranch. I looked to see if Kelvin and Kory were on one of them. Couldn't tell. But, at least some of the men were out of there.

"Here we go," said the pilot. "Hang on."

The pilot pushed the yoke forward and down we went. Lower...lower...lower...

Touch down.

And, it was smooth. Not the typical shake and shimmy you get with commercial airlines. This craft was small, sturdy, and tight. No wonder people spent fortunes on them.

The jet engines reversed to slow our momentum. I saw planes parked haphazardly along the sides of the runway. We bounced over the soft terrain as we passed the control tower. The end of the runway was two hundred yards ahead. The pilot appeared confident. The plane slowed. There was just enough room, as he had expected. I relaxed a little.

Our wing clipped the tail of a plane parked to the right of the runway.

And, all hell broke loose.

80

Glass cracks spider-webbed across the windshield. The plane teetered hard, the left side dropped. The pilot lost control and the yoke jerked wild. His head smashed against the side of the cabin.

I grabbed my seat. The seatbelt held me tight. But, I ducked forward, head between legs and just about did kiss my ass goodbye.

The windshield shattered and glass exploded into the cabin. I felt the gust of warm air from outside.

The plane swerved left, guided by the wingtip cutting through the runway sod. Then, it whipped hard and smashed into another plane. It made a monstrous sound as our momentum took us up the berm in a turning arc. The wing buckled at the jet body. The plane barrel rolled over and hammered the ground with a final devastating crash.

"Hello?" called a voice.

I blinked my eyes open. It took a moment to realize I was stunned and stuck hanging upside down, still strapped to the seat. My face was heavy with the rush of blood. And, it took extra effort to feel my arms, which had been dangling below my head.

Who just said 'hello'? They were coming for me. I had to go!

I pressed my seat buckle and dropped. Despite twisting my shoulder in an odd manner, I was able to hang on to the seatbelt and keep from falling onto the pilot's mangled corpse. I kicked wide to straddle him before putting all my weight down.

"Get the door open. Quick!" said the voice outside. other voices murmured.

The door to the plane jiggled on its hinges. They were trying to pry it open. My exit was cut off. But, the windshield was wide open. Jagged glass bits formed razor sharp teeth around its edges. Looking out, I saw it wasn't far above the ground.

I pulled on the partly open cockpit door. As I closed it, I saw the Mexican girl lying dead on the cabin roof. I hoped she had been out of it when we crashed. I didn't care about the other guys. Not even the man in the expensive suit sprawled out dead in the aft cabin. Its door had split opened during the crash.

I locked the cockpit door. Then climbed up the bend of the cockpit roof. My feet slipped on glass and I braced my foot on the ceiling light. It was enough to get me up to the edge of the windshield. I dropped over and landed on the grass, which was littered with plane debris.

I crawled to the side of the plane. There they were. Five of them storming into the hull of the craft as the cabin door buckled open. That cleared the path for me and I ran.

God, it hurt. My head felt like it was still being swung around inside the tumbling plane. Twice I had to slow down to steady my balance. I couldn't imagine what the hospital bill was going to be after all this.

I dashed behind the control tower. A pair of control tower guys muttered in disbelief at what had happened. "Guy's a psycho flying in like that..." said one of them.

No time to wait and debate. I snuck past the mutterers and stepped into the control tower. Not much to it inside; just a small waiting area and several flights of stairs.

And, no girls. Ilsa wasn't here.

A sickening thought hit me. What if she was on the plane that had taken off as we were coming in? The one we almost crashed into.

I stepped out of the control tower and ran across a dark part of the runway. To my right was the quiet prairie night. To my left, chaos. That's where I needed to go.

Under the trees, along the path, cutting through the night.

No one near the offices. Few people by the pool. Where did everyone go?

Frantic Kith staff skittered across the scene. They were trying to put the blaze out. Some had fire hoses.

Had all of Carlos' men left the property? I recalled seeing the trucks driving away from the ranch as the plane flew over. I didn't see any of them here now. No time to worry about it.

I had to act now.

Pick up that phone.

Click online.

Ask your operator.

Just make it happen.

Something caught my eye. Far side of the blaze. A gaggle of girls. And, one big son of a bitch: Opae.

He was corralling the ladies towards some unknown destination. Taking them off the ranch? Sending them to massage parlors? It wouldn't do to have slaves found at Rogers and Kay's ranch if the authorities showed up.

I ran after them. Enough hell had broken loose that I could cut right through the commotion. Didn't give a damn if they saw me. They'd have to catch me.

The heat from the house blazed on my face as I sprinted down the winding path. Up ahead, Opae and the girls' appeared in and out of the firelight. I couldn't decipher just what they were doing. Only that they were doing it straight ahead.

Past the house, I staggered down the grass incline, which had become damp from fire hose water run-off, careful not to slip. But, I slipped anyway. My slide turned into a tumble down the hill.

When I sprang up and looked around there was no trace of Opae and the girls. Where the hell…there! Muddy footsteps on the sidewalk. I glanced around. There were three directions they could have gone—into the stables and shacks, beyond them, or winding in the opposite direction around to the front of the house towards the main ranch entrance.

No sign of action beyond the stables. But, what about inside them? That was the most dangerous place for me.

A deep breath. I ran to the closest stable. Fuck it, kick the door in. Nothing doing. I had to pull it open. Empty inside.

Stable Number 2. The side entrance had been left half-open. I crept and listened. No sound. I glanced inside as I dashed across to the other side of the doorway. No way a gaggle of girls, no matter how drugged up, could stay that quiet and still.

That left two small shacks and the junkyard beyond them. Shack #1, door closed and locked. Shack #2, door ajar. I took a position behind the door, hinge side. No sound inside. My plan was to yank the door open but not step in the doorway. Let them shoot first with me out of the way.

I grabbed the handle. 1...2...3...pull!

A loud burst and a blast.

But, not the firearm type. It was an engine, a truck rumbling to life on the far side of the shack.

I ran around the shack and saw a familiar sight—the slave truck from the side of the highway. Opae was locking it up. The girls had to be inside.

Not again.

I charged fast and tackled the big bastard as he reached to close the padlock dangling from the truck doors. I knocked him to the ground. It didn't stun him. With one hand, he threw me off and scrambled up. He was fast for his size. Before I could get to my feet, he was up and kicking my ribs. I fell back. My wind puffed out. I clutched my chest and tried to stabilize my breathing. Didn't happen before his big fist pounded down on my shoulder. My arm went numb and I fell to the ground. Two strikes and he just about had me down and out.

The herculean beast stepped into view. His hands were tightened into claws. The fiery backdrop framed him up like an albino demon rising from hell. And, his face was filled with rage.

Somehow, in that split-second, it occurred to me that a guy like him—a freak by society's standards—had found his first safe place here at the ranch. And, I'd just helped burn it to the ground. In that moment, I understood his rage. But, I didn't accept it.

I swung my knife. It sliced his calf just above the boot line. He screamed, but more in anger. Blood seeped through the denim.

I swung again.

He stomped on my arm and pinned it to the ground. He bent down and took my knife by the blade, threw it aside, and unsheathed his own, larger blade. He slashed it through my calf. Payback.

The pain was amazing and awful.

He pressed the blade's blood-wet steel against my face. I felt his hot breath on the back of my neck.

"My blade hungers for your flesh," he said in a snarling, gravelly voice that would terrify a corpse. He seized me up by the neck and slammed me into the semi trailer.

Clink, clink.

His arm swung past in a flash. The solid weight of chain thumped against my chest as he pulled it tight around my throat. My left arm was still numb. With my right, I reached up to stop the chain from strangling me. The links pinned my hand against my throat, and all I could do was flap my elbow.

The chain choked away my air as Opae lifted me off the ground. He swung me against the back of the truck. My head bounced off the rear doors. My body dropped to the ground.

I was in bad shape. Opae knew it. Otherwise, he wouldn't have turned from me to make matters worse: He tied the chain—clinking and clanking—around the low step of the trailer.

He unsheathed his knife and leaned in to start scalping.

81

The cold blade pressed against my forehead. Just the weight of it broke the first layer of skin.

Opae snarled and recited words I couldn't understand. But, the – tchees and chays in his words led me to believe he was speaking the native tongue of Seminole Indians.

He slid the blade. The cut stung. Blood got in my eye. Oh dear God…

Another explosion.

People were fleeing this way.

Opae looked at me with disappointment. I would have to wait. He kicked me with his tattered, leather boot. The same boot that crunched gravel and grass as he hurried around to the truck cab.

"Any of you ladies wanna give me a hand?" I said towards the trailer's locked doors. It was bad humor, movie style.

The engine revved and the truck shook. Opae wasted no time. The wheels started to roll and I started to drag across the ground.

How fitting.

I'd spent the past week trying to drag the Club's horrible truth into the light...and now they're gonna drag me dead with the very truck that started it all.

I grabbed the metal trailer step and tried to pull myself up. The effort was enough to relieve the chain's pull on my neck. But, the drag from the ground worked against me. I released and fell back into full, choking drag.

The truck sped up.

The wheels hit a pothole. The trailer shook and yanked me off the ground like a whip getting cracked. If my hand hadn't been stuck in this chain, my neck would have snapped and that'd be that.

The road yanked off one of my shoes. My heel burned against the asphalt until I crossed it over the other leg. We were on the main road now. I could see the ranch house shrinking in the distance. We'd soon reach the highway. And, if I wasn't fully up on the truck by then...

I grabbed the step with all my might and pulled my body close. My head rose above the step. The chain slackened just enough...

Thirty miles-per-hour.

...just enough to shake my stuck hand loose. I grabbed for the step. My hand was numb to tingles and I could barely hold on. My other arm was weakening. I re-clutched my muscle. It kept my head up only a moment. I had to relax it. The chain pulled hard on my neck. I lifted my shoulders to lessen the pressure while my arm recuperated. I wiggled the fingers on the other hand to get the blood flowing.

Forty miles-per-hour.

Opae wasn't slowing down. I imagined him watching me in his side view mirror with salacious glee.

My back scraped the ground. I was losing.

I pulled up with both arms. Got my head above the step, and had enough slack to throw an elbow over it so I wasn't dangling by my neck. I was half way off the ground but my head was still stuck in the chain. My feet were still dragging. The rubber of my shoe was about scraped off.

I worked the chain, unable to see how he had tied it to the truck. Just guessing, my fingers felt along the links. I found the knot. My fingers pulled. Too heavy. Try again. I leaned into it, moving my neck closer to offer more slack.

That did it.

I yanked the chain. The links slid out of the knot. As the weight of the loose chain increased, it pulled faster. It ricocheted off the pavement and whipped the bottom of the truck, inches from my face, before dragging out behind the back of the truck. I set my feet on the chain. Still dicey, but at least I was off the ground. For now.

But, there wasn't enough slack to free my neck. *Come on!*

I twisted and turned. Nothing. I couldn't see what it was caught on. The chain under my feet was helping. But, how long would that balancing act last? Sparks popped off the dragging metal.

The truck slowed to a stop.

I looked ahead, under the long chassis. We were at the highway intersection. The truck was angled to the left, pointing west. Not much civilization in that direction. We'd be in for a long ride. Make that a long drag. I had to do something before he hit full speed or it was over.

I yanked the chain with all my might. I leveraged my knees against the pavement and reared my body back. Nothing. I reached for whatever the chain was latched on to. Couldn't find it. Found it. Couldn't budge it.

The truck hissed.

I slapped the back of the trailer doors. No answer.

The truck inched forward.

I walked on my knees to keep pace. They were going to rip off if I weren't on my feet by the time he accelerated.

I heard a car in the distance. Approaching. Passing.

The truck rumbled.

The truck moved.

Come on!

The truck pulled onto the highway. I started dragging again. The truck's turning radius swung me onto the road shoulder. When it straightened out, I swung the other way.

Lookout!

A car whipped past the truck just as I swung out of the opposite lane. I drew my legs to my chest. My ass barely missed the car. Road debris crackled against my skin as I swung back behind the truck.

I was losing strength.

Fifty miles-per-hour.

Everything - the stress, the night, the fighting, the pain - it was all taking its toll.

My bill was coming due.

Sixty miles-per-hour.

My arms felt ropey. The weaker I grew the more the chain tightened around my throat. My vision narrowed. Focus faded. My legs stopped kicking. Everything was turning dark.

It had been a good fight.

But, they won.

I lost.

82

The truck broke hard, skidded, and stopped dead.

The abrupt stop shook the trailer with such force and fury that the rear wheels lifted off the ground. And, the impact was enough to shake my chain off whatever had been holding it as I swung underneath the axle.

I hugged the pavement as the trailer tires slammed the ground around me.

My heart almost burst. My senses took a moment to return. I felt like road kill.

Steam hissed.

I willed myself into action. Even if that action was mustering the energy to get on my knees and crawl over shattered bits of glass and road debris

"You son of a bitch," said a voice. Opae.

To who? Someone had screwed things up for him.

I reached the grass. The sod was sweet, soft relief on my knees. The crumpled hood of another truck peeked around the hull of the semi. An accident?

Opae's feet dropped into view and walked towards the front, of the semi. How soon 'til he came looking for me? I crawled towards to the impact point between the two vehicles. I didn't dare look away.

Opae's feet disappeared behind tires.

"Back this thing up, goddammit. I gotta move this load," said Opae.

I pushed up from the ground, wobbled on my legs, got my balance. With caution, I walked closer to the collision point.

Gun shot. Roaring.

I startled and dropped to the ground.

Opae fell onto his back. A large, red blossom of blood dotted the front of his half-buttoned denim shirt. He contracted in an effort to pull himself up. But, all life went out of him. His white hair was stained pink.

"Hello?" I said.

"Hey, Walt." DG appeared around the front of the truck. "You okay?"

I was never happier to see him.

83

DG, still weak and a bit winded, helped me roll Opae out of the road and into the ditch. Now, he was sitting in the cab of his truck, resting. He told me he had borrowed it from a man at the hospital farm, whom he had told outright there was a chance it could be destroyed and that he would replace it with this year's model, top of the line, full package. The man tossed DG the keys with little hesitation.

The truck had a CB radio and he had been able to communicate with the other trucks in the rescue party. He'd had to ask them to mix a few English words in between the Spanish ones. He got the word that Carlos and his men had blown up the house and were rolling out of there. But, they didn't know what had happened to me. DG asked for directions to the ranch and that's where he was headed when he came across Opae's semi. He knew it was the right semi when he saw me swing out into opposing traffic. Then, he stopped the semi the fastest way he knew how.

So, here we were.

I climbed out of the cab and went to the rear of the truck and pulled the trailer door open. Anxiety tightened my chest. I was worried what I would find inside, how I would find them.

The moon was west of the wreck and didn't shine much light inside. And, there were no street lamps. A wave of heat and human odor wafted out.

The first face I saw was soft and sweaty with closed eyes and lying on the floor of the trailer. She was Mexican. Long, black hair wrapped haphazardly around her face.

I reached down and opened an eyelid.

She stirred. Good.

"Ilsa?"

No response.

I wanted my eyes to adjust faster and reveal the details inside the darkness. I put a foot on the same step rail I had been choking on not five minutes ago, grabbed a handle, and pulled myself up to stand at the edge of the trailer.

More girls started stirring. It was tough to tell if they were reviving from passing out or still in a drug haze. I'd take either. At least they were alive.

I moved into the trailer, careful not to step on any of the girls. I could now see shoulders and knees and arms slithering across the floor as they stretched. The cool air from outside had brought a wake up call.

And, then her face appeared in the blue light of the night.

Ilsa.

84

The sounds of passing cars, crickets, and frogs in the night all faded.

She looked different. The trauma and exhaustion of the ordeal, which I knew to be kidnapping, at least, had taken their toll. And, they had drugged her. There was no doubt about that now. Filthy, bags under her eyes, clothes tattered. And, she was beautiful.

My Ilsa.

I hugged her—grateful, consoling, relieved. I loved that she gave me a weak hug back. Her body seemed to melt into mine. I kept her standing more than she stood. She needed food, rehab.

I looked her over. No bruises, no visible damage. Wait. Swelling on the side of the face. Bastards.

"Come on, let's get out of here," I said.

I turned to lead, my hand holding hers, guiding her through the tangle of bodies.

All of these girls needed help. But, Ilsa first. I wasn't going to apologize for that. None of these other girls' fathers, husbands, or brothers would. Ilsa first. The rest, not far behind.

I sat Ilsa at the edge of the truck. She was shaky as she lowered herself down. Her eyes widened at seeing nature. Even the short time in the dark of the truck had stifled her senses enough to add brilliance to the night. With her settled, I hopped down and got a preview of which body parts were going to hurt most in the coming days.

Ilsa sat with her hands flat on the floor of the trailer, as if holding herself up like a fragile, unsteady bird on a perch. I slid my arms around her waist, pulled her down, and gave her a moment to get steady on her feet.

"DG's going to give us a ride."

She gave a vacant nod.

I glanced at the girls in the truck. Several were sitting up now, shaking off the internal cobwebs. I couldn't recall--DG's truck was big, but could it transport all of them? Where would we take them?

Questions to answer later.

"Come on." I took Ilsa's hand and led her around the truck.

Click.

"That's far enough."

85

It was Rogers.

He had a gun to my face. DG was motionless on the ground behind him. Beyond that was a car, a Mercedes. No hazard lights flashing.

The nightmare refused to end.

"Get in the goddamn ditch." He said it with venom and moved towards me, pistol first.

I walked backwards.

He slapped Ilsa hard as he passed.

She dropped to the ground and clutched her cheek.

I charged him.

He pulled the gun's hammer back and stopped me short. "No," he said, seething. Hate was in his eyes. It was clear he was tired of me.

If he got me down in that ditch I'd have no options. I stepped onto the patch of grass just before the ground sloped down.

"You gonna take all these girls home by yourself?" I said.

"They're mine aren't they?" he said.

Ash was smeared across the side of his face.

"Get a little close to the fire, Rogers?"

"Not as close as you're gonna get to the flames of hell."

"I'm not the bad guy here."

"You're the dead guy."

Bam!

I dove to the side and he missed.

Bam!

I rolled down the hill and he missed again.

He turned to aim.

A glint of light. Something moved through the moonlight.

Ilsa!

She'd found the chain on the ground and whipped it down hard on Rogers' arms. He grunted so hard his dentures slipped from his mouth and tumbled into the dirt.

He also dropped the gun.

I trudged up the incline but slipped.

He looked unsure whether to go for the dentures or the gun.

He went for the gun.

Ilsa got it first.

And, she fired. Almost point blank to his face.

His body flopped forward onto the grass. The momentum rolled him into a ball that splashed at the bottom of the soggy ditch.

Now, he was gator meat.

86

Ilsa smiled as her head broke through the surface of the water. It was the first sign that life could possibly return to normal. The cool water of the Rainbow River had that kind of recuperative power. But, full recovery would take a long time.

Whatever the Kith had drugged her with was slow to flush from her system. Her body hungered for a fix, but of what we didn't know. Detox was hardest at night. She was getting there.

There was also the trauma. Her mother had died. Ilsa had been kidnapped. She'd been sold at a slave auction. Trafficked in a human cargo truck. And now, she was a murderer. I knew how difficult that could be to wrap one's head around. Both of our lives were forever changed. Again. If the Kith had ended for good with Rogers Aufderheide's corpse spilling into a ditch then we could make do with the resonant collateral damage.

But as far as I knew, Oren and Rance were still alive. There were no guarantees the Kith were over. It was bittersweet knowing I'd won the battle but probably not the war.

DG's sage advice was for me to presume they would come back, but not for a while. He knew how underground operations worked. The Kith had rebuilding to do. Their patrons were spooked by the commotion, by the terrifying proximity of being exposed. The Kith would have to re-build that trust, work on themselves before they came after me.

That sounded good coming from the man I could truly call my best friend. DG had saved my life too many times to doubt him. But, living with that kind of paranoia in the meantime seemed an impossible task.

That's why I drove to Orlando as soon as I read the news. The gubernatorial race had been thrown into chaos. The Democratic candidate and challenger, Emilio Abrantes, was dead. His plane crashed last night at a private ranch airport located just outside of Sebring, Florida.

I was on that plane.

Abrantes was the unseen man in the back.

He was a member of the Kith.

And, to think I was set to vote for him.

But, the crash wasn't last night. The Kith had used their considerable influence and connections to change the reported date of the crash from seven days ago to two. Enough time to clean the scene, fix the story, and cover their ass.

Tonight in Orlando, the Democratic Party was set to announce that Buddy Simon, the man intended to be Abrantes' Lieutenant Governor, would be running in Abrantes' place. Election night was two weeks away.

Buddy Simon was Kith, too. I'd seen him. That night at Hal Bodeker's place. He was the man who had said he'd need an extra plate for the girl buffet. I didn't know who he was at the time.

I walked through downtown, blocks from the park where the Simon announcement was due to take place. Techs had set up a stage and public address system. The news crews had already arrived. Security was in place. Crowds were gathering.

Knowing Simon's connection to the Kith I was hoping to find Oren and Rance in Orlando.

But, Rance found me. I had passed the restaurant where he was eating. He recognized me through the front window and stepped out to wave me back inside. What choice did I have?

Rance offered me a seat. He was polite, smiling, charming. Not the cold-blooded creep from the other night. Too weird.

"What brings you to Orlando, Walt?" he said.

"Politics."

"Didn't know you were an enthusiast."

"I care about Florida."

"So do I." Rance cut a bite of steak. It was bloody.

"Are we just going to bullshit each other as if your little shindig the other night didn't happen?"

He laughed to himself.

"Small talk is such a dumb habit. I really need to stop being so considerate," he said.

"You already have that down."

"Good point." He took another bite, a sip of wine, and wiped his lips. He leaned in, elbows on the table and folded his hands under his chin.

"We had a lot going on the other night. You really stopped by at a bad time. Sorry if we weren't very hospitable."

"You tried to have me killed."

"For like the fiftieth time, right?" He smirked. Glad he was in on the joke. But, his schtick was tiring.

"Look, I won't keep you. I'm not mad at you anymore for the simple fact that you can't do anything to stop us. Not now."

"Because of Simon?" I said.

He nodded.

"What if he doesn't win?"

He waved off that concern as he leaned back in his chair and ate the last bite on his plate. The waiter must have passed behind me because Rance air penned for the check.

"You don't think we have both parties covered?"

Actually, I hadn't. I was annoyed thinking about it now.

"If Simon wins, terrific. That puts one of our guys in the top office. If Vissel wins, we've flipped the Lieutenant Governor to push our interests."

"What are your interests?"

The waiter brought the check and left.

"We just want to be left alone," he said. "That's all."

"So, you can indulge your inner libertine."

He nodded, giving me silent credit for knowing what a libertine was.

"We're not going to start feeling bad about it. So, we're just going to make sure everyone lets us do our thing."

"Making the most of it," I said.

"Making the most of life," he said. This guy had an anger trigger. And, it sounded close to getting pulled.

He signed the bill, took his credit card, and closed the leather book with a flip.

"This Maximum Freedom bit never impresses because it always comes from entitled pricks who are too bored with their good fortune to appreciate it."

"Everyone is entitled," said Rance. "There are no rules except those you put on yourself."

"One of Razook's inspirational quotes?"

"He's a great man who has helped so many."

"Hard to believe having seen stacks of dead immigrant clothes in your Groveland warehouse."

"Get off your high horse, Walt. You're a murderer, too. We have the bodies to prove it."

"Saving them for a special day?"

He was about to say something but stopped. He smirked. "I see why Oren was so impressed with you."

"Lines like that are usually followed by an offer to join you creeps," I said.

He shook his head. "Not this time. But, I will offer a truce."

"Tempting. But, how could I ever trust you to leave us alone? And how—"

"How could you live with yourself knowing we'd still be out there doing all the ugly things we do?" he said, beating me to the punch.

"Correct."

"That's for you to figure out." The lighthearted expression he'd had a moment ago was replaced by a grim façade. "In two weeks, we'll own the Governor. Our influence will grow. We'll do exactly as we please. And, we will win. You know it's true. So, make your mind up quick. Do you want to live to see it? Because I will give you my word right now that you and Ilsa and your friends will be forever safe from us. Otherwise, we can make it all end very fast for you."

He had me. I didn't want to die. Didn't want any harm to come to--

"The best deals involve compromise on both sides," said Rance. "I believe we've found a fair middle ground, Mr. Asher." The man I'd come here to stop, or more likely kill, held out his hand.

I shook it.

"Deal," I said.

"Good. Let's get the fuck out of here. Party's about to start."

The sun was setting. Orange light filtered in between the high rises. The air was cool and crisp.

I wasn't sure whom I hated more for the compromise, me or Rance. It was something to think about. The only consolation was knowing I could always void the terms of agreement. Maybe I would.

He looked to me as we walked past the front of the restaurant. I glanced back at our table. Still messy from eating. Scene of the crime.

"As a good faith gesture, how about you let me get you into the show as a VIP?" said Rance.

"No thanks. I'm going home," I said. I hadn't decided it until I said it.

"You sure? You love Florida. This is Florida history happening in real time."

"I'll skip it."

"At least take a look at the set up. There's media from all over the world." He stopped to let me catch up.

Wait a minute.

His knife wasn't on the--

Rance threw his arm around my neck and dragged me into the alley. He was big and strong.

And, he had the knife. Setting sunlight reflected off it. He stabbed up, but missed my chest. The blade speared under my armpit.

I dropped to my knees and pulled out of the headlock. He spun and slashed. I rolled. He missed. I flipped onto my backside. Found a broken, jagged concrete block and raked it across his head.

He hit the ground hard, face-first. Blood leaked onto the gravel. White dust landed on the dark fabric of his sport coat.

Rance was dead. The top of his head was peeled from his skull like an old, drooping Band-Aid.

No time for satisfaction. I needed to leave. Better to exit at the far end of the alley. Go!

Two steps.

Wait.

The knife on the ground. Cast aside while dying.

I looked back at the body.

I got a notion.

They were never going to leave me alone. Ever. So, why should I leave them alone?

I picked up the knife and hurried back to the body. Rance's cleaved head continued to spill in the golden hour light. I knelt down, clutched the blade, and wondered how Oren would react when he received his good buddy's scalp in the mail along with a note that read:

This is not over.

294

Get Your FREE Copy!

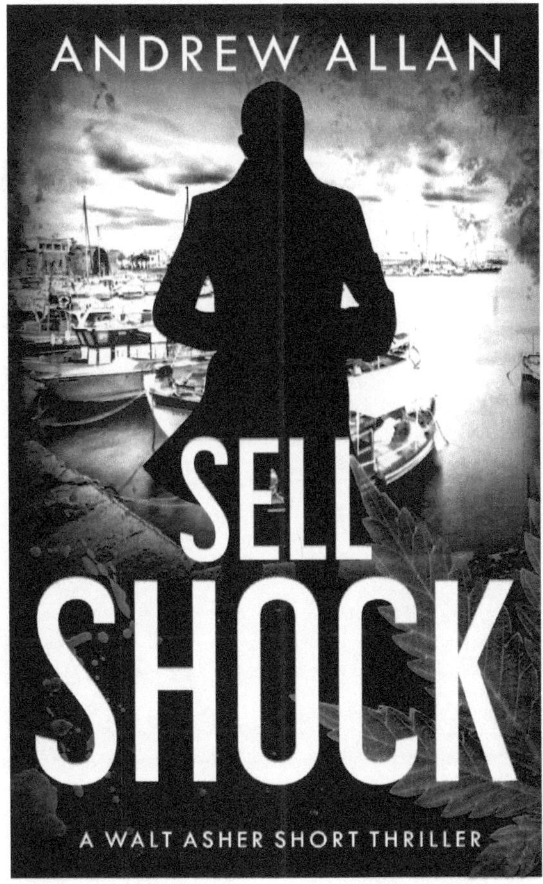

Want more Walt? Your FREE copy of SELL SHOCK, a Walt Asher novella, is waiting for you now at **www.andrewallanbooks.com**. Just sign up for the free VIP mailing list to receive yours today. You'll be among the first to get updates about new releases, exclusive promotions, and members only content.

Sign up today at:

www.andrewallanbooks.com

ANDREW ALLAN

The Book Blasters are my V.I.P. Readers. A big, whopping, alphabetical order thanks goes out to…

Brian Anderson • Bruce Avery • Dr. Tom Barnard
Sheri Brennan • Joe Elliott • Mike Hart
Walt Hunt • Angie LeBlanc • Roxy Long
Michael Nethery • Chris Nicholls • Jay Williams
Lee Zak • Maurice Dykes • Robert Hinkle
Jay Lamborn • Lisabeth Racine • Peter F. Bennett
Banacek • Connie Gisone • Ken Lingenfelter
Judy Johnson • John Evans • Adele E.
Nicole Burns • Sheri Reed • Chuck Haley

…and all the other Book Blasters who have thrown their support behind me and my books. Your reading, feedback, reviews, dedication, and friendship are sincerely appreciated. You rule!

ANDREW ALLAN

Yes, it's true. Andrew Allan really is a top infomercial writer and director. But wait, there's more! He also makes wild cult movies, runs DailyGrindhouse.com, and lives with his wife and three children in Clearwater, Florida. He also loves to hear from readers at AndrewAllanBooks.com. You'll probably find a free book by Andrew while you're there.